The Golden Stairs

THE GOLDEN STAIRS

AL & JOANNA LACY

Multnomah® Publishers
Sisters, Oregon

THE GOLDEN STAIRS
published by Multnomah Publishers, Inc.

© 2006 by ALJO PRODUCTIONS, INC.
International Standard Book Number: 1-59052-561-2

Cover design by The Design Works Group, Inc.

Scripture quotations are from *The Holy Bible,* King James Version

Multnomah is a trademark of Multnomah Publishers, Inc.,
and is registered in the U.S. Patent and Trademark Office.
The colophon is a trademark of Multnomah publishers, Inc.

Printed in the United States of America

For information:
Multnomah Publishers, Inc., 601 N. Larch St., Sisters, Oregon 97759

Library of Congress Cataloging-in-Publication Data
Lacy, Al.
  The golden stairs / Al and JoAnna Lacy.
      p. cm. — (Dreams of gold trilogy ; bk. 3)
  ISBN 1-59052-561-2
  1. California—History—1846-1850—Fiction. 2. Gold mines and mining—Fiction. I.
Lacy, JoAnna. II. Title.
  PS3562.A256G65 2006
  813'.54--dc22

                            2005025583

06 07 08 09 10 11 12 — 10 9 8 7 6 5 4 3 2 1 0

With much love we dedicate this book to our special fans,
Nancy Barlament, who is our pastor's wife,
and their daughters Amber and Mandi.
The Lord bless you!

EPHESIANS 6:24

PROLOGUE

In this trilogy we call Dreams of Gold, we will tell the stories of three major gold strikes that took place in North America in the nineteenth century and changed this continent forever.

The first is the California gold strike in the late 1840s. The second is the Black Hills gold strike in the mid-1870s. The third is the Yukon gold strike in the late 1890s.

Gold is referred to very early in the Bible:

> And a river went out of Eden to water the garden; and from thence it was parted, and became into four heads. The name of the first is Pison: that is it which compasseth the whole land of Havilah, where there is gold; and the gold of that land is good.
>
> GENESIS 2:10–12

Many people ask why man has valued gold so highly, practically ever since he has been on the earth. There are several reasons. Gold is good and highly prized because it is warmly beautiful. It is enduring, for it never dissolves away. Under all circumstances, it retains its beauty.

Strong acids have no effect on it. Gold is the only metal that is unharmed by fire. In fact, each time gold goes through fire, it comes out more refined than before. It can be melted without harm, and it is marvelously adapted to shaping.

Finally, gold is prized so highly because of its scarcity. Being rare makes it valuable and much sought after. Hence, when gold was discovered in California, the Dakota Black Hills, and in the Klondike region of Yukon Territory in Canada, multitudes of gold seekers rushed to these places to make their fortunes. In this trilogy, we tell some of their stories.

Gold is also mentioned at the very end of the Bible. In the book of Revelation, the most precious of metals is portrayed as constituting the New Jerusalem, with even its street made of gold so pure that it is transparent as glass. An angel was giving the apostle John a tour of the city in a beatific vision, and even used a reed of gold to measure the city and its gates and walls.

And he that talked with me had a golden reed to measure the city, and the gates thereof, and the wall thereof.... And the building of the wall of it was of jasper: and the city was pure gold, like unto clear glass.... And the twelve gates were twelve pearls, every several gate was of one pearl: and the street of the city was pure gold, as it were transparent glass.

REVELATION 21:15, 18, 21

In between the beginning and the end of the Bible, gold is spoken of so many times that one must use a concordance to find all the references.

So often in the Bible, gold and the less precious metals are linked with money and other possessions that make men rich, and the pursuit of riches is tied to greed and covetousness, which destroy lives. Riches are also spoken of in the Bible as often deceptive, unsatisfying, hurtful, and uncertain. Repeatedly in history, many of the supercilious wealthy have lost their fortunes in the blink of an eye.

These truths are shown in the trilogy. Let each of us take note of what the Spirit of God told Paul to write to Timothy, his son in the faith:

> Charge them that are rich in this world, that they be not highminded, nor trust in uncertain riches, but in the living God, who giveth us richly all things to enjoy.
>
> 1 TIMOTHY 6:17

INTRODUCTION

Scientists tell us that gold collects in long fractures deep in the rock that makes up the earth's crust. These long veins of gold are called *lodes*. Little by little the earth's crust buckles and splits, and rocks with veins of gold protrude through the surface. Over the course of many centuries, sun, wind, ice, rain, and rivers and streams erode the rock, exposing the gold.

Because this precious metal is so heavy, it settles in stream beds, where it is easily spotted, especially when the sun is shining on the water. This process takes many years—sometimes centuries—and has happened in only a few places on earth. The Klondike, a vast region of mountains, valleys, rivers, and creeks in the Yukon Territory of Canada near Alaska's eastern border, is one of those places.

In 1849, the same year as the California gold rush, a Russian engineer named Peter Doroshin found a small amount of gold in Alaska...the first time ever, as far as anyone knows. Shortly thereafter, word came from Canada's Yukon region that a couple of fishermen had found small amounts of gold in the Yukon River.

Word of these discoveries spread, and a few years later, men who had not struck it rich in California drifted north, seeking gold. Year after year, a little gold was found—some near Juneau in southeastern Alaska, some in central Alaska, and a small bit in the Canadian Yukon—but soon the excitement waned, and interest in gold in the far north waned with it. Only a small number of hopeful miners continued to search for gold. For years they worked the hills and streams of Canada that fed the Yukon River, including the Klondike River and its tributary streams, but found very little of the precious metal.

In the early 1890s many countries in the world experienced a dreadful economic collapse. A financial crisis erupted in the United States on May 4, 1893. Banks were forced to close. Railroads and various businesses failed. A great many people lost their jobs. The New York Stock Exchange went into panic. Stocks plummeted and foreign trade declined sharply.

The "Panic of '93" was just over three years old when, deep in Yukon Territory, a California fisherman named George Washington Carmack discovered a large deposit of gold in Rabbit Creek on August 17, 1896. He staked his claim legally and began to find more and more gold. Rabbit Creek was renamed Bonanza Creek.

Other gold seekers—both Alaskan and Canadian—learned of Carmack's strike and staked claims on Bonanza Creek, also.

During the winter of 1896–97 the miners worked the frozen mud, sand, and dirt along the banks of the creek. Soon, miners were also finding gold in both the Klondike and Yukon Rivers, and in the hills and creeks due east.

Dawson City, a small Canadian town just fifty miles from the Alaska border, was situated on the confluence of the Klondike and Yukon Rivers. More miners crowded into the area during the early wintry months of 1897, and in that time Dawson City's population grew from some six hundred to nearly two thousand. With little food available in the Dawson

City grocery store, the miners had to work with hunger pangs in their stomachs.

Finally spring came, and the ice in the rivers began to melt. Two ships arrived to bring food and supplies and to take passengers back to the United States. The miners piled their gold into the holds of the *Excelsior*, heading for San Francisco, and the *Portland*, heading for Seattle.

On July 15, 1897, the *Excelsior* pulled into the harbor of San Francisco Bay. Newspapers ran stories about the gold brought off the ship from the Yukon gold fields just east of Dawson City. It was the same when the *Portland* arrived in Seattle.

Huge headlines in the San Francisco and Seattle newspapers announced "GOLD! GOLD! GOLD!"

Word spread fast in the United States and its territories, and a listless nation in the grip of financial depression traded its doldrums for the excitement of the gold strike in Canada's Yukon Territory. From all corners of North America, ordinary people turned toward the cold, dark, remote land that held the stuff of their dreams.

Two basic routes from southern Alaska to the Canadian gold fields near Dawson City were established over the towering, snow-laden Coast Mountains, which extend for nine hundred miles north from west British Columbia into southeastern Alaska. The one used most by far was Chilkoot Trail, which went over Chilkoot Pass, out of Dyea, Alaska. It was extremely steep, and the snow was deep year round, with very little melt off in the summer. Pack horses could not be used. The trail from one side of the pass to the other was thirty-three miles long.

The other route was White Pass Trail out of Skagway, Alaska, which was neither as high nor as steep as the Chilkoot Trail but was twelve miles longer. It was a torturous trail full of giant boulders, sharp rocks, fallen trees, and sheer cliffs. The trail soon became littered with horse carcasses, and the Canadians labeled it "Dead Horse Trail."

As gold seekers came by the hundreds, the steep, snowy, icy Chilkoot Pass was chiseled with actual stairs in the ice by two men who charged each person a toll for using them. Thus, the path to the gold fields was dubbed the "Golden Stairs."

The Canadian police force—called Mounties because they traveled on horseback—required each person crossing the Canadian border to seek gold in the Klondike to bring a year's provisions and plenty of warm clothing. The equipment required by the Mounties, called a miner's outfit, cost from $250 to $500 in San Francisco or Seattle.

Many men brought their wives and children with them, and some women even came alone to make their fortune. Quite often, when prospective miners—male and female—reached the base of Chilkoot Pass and eyed the steep stairs chipped in the ice, they were so disheartened that they sold their outfits for ten cents on the dollar and bought a ticket back to San Francisco or Seattle.

The others pressed on. An unbroken line of men, women, and children carrying packs of fifty to a hundred pounds headed up the icy stairs toward a dream of gold. Some hired Chilkoot Indians as packers. The Indians, known for their strength, often made more money than the miners they helped.

At the top of Chilkoot Pass, the climbers stored their goods, made their way back down the stairs, and started over again with another heavy bundle. Because climbing the icy stairs was so strenuous, most people could make no more than one trip a day. It took from twenty to forty days to carry the average outfit over the pass.

In spite of the extreme difficulty, great numbers finally made it to Dawson City and the gold fields. Some became quite wealthy while others barely made enough to pay for their tickets back to San Francisco or Seattle.

Robert Service, a well-known poet of Lancashire, England, migrated to Canada in 1894. He was employed by the Canadian Bank of Commerce in Victoria, British Columbia, and stationed in the Klondike region of Yukon Territory during the gold rush years. Though many miners struck it rich, Robert Service saw that the wealth failed to satisfy their hearts. His observance led him to write and publish this poem:

> I wanted the gold, and I sought it;
> I scrambled and toiled like a slave.
> Was it famine or scurvy—I fought it;
> I hurled my youth into a grave.
> I wanted the gold and I got it—
> Came out with a fortune last fall—
> Yet somehow life's not what I thought it,
> And somehow the gold isn't all.

God's Word echoes these same thoughts:

> Then I returned, and I saw vanity under the sun. There is one alone, and there is not a second; yea, he hath neither child nor brother: yet is there no end of all his labour; neither is his eye satisfied with riches.

> ECCLESIASTES 4:7–8

The Lord Jesus spoke of this type of person: "So is he that layeth up treasure for himself, and is not rich toward God" (Luke 12:21). And King David wrote under the inspiration of the Holy Spirit:

The fear of the LORD is clean, enduring for ever: the judgments of the LORD are true and righteous altogether. More to be desired are they than gold, yea, than much fine gold.

PSALM 19:9–10

ONE

It was Friday, February 11, 1898. At the California State Prison just outside San Quentin on San Francisco Bay, twenty-nine-year-old Jess Colgan stood at the barred window of his cell, staring across the prison yard, beyond the oppressive walls toward the city.

It was a typical winter's day. Fog hung low over the city and the bay, and rain fell steadily from the gloomy sky.

San Quentin was shrouded in a gray cloak, hiding her face from the world.

Jess Colgan popped his right fist into his left palm and said in a low whisper, "Only three more weeks, then I'm off to the gold fields to make my fortune. Nothing is going to stand in my way. Nothing!"

Jess heard footsteps in the corridor, and a key rattled in his cell door. He turned around to see two guards with a prisoner dressed in prison stripes. The guard who had unlocked the door motioned for the young man in the striped clothing to enter. As he obeyed, the guard looked at Jess and said, "New cellmate for you, Colgan. His name's Fred Matthis."

The door clicked shut, the guard turned the key in the lock, and both guards walked away.

Matthis extended his right hand. "Glad to meet you, Colgan. What's your first name?"

"Jess," replied Colgan, shaking his new cellmate's hand.

Matthis looked at the two bunks in the cell. "Which one's yours?"

"The lower one."

"Okay. I'll take the upper. Mind if we sit down on yours and get acquainted?"

Jess smiled. "Not at all."

As they sat side by side, Matthis said, "I'm in for twenty-five years for manslaughter. How about you?"

"I've been here for almost seven years...for robbing a bank in San Jose."

Matthis raised an eyebrow. "Tracked you down and caught you, eh?"

Jess shook his head. "No. I was wearing a mask when I entered the bank, and was about to get away with a moneybag containing thirty thousand dollars when the county sheriff and a deputy just happened to be coming into the bank as I was dashing for the front door. They whipped out their guns and forced me to surrender. The judge sentenced me to seven years." Jess let a smile curve his lips. "I'll be getting out next month...Thursday, March 3."

Matthis's brow furrowed. "Why'd you take such a chance robbing a bank? Were you not employed?"

"Not gainfully. My father owns a chicken farm across the bay just outside of Oakland. We never had much money in my growing-up years, and I had to wear the tattered, hand-me-down clothes of my older brother." Jess's features twisted in anger. "I hated the way people looked at me. I swore that when I grew up, I'd make a lot of money and be rich. I'd never been able to get a really good-paying job since graduating from high school. All I knew about was feeding chickens and cleaning out chicken houses. So I decided to rob the San Jose Bank. I would wear a mask and get my hands on some *real* money." He sighed. "That thirty thousand dollars would've been wonderful. But now, I'm penniless."

"So what are you gonna do when you get out of prison?" Matthis said.

Before Jess could answer, a guard stepped up to the barred door and said, "Colgan, you've got visitors. Your parents."

Jess rose from the bunk and looked at Matthis. "My dad and mom take a ferry across the bay twice a month to visit me."

As the guard unlocked the cell door, Matthis said, "You've got good parents, Jess. My parents already told me they'd never come see me here at the prison."

Jess stepped into the corridor and looked back through the bars. "I'm sorry about that, Fred."

The guard led Jess down the long corridor to the visiting room, and he sat down at a barred window with his parents facing him. When Jess looked at them, he thought they looked far older than they actually were. His mother's hair was now more silver than light brown, and most of his father's hair was already gone.

Maybelle Colgan's old dress was clean, but the pattern was faded beyond recognition. Her hair was pulled back in a bun, which seemed to accentuate the deep worry lines etched in her brow and at the corners of her eyes.

Lawrence Colgan's overalls had seen better days, but they were clean, and the plaid shirt he wore was pressed. Both parents' eyes showed excitement as they looked at Jess.

"Oh, honey, only three more weeks and you'll be free!" Maybelle said.

"Yeah, son, only three more weeks," Lawrence said. "Then I'm going to try to help you find a job."

"I'm sure your dad will be able to do it," Maybelle said. "He knows lots of business people."

Jess let his eyes settle on his father's face. With a softness in his voice, he said, "Dad, I appreciate your wanting to help me find a job, but..."

"But what, son?"

"Well, I've got other plans."

"What do you mean, other plans?"

"Well, I've been reading in the *San Francisco Chronicle* about the gold strike in Canada's Yukon Territory, and how thousands of gold seekers are going there from all over to make their fortunes. My plan is to go up there and make my fortune in gold."

Maybelle blinked. "I thought the prison officials wouldn't let the prisoners have newspapers."

"They won't *provide* newspapers, Mom, but they allow us to have them if some visitor brings a paper to us."

"Oh."

"An ex-con that I got to know in here comes to see me once a week. His name's Bernie Brodak. He always brings me the latest editions of the *Chronicle*. Bernie's been out almost two years and has a good-paying job working at the docks for an uncle who owns a ship-building company. After I'd read about the Yukon gold strike in the papers, I told Bernie of my desire to go up there. When I get out next month, Bernie's going to give me the money I need to get there."

Lawrence rubbed his jaw. "Son, it'll take a real chunk of money to do what you're talking about doing. You'll have to have sufficient food and plenty of warm clothing and miner's equipment, let alone the cost of a ticket to sail there from here. Is Bernie aware of the cost?"

"He is, Dad. He and I have discussed it, and Bernie's going to give me twice as much money as the highest estimate."

"Why is Bernie so willing to do this for you?" Maybelle said. "I know you're good friends, but we're talking about a lot of money here."

Jess smiled. "Mom, I saved Bernie's life a few years back when a convict who had it in for him tried to kill him in the prison yard. I was close by and went to Bernie's rescue. I had to pound the man into unconsciousness to keep him off Bernie."

Lawrence and Maybelle looked at each other in amazement. Lawrence said, "Jess, we didn't know about this. But I'm sure proud of you for rescuing your friend."

"No wonder Bernie wants to help you fulfill your desire to get to the Yukon," Maybelle said.

Lawrence frowned. "Son, did that convict become a threat to you afterward?"

"No. He tried to escape from the prison a few days later and was shot to death in the attempt."

"Oh, I see. Have any of the inmates ever tried to hurt you?"

"No inmate ever has, Dad, but a little over a year ago, I had a run-in with a guard when I was in a chain gang, working outside the prison walls. His name was Howard Ziegler, and because he was supposed to be tough, he expected the convicts to be afraid of him.

"One day Ziegler ordered me to lift a huge rock and carry it several yards to a different spot. He knew that no one man could ever lift that rock, much less carry it somewhere else. I told him I'd need help. His temper flared. He demanded that I pick up the rock and move it to where he had indicated. When I told him I couldn't do it alone, he told two other guards to grab me and strip off my shirt. Then he told them to put me facedown on the ground and hold me there. He then beat me with a whip."

Maybelle gasped and shuddered.

"Son, why didn't you tell us about this?" Lawrence said.

"I didn't want to worry you and Mom, especially since I had more time to be in here."

Maybelle thumbed a tear from her eye. "Son, do you have scars on your back from the beating?"

Jess unbuttoned the top buttons of his shirt, turned his back toward his parents, and pulled the shirt collar down a few inches. When his parents saw the scars, they both gasped.

"The scars go all the way to my waist," Jess said, looking at them over his shoulder.

Lawrence's features were gray. "Did you get any medical care?"

"Ziegler took me to the prison doctor, but the incident never got to the warden's ears. The prison doctor was afraid to report it to anyone, especially the warden. He knew if he did, Ziegler would do something drastic to him."

"Well, he should've reported it to the warden anyway!" Lawrence said. "And the warden should do something about that no-good Howard Ziegler!"

Jess shrugged. "They're gone now, Dad. The prison has a new doctor and a new warden, and Ziegler and the two guards who held me down are gone. Not long after my beating, Ziegler and the two guards beat another prisoner and got caught in the act by the warden himself. He fired them on the spot."

"Well, I'm glad for that," Lawrence said.

Jess drew a shaky breath. "If I ever see Howard Ziegler again, I'll kill him!"

"Jess, don't talk like that!" Maybelle said.

"Your mother's right, son," Lawrence said. "If you killed Ziegler, you'd hang for it. You've got to get him out of your mind."

Jess bit his lower lip and drew another shaky breath. "I'll put my mind on my future, Dad. I'm really going to enjoy prospecting for gold. And when I strike it rich, I'll give you and Mom lots of money so you can retire comfortably."

"Your mother and I appreciate your desire to do that for us, son, but we really don't want you going way up there in the cold northland. Just let me try to help you get a good job right here."

Jess shook his head. "My mind's made up, Dad. I'm going to Canada to get rich. When I'm released from prison on March 3, I'll come home and stay with you until I can get reservations on a ship from San Francisco Bay to Alaska."

"Jess, you have a right to make your own decision about what to do with your life," Maybelle said. "Your dad and I will be glad to have you back home for whatever time you'll be here."

"We really don't want you going so far from us, but your mother's right." Lawrence drew a deep breath. "We'll be back to see you as usual in these next few weeks, and on March 3, we'll be here to take you home."

Jess let a smile curve his lips. "Thanks, Dad."

Lawrence smiled back and rose to his feet. "Well, Maybelle, we'd best be going."

Maybelle looked at her son through the bars. "I love you, Jess."

"I love you, too, Mom. See you next time."

The Colgans watched their son as he walked to the door of the visiting room. A guard was at the door to the corridor and opened it, and his parents kept their eyes on him until he passed from their view.

Lawrence and Maybelle stepped out of the prison building into the falling rain and headed toward their wagon. Lawrence noticed that Maybelle was wiping tears with a handkerchief. As they drew up to the wagon, he placed an arm around her shoulder and drew her close to him. He held her tightly for a moment, then helped her onto the seat.

Maybelle was still dabbing at her eyes when he settled on the seat beside her. "I wish things were different, dear," he said softly as he put the horses into motion, "but we'll just have to let our boy do what he thinks best."

Maybelle reached down and pulled up a blanket from the floor and placed it over their laps. She then gazed forward at the fog-enshrouded road.

Lawrence took hold of Maybelle's hand. "I know you're disappointed with Jess's decision to go to Canada, honey, and I am, too. But we both know there's nothing we can do about it. It's his right, as you said. He has to make his own way in life, along with his own mistakes and choices. He knows we love him, and that there's always a place for him here in our home."

Maybelle nodded and sniffled. "Yes, honey, but he knows nothing about gold mining. He's never been out of this country. He has no idea what he might face up there. There's no telling what hardships and obstacles he may have ahead of him." She took a deep breath. "But life goes on, and though I'll worry about Jess, I'll do my best to handle it."

"I know you will, sweetheart. And as for us, we still have each other, a roof over our heads, and a warm fire waiting at home. I wish I could give you a nicer house, but for now our little place will have to do."

"It'll be fine. We have so much to be thankful for, dear."

Just then, there was a break in the fog, and a small ray of sunshine poked its way through.

Lawrence looked up at it and a smile creased his face. He squeezed Maybelle's hand. "See that sunlight up there?"

She looked up, and a smile touched her lips. "Mm-hmm. Beautiful, isn't it?"

"Sure is. And you're right. We do have a lot to be thankful for."

TWO

That night, Jess Colgan lay on his bunk, thinking about the riches he was going to find in Canada. Lanterns burned at both ends of the corridor, giving off just enough light so the men behind bars could see to get around in their cells.

Fred Matthis was already asleep on the bunk above Jess, and snoring lightly.

Jess pictured himself in Yukon Territory on a bright, sunny day, swinging a pick, digging in the ground with all his might. Suddenly in his imagination, he felt the pick strike something solid. He dropped the pick, fell to his knees, and scooped up chunks of moist dirt in his hands. In the dirt were shiny nuggets that sparkled and seemed to smile at him. "Gold! Gold!" he shouted.

Above him, Fred rolled over on his bunk, snorted, then leaned his head over the side and looked down at Jess. "Hey, man, what's going on down there?"

Jess was about to explain when a guard stepped up to the barred door. "What's goin' on in here?" he demanded. "What's the shoutin' about?"

Jess cleared his throat. "I...I'm sorry. I, uh...was dreaming. Sorry to disturb you." He looked up at the face hanging over the edge of the top bunk. "Sorry, Fred. I didn't mean to disturb you, either. I won't do it again."

"Good," the guard said. "I'm sure the rest of the inmates will appreciate that."

As the guard walked away, a voice came from the adjacent cell to the north: "Where'd you find the gold you were yellin' about, Colgan? In your teeth?"

"Sorry, Ralph," Jess said. "Go back to sleep. I won't bother you again."

When all was quiet again, Fred whispered, "Jess, you must've been dreaming about digging gold in Yukon Territory."

"Well, to tell you the truth, I was *thinking* about that very thing. I just wasn't asleep. I got so excited when I pictured myself finding gold—well, it just came out."

A few seconds passed, then Fred whispered, "Jess..."

"Yeah?"

"Wish I was going to Yukon Territory with you."

"That would be fine with me, but short of a prison break, you won't be doing that."

Fred sighed. "Yeah. And that won't be happening. I'm not going to try anything that stupid."

Soon Fred was snoring again, and after thinking about the gold fields in the Yukon for a while, Jess also fell asleep. Shortly thereafter, he dreamt about the day he was in the chain gang in the woods outside San Quentin Prison...

Guard Howard Ziegler had guard Rex Wilson remove the chain from Jess's ankle, saying he had a special job for this convict.

Jess looked at Ziegler while Wilson was unlocking the ankle cuff and asked, "What special job is that, Mr. Ziegler?"

Ziegler pointed to a large rock near a tree. "See that rock over there? It needs to be moved. Pick it up and carry it over there by that fallen, dead tree."

"Why does it need to be moved over there?" Jess said.

Ziegler's face reddened. "Because I said so! Now do it!"

Jess licked his lips. "It's too big and heavy, Mr. Ziegler. I'll need help to get it over there."

"You'll do it yourself, Colgan! Now get it done!"

Jess's voice trembled as he said, "Mr. Ziegler, I'm telling you I can't do it alone."

Ziegler turned to the guard who had just unlocked Jess's ankle from the chain that bound him to the other inmates and barked, "Wilson, you and Ellsworth strip his shirt off!" To another guard, he snapped, "Barnes, go to the wagon and bring me my whip!"

Jess's heart pounded as Wilson and Ellsworth removed his shirt.

"Put him facedown on the ground!" Ziegler commanded.

Jess was flung to the ground and held there by the two guards as guard Gordon Barnes came running back and handed Ziegler his bullwhip. Ziegler snapped the whip twice in the air, then stepped toward the spot where the guards held Jess on the ground.

Eyes bulging, Ziegler stood over the helpless convict and growled, "I'll teach you not to argue with me when I tell you to do something, Colgan!"

Suddenly the whip came down across Jess's bare back, and he shrieked. Then the whip was lashing his back repeatedly. It felt like streamers of fire, and Jess could feel the blood flowing from the torn flesh of his back...

∾

Suddenly Jess was awake and could hear himself moaning. He was breathing hard and sweating all over. He felt the framework of the bunk bed move, and from above him, heard Fred Matthis's heavy whisper, "Jess, you all right?"

Jess drew a shaky breath and said, "Yeah. I'm all right. I...was having a nightmare. Sorry I woke you up."

"That's okay. You sure you're all right?"

"Yeah. I'm fine. Go back to sleep."

The next morning, after the inmates had been in the prison yard just over two hours for exercise, they were taken back to their cells.

Jess and Fred were sitting on the bottom bunk in their cell, talking about Jess's nightmare the night before, when a well-dressed man stepped up to the cell door with a guard beside him, smiled, and said, "Good morning, Jess. And good morning to *you*, Mr. Fred Matthis."

"Morning, Chaplain," responded Jess, his voice less than warm. "Fred, this is Chaplain William Glaxner."

Fred stood up and nodded. "Chaplain."

Glaxner smiled. "Mr. Matthis, since you're new here, I'd like to get acquainted with you. Will you come with me to a meeting room where you and I can talk? I always like to get to know the inmates so I can help them any way I can, if they'll let me."

As the guard placed a key into the door lock, the chaplain looked at Jess and said, "I'd like to talk to you after I spend some time with your cellmate."

Jess regarded him carefully. "What do you want to talk about?"

"I heard something from some of the inmates in another cell-block about your plans to go to Yukon Territory. I'd like to discuss it with you."

Jess nodded, his lips drawn into a thin line.

"Good," Glaxner said. "See you in a little while."

Jess watched as Fred, the chaplain, and the guard walked down the corridor and passed through a steel door.

Just over an hour later, the same guard brought Fred to the cell, and Jess noted that his cellmate was smiling. The guard unlocked the barred door and said, "Colgan, Chaplain Glaxner is waiting for you in his regular meeting room."

"What are you so happy about?" Jess said as Fred stepped into the cell.

Fred's eyes were bright as he said, "Jess, Chaplain Glaxner just showed me from the Bible how to have all my sins forgiven— even my crime of manslaughter—and how to go to heaven when I die. I just received Jesus Christ into my heart as my Saviour!"

Jess only stared at Fred, then walked with the guard down the corridor. When the guard ushered Jess through the door of the chaplain's meeting room, Glaxner was standing there, waiting for him. He gestured toward the small table where they had sat together before. The guard excused himself and left.

As they sat down, facing each other over the table, Jess noted the Bible on Glaxner's side of the table.

The chaplain met Jess's cool gaze. "Jess, did Fred tell you what happened when he and I were together?"

Jess nodded. "He did."

"What about you, Jess? I've talked to you many times about being saved. Don't you want to open your heart to Jesus like Fred did?"

Jess sighed. "May I remind you, sir, that I have told you over and over that I will tend to the next life later."

Glaxner started to say something, but Jess cut him off. "Right now, Chaplain Glaxner, I am only interested in getting rich in *this* life. I've lived in poverty all my life. When I get my hands on that Canadian gold, I'll be rich and superbly happy."

Glaxner leaned closer to the convict. "Jess, let me tell you something that a very wise man said one time. He said, 'Money never made a man happy, nor will it ever. There is nothing in its nature to produce happiness. The more money a man has, the more he wants. Instead of filling a vacuum, it *makes* one. If it satisfies one desire, it doubles and trebles that desire another way.' And he was right, Jess. Riches don't satisfy a person's heart."

Jess's brow furrowed. "You don't think so?"

"I *know* so. Besides, riches are so uncertain. A man who becomes rich never knows how long he will stay that way. He lives in constant fear of losing his fortune. Your greatest need is the same as that of all other human beings. You need to make Jesus your Saviour and take hold of *real* riches…*eternal* riches."

Jess shook his head. "Chaplain, I'm really not interested in hearing any m—"

"I'm trying to help you, Jess. Listen to me. A preacher I heard once said, 'No man can tell whether he is rich or poor by looking at his bank account. It is the *heart* that makes a man rich. He is rich according to what he *is*, not according to what he *has*.' And that preacher was right. If you become a child of God by the new birth, you'll be truly rich. Without Jesus Christ, Jess, you're a pauper, no matter how much money you have in the bank or in your pocket. Jesus said, 'Take heed and beware of covetousness: for a man's life consisteth not in the abundance of the things which he possesseth.'

"What a tragedy, for a man to live for what money he can pile up in life, then to die and spend eternity in hell. Being wealthy is no sin if a man has come by it honestly, but to make that wealth his god is dead wrong. That is idolatry, and will only land him in hell when this life is over."

Jess Colgan's features stiffened as he extended his open hands toward the chaplain and said, "Right now, all I can think about is holding gold nuggets in these hands. I'm going back to my cell."

Glaxner quickly took hold of both hands and squeezed them tightly. "I know you would rather leave than listen to me anymore. But believe me, I'm trying to help you."

"I'm going back to my cell."

The chaplain squeezed Jess's hands harder. "Will you let me tell you a story before you go?"

Jess let the tension ease from his body, nodded, and said, "All right, Chaplain, I'll listen to your story."

Glaxner let go of Jess's hands. "Thank you. I appreciate that. Have you ever heard of Midas, the king of Phrygia in Greek mythology?"

Jess nodded. "I recall hearing the name somewhere. Probably in high school."

"Have you heard of the mythological Greek god Bacchus?"

"No."

"Well, in Greek mythology, Bacchus was the god of fruitfulness. The Greeks tell of the day that Bacchus was feeling generous and offered King Midas his choice of a gift...a natural capability that no one else on earth possessed."

Jess's brow furrowed. "You mean like an ability to do impossible deeds?"

"Yes, that's right. Well, King Midas was pleased at the offer from this esteemed Greek deity. He asked Bacchus if he might be gifted so that whatever he touched would be changed to gold. Bacchus consented, though he was inwardly disappointed that King Midas had not made a wiser choice.

"Midas went his way, rejoicing in his newly acquired power,

which he hastened to put to the test. He found the twig of an oak tree lying on the ground and picked it up. He could scarcely believe his eyes when the twig instantly turned to gold in his hand."

Jess grinned.

The chaplain went on. "Midas was excited. He bent over and picked up a stone from the ground. Instantly, the stone turned to gold. He touched a dirt clod, and it did the same. Midas then went to an apple tree, plucked an apple from a branch, and it immediately turned to gold."

Jess grinned again. "Wow."

Glaxner grinned, too. "Midas's joy knew no bounds. When he arrived at his palace with the items of gold in his hands, the servants had set a splendid meal on the table. The hot, fresh-baked bread looked and smelled so good. He picked up a slice of bread, and to his dismay, it hardened in his hand, turning to gold. He dropped the bread and put a morsel of meat to his lips. It defied his teeth by turning to gold. He picked up a cup of water. The cup instantly turned to gold. He took a drink, but the water choked him as it flowed down his throat like melted gold."

Jess shook his head slowly and rubbed the back of his neck.

Glaxner went on. "Fearing starvation, Midas dashed out of the palace and ran to the spot where he had seen Bacchus earlier and found him there. He held up the gold that had been bread and meat and asked Bacchus to take back his gift. Bacchus said, 'Go to the Pactolus River, trace the stream to its fountainhead, and there plunge your head and body in, and wash away your greed and its punishment.'

"When this was done, Midas no longer wanted wealth and the splendor he had sought in it. He was satisfied to go on through life as before."

Jess shook his head and rose to his feet. "Chaplain, that's only a story somebody made up. Like I told you, I've lived in poverty all my life. That's going to change. More than anything else, I want to be rich. Filthy rich. I'm going to go to Yukon Territory and make a fortune, and I won't mind bragging about it when I do. Nobody is going to change my mind."

Glaxner stood up, looking Jess straight in the eye. "But if you do that, money will be your god. When you die, Jess, you'll leave your riches behind and end up in hell because you rejected the Lord Jesus Christ."

Jess simply stared at him.

"Jess, in His Word God says, 'Charge them that are rich in this world, that they be not highminded, nor trust in uncertain riches, but in the living God, who giveth us richly all things to enjoy.'" As he spoke, the chaplain rounded the table and stepped up close to Jess.

Jess opened his mouth to make a retort, but Glaxner quickly said, "Jess, the only way you can trust in the living God is to repent of your sin, put your faith in His Son, and make Him your Saviour. Only in Jesus Christ can you find true riches."

Jess started to say something again, but Glaxner laid a gentle hand on his arm and said, "I implore you…put your trust in Jesus Christ, the living God, not in your proposed god of gold. Eternity is coming."

Jess jerked his arm from Glaxner's hand. "I told you, Chaplain, right now I'm only interested in *this* life. When I get my hands on that gold up there in the Yukon, I'll be rich and happy!"

Tears misted Chaplain William Glaxner's eyes. "That's what Midas thought, Jess, about the gold he was going to hold in *his* hands."

Jess gave a sharp huff, stomped to the door, and called for a guard to let him out.

THREE

It was Sunday morning, February 13, under a clear, bright San Francisco sky. In one of the city's Bible-believing churches, Pastor Wayne Dukart left his chair after the song leader had just led the congregation in a rousing gospel song, and stepped up behind the pulpit.

"At this time," Dukart said, "I need for our assistant pastor to summon his family to the platform."

Sitting in a chair on the platform next to the song leader, Assistant Pastor Tom Varner rose to his feet, walked up beside the pastor, and smiled down at his wife and children, who sat on the second pew in the center section. He motioned for them to come to the platform.

All eyes in the auditorium were on Peggy Varner as she led their nine-year-old son, Johnny, and seven-year-old daughter, Rebecca, up the steps and onto the platform. Tom guided them to stand close to the pulpit, then stood next to Peggy, with the children in front of them.

Pastor Dukart said loud enough for all to hear, "I want to remind all of you of the burden the Lord has laid on the hearts of

Tom and Peggy to go as missionaries to Dawson City in the Yukon Territory of Canada and plant a church. Most of you read your newspapers well enough to know that Dawson City is growing by leaps and bounds because of the gold rush up there. Tom and Peggy want to bring as many people as possible to salvation in the Lord Jesus Christ."

There were amens heard all over the auditorium.

The pastor smiled. "Folks, before the Klondike gold rush began barely over a year ago, Dawson City's population was some six hundred. Now, it's almost two thousand and growing fast. In the nearly four years that Tom has been assistant pastor here, he has won a great number of souls to the Lord. Many of you here today came to know Jesus through Tom's ministry."

Hands were waved as more amens were heard.

"I also want to remind you that for several months the church has been praying about sending the Varners to Dawson City, and now it's time to make it official. We will take a vote in a moment, but before we do, I want you to understand that Dawson City has mail service, and it has a bank. So the Varners will be able to receive our support checks and bank them."

The vote was then taken, and it was unanimous for the church to send the Varners to Dawson City and to support them at $150 a month.

"The Varners knew we would send them, without question," Pastor Dukart said, smiling broadly. "They already have plans to leave for Yukon Territory and Dawson City in early March."

There was laughter, then the pastor turned to his assistant and his wife and said, "Tom…Peggy…come and say whatever you want to the people."

Tom motioned for Peggy to go first. Moving up to the pulpit, Peggy thanked the church for their generosity in paying their way to Dawson City and for the monthly support. She asked that they pray for them daily, then stepped back and moved to Johnny and Rebecca, laying a hand on each shoulder.

Tom stepped up to the pulpit and said, "My dear Christian friends, I want to underscore what Peggy just said to you about your generosity in paying our way to our new mission field, and for the monthly support. Yes, please pray for us every day. I know the church won't be able to help us with the cost of erecting a building in Dawson City. I only ask that you pray for the Lord's blessing on the new church that will be started there, and that with us, you ask the Lord to provide a place for us to meet until the church grows enough that we need a building."

Again, many amens were heard throughout the crowd.

Following the offering and a women's trio, which sang "Alas! And Did My Saviour Bleed?" the pastor surprised the people by announcing that his assistant was going to preach the morning sermon. Tom Varner, having asked the trio to sing this song, stepped to the pulpit and preached a sermon on the precious blood of Jesus Christ. When the invitation was given, several Christians came to the altar just to thank their Saviour for the blood He had shed for them on the cross. A few adults and young people came to receive the Lord Jesus as Saviour.

When the service was over, the church members passed by the Varners, who stood at the foot of the platform at the pastor's request. The people told Tom, Peggy, Johnny, and Rebecca that they would faithfully pray for them and for their success in Dawson City.

Later, when the Varners arrived at the rented house the church had been providing for them, there was much excitement about their upcoming ministry in Yukon Territory.

"I can't wait!" Rebecca said. "I want to see some Eskimos!"

"Eskimos are fine, little sis," Johnny said, "but I want to see some Canadian Mounties!"

Rebecca's eyes showed a touch of playful orneriness. "If you do something bad when we get to Canada, you'll see some Mounties, all right!"

Johnny made fists and put them on his hips. There was mock anger on his face as he said, "Well, as naughty as you are, you'll no doubt see the inside of a Mountie jail!"

Rebecca laughed, as did her brother and their parents.

Peggy was glad to see the happiness and excitement on the faces of her husband and children. She felt the same way, but a tiny touch of fear invaded her heart at the thought of giving up their home and friends in San Francisco to head into the unknown. She always wanted the family to do whatever the Lord led them to do, but this was a big step.

Rebecca went to the kitchen with Peggy to set the table while her mother prepared Sunday dinner. While Peggy worked at the stove and the cupboard, the little touch of fear still needled her heart. Suddenly a phrase she had read one time in a devotional book came to her mind: *"Courage is fear that has said its prayers."*

She told herself she would try to remember this and get her courage from the times she would spend with the Lord in prayer.

When dinner was ready, Peggy sent Rebecca to the parlor to advise Tom and Johnny. Moments later, the Varner family sat around the table holding hands while Tom thanked the Lord for the food and gave praise to Him for calling them as missionaries to Yukon Territory.

A peace that Peggy had not felt before found its way into her willing heart, and finding a home, it would there abide.

On Monday, February 14, at the Victorian Hotel in San Francisco, assistant manager Margo Fleming had a young lady in her office who was applying for a job as a maid. Jane Wheeler was eighteen years old, and Margo liked her pleasant personality. Jane had just said that she liked talking with a woman about the job, but that she had expected a man.

Margo, who was thirty-eight years of age, said, "Well, my dear, Mr. Clyde Ames, the hotel's manager, is in Chicago at a meeting of the corporation that owns the Victorian Hotel, along with twenty-three other hotels all over the country. I'm doing Mr. Ames's job for him in his absence."

Jane nodded, brushing her long blond hair from her eyes. "I'm curious. How did you ever get to be assistant manager of the hotel in a man's world?"

Margo explained in brief that she started as a maid after her husband, Norman, was seriously injured on his job. The injury crippled him for life less than a year after they were married, which had been eighteen years ago.

"As a maid, Jane, I worked very hard, showing Mr. Ames that I could handle any assignment he gave me. Soon, I was promoted to head maid, though most of the other maids were older than I."

Jane smiled. "Good for you."

"Shortly after I was put in charge of the maids, Mr. Ames's secretary resigned because her husband was being transferred to Los Angeles. Mr. Ames hired me in her place. I did that job until the assistant manager's job came open five years ago. I replaced a man when I was given the promotion."

"That's great, ma'am. I'm glad for you."

"Thank you. Well, from everything I see here on your

resume, you've been a busy girl since you were orphaned at fifteen. It's hard work here, I want you to understand."

"I'm not afraid of hard work, ma'am. I promise, if you give me the job, I will be a good employee." Jane eased back on her chair. "Who knows? Maybe one day I can follow in your footsteps and be an assistant manager of a nice hotel like this one."

Margo's eyes brightened. "I hope it happens, dear. Well, let's make it official. You're hired."

"Thank you, Mrs. Fleming. This makes me very happy." Her eyes fastened on a newspaper that lay on Margo's desk with the front page in view. "Ma'am…?"

"Yes?"

"I couldn't help but notice the front page of the *San Francisco Chronicle* there on your desk. I see it carries a story on the latest news of the big gold strike in Canada's Yukon Territory."

Margo glanced at the paper, then looked back at Jane.

"I noticed that the headlines say thousands of people are going there and that they tell of the fantastic growth of Dawson City."

"Yes, quite a bonanza going on there in the Klondike," Margo said.

"I read an article in the *Sacramento Journal* recently that said that experts in Canada expect the gold strike to go on for many years, and they believe Dawson City will grow to forty or even fifty thousand. Mrs. Fleming, I'm sure, as well as you have done in the hotel business, you could go to Dawson City, open your own hotel, and get rich."

Margo grinned. "Well, Jane, it just so happens that Norman and I are going to Dawson City next month to open up our own hotel. I've already told Mr. Ames that we're going."

Jane's eyes widened. "Really?"

"Yes. Norman is confined to a wheelchair, but we're going to make it in the hotel business up there in spite of that."

Jane chuckled. "I was closer to the truth than I even imagined, wasn't I?"

"Guess you were. Norman and I both see the potential in Dawson City that you just spoke about, and so do my parents, who live in Minnesota. Norman and I have had a tough time financially ever since his accident, but my parents are quite well-off. They've loaned us the money to buy land in Dawson City and have a nice-sized hotel built. Mr. Ames understands our desire to go into the hotel business, and he, of course, is now looking for a new assistant manager."

Margo stood up and said, "Well, since you are now one of the Victorian Hotel's maids, I'll take you to meet the head maid. She'll provide you with a couple of uniforms, introduce you to some of the maids, and you can then go to work."

Jane rose to her feet, her eyes dancing. "Let's go!"

After taking Jane Wheeler to the head maid, Margo Fleming went to the hotel's front desk to fill in for the desk clerk, who had a doctor's appointment. She had been sitting there no more than five minutes when a young family came into the lobby and approached the desk.

Margo smiled and said, "May I help you?"

"Yes, ma'am," said the man. "My name is Dale Burke. This is my wife, Elaine, and these are our children, Barry, Susan, and Ernie. We're from Nebraska, and we're going up to Yukon Territory in Canada to get in on the gold strike."

Margo's eyes lit up. She quickly shared with them that she and her husband were planning to go there to open a hotel in Dawson City.

"Well, isn't that something?" Dale said. "I hope you and your husband do well in Dawson City, ma'am. We're booked to sail to Skagway, Alaska, on the steamship *Alaska* on March 20. We got here early because we decided to come with a wagon train that was headed for San Francisco, and thought it was better and safer to come with a wagon train than to travel by ourselves."

"You were wise to do so, Mr. Burke," Margo said. "It just so happens that my husband and I are also booked on the *Alaska* on that same day. However, we're going to Dyea, Alaska. We're going to go over Chilkoot Pass on the Chilkoot Trail."

Dale nodded. "Well, we're going to go over White Pass Trail out of Skagway because it's not as steep as Chilkoot Pass, though it is longer."

"Norman and I were advised to go over the Chilkoot Trail because of the Golden Stairs. Norman is crippled and has to travel in a wheelchair. We were told by the shipping company that there are Chilkoot Indians on the pass who will help travelers carry their baggage over the pass. For a price, of course. But it'll be worth the cost to have them carry my husband up the Golden Stairs and over the pass."

"So the Golden Stairs are actual stairs that go all the way from the base of Chilkoot Pass to the top?"

"Well, not quite at the base. The stairs start at a relatively flat area above the base called the Scales. Norman and I read that one trip up the Golden Stairs is like climbing the Statue of Liberty four times. Some gold seekers recently were so disheartened when they saw the stairs, they sold their outfits for ten cents on the dollar and bought tickets back home."

Dale chuckled. "I guess climbing those stairs isn't for sissies."

"No, but from what we've read, it's still better than climbing White Pass Trail, even though it's not as steep. It's a harrowing trail with huge boulders, countless sharp rocks, dead trees lying on the path, and dangerous cliffs."

Margo noticed a defeated look on Elaine Burke's face but said nothing.

Dale shrugged his shoulders, grinned at Elaine, and said, "Well, honey, I guess we'll just stick to the original plan and hope for the best." Then to Margo: "We need a room for the five of us until March 20, ma'am."

Margo nodded. "I can take care of you, all right. We have small beds on wheels made for children. We'll put three of those in your room."

"Great! Sounds like we came to the right place."

After the paperwork was done, Barry stepped up to his father and said, "Papa, will you take me and Susan and Ernie out on the street so we can see the fishermen's wagons that are passing by?" He pointed toward the large window on the street side of the lobby. "See 'em?"

Dale turned to Elaine. "You want to go with us?"

"I'll wait for you."

"Okay. Well, children, let's go see the fishermen and their wagons!"

Dale hurried the excited children outside.

"That Barry has a fascination for any vehicle that's pulled by horses," Elaine said with a weak smile as she turned to Margo.

"Sounds like he's all boy." Margo paused. "Is there something wrong, Mrs. Burke?"

"What do you mean?"

"Well, woman to woman…I believe I detect that something is bothering you. Want to talk about it? I'm not trying to be nosy, but if there's anything I can do…"

Tears welled up in Elaine's eyes and her lips trembled as she said, "I really don't want to go to the gold fields up north. I didn't want to leave our home in Omaha. Dale had a good job as an accountant in the largest dry goods store in Omaha and was paid

45

a good salary. But as he read in the newspapers about the gold strike in Yukon Territory, and that some of the miners up there were striking it rich in a big way, he caught the gold fever, if you know what I mean."

"Yes, I do."

"Well, he came home one day and told me about what he had been reading in the newspapers. He said he was going to quit his job, and our family was going to the Yukon to make our fortune in gold."

"A bit sudden, without any previous warning at all, I take it."

"Right." Elaine pulled a handkerchief from her purse and dabbed at her wet cheeks. "I…I begged Dale not to do this. I told him it would be too hard on all of us, especially the children. But the gold fever deafened his ears and blurred his good sense. We have enough money to get to Dawson City, and even purchase or build a house." She sniffed and dabbed at her tears once more. "Even…even though I was against our going to the Yukon from the beginning, I felt I should be in subjection to my husband, so I've never tried to stand in his way."

Margo walked around the end of the counter and put her arm around Elaine's shoulder.

Elaine dabbed at her eyes with the handkerchief, trying to gain her composure. "Mrs. Fleming, I know this venture is exciting for Dale and for the children, but of course, they're too young to really know about the hardships we may be facing. We had such a good, satisfying, well-organized life in Omaha. Barry and Susan had a good school. All of our family is there, except now, for the five of us. I'm reconciled to the fact that we are on our way to the gold fields, but as you can see, I'm not terribly happy about it." She excused herself and blew her nose into the handkerchief.

Margo said, "You *did* marry Dale for better or for worse, didn't you?"

"I did."

"Well, maybe this 'worse' you're experiencing is going to turn to 'better.'"

"You really think so?"

"I do."

Suddenly, Elaine clapped a palm to the side of her head. "Your reminding me that I married Dale for better or for worse just brought back something else I also vowed—*Whither thou goest, I will go.*"

Margo smiled. "Well, that's what you've done. Why not make the best of it?"

Elaine's eyes brightened. "Yes, I have done that, haven't I? Here I am...on my way with my husband to the Canadian gold fields. Then, Mrs. Fleming, I *am* going to make the best of it. I do want my husband to be happy and content in his gold-mining work, and I'm glad that he wanted the children and me to come with him. Whatever happens—*for richer or for poorer*—I'm supposed to be with Dale, no matter what happens. We still have each other. He's a strong and wonderful husband."

Margo hugged her. "Good for you, Elaine. That's how I feel about Norman, too. He's in a wheelchair, yes, but he's still my support and encouragement in life."

The two women smiled at each other, a bond of friendship between them.

"Elaine, maybe you and Dale are going to become very rich," Margo said.

"I certainly hope so."

FOUR

Late in the afternoon on Wednesday, February 16, a cold, brisk wind was blowing across San Francisco Bay under a clear blue sky—a pleasant change from the normal foggy days at that time of year in the Bay Area.

Forty-one-year-old widow Flora London stood on the docks, watching a big cargo ship sail into the bay and head for the dock where she was standing. Several dock workers were there, prepared to unload the freight the ship was carrying from Japan.

Two husky dock workers were moving past the trim, petite lady. As she pulled the collar of her worn black wool coat up around her face, the two men stopped and smiled at her. One of them said, "Are you sure you're at the right dock, ma'am? This is where cargo ships drop anchor to be unloaded. No passenger ships use these docks in this section."

Flora smiled in return. "I'm aware of that, sir. My son, Jack, is a sailor aboard that ship."

"Oh. Sorry. We just thought you might be expecting to meet someone on a passenger ship."

"That was thoughtful of you. Thanks."

Both men nodded, touched the brims of their caps, and moved on.

As the ship drew nearer, Flora thought of the years of poverty that she and Jack had gone through since he was a teenager, and she was glad he had this well-paying job.

Black billows of smoke swirled out of the ship's two smokestacks as the vessel glided up to the dock, its bell clanging. A thrill of joy filled Flora's heart when she spotted her twenty-two-year-old son standing at the deck railing, and she waved excitedly at him.

Jack London took off his cap and waved it at her. The wind toyed with his thick, dark hair.

The gangplank was now being lowered to the dock, and Flora hurried to where it would touch down. A moment later, Jack was on his way down the gangplank, carrying his sailor's canvas bag of clothing and personal supplies. When he stepped onto the dock, Flora opened her arms to him.

Jack bent low, embraced her, and kissed her cheek. "It's good to see you, Mama."

"Welcome home. I've missed you so much."

As mother and son walked along the lengthy dock toward the ferry that would take them across San Francisco Bay to Oakland, Flora said, "So, what did you think of Japan?"

"Well, it was different than any other place I've been, but I found it quite interesting. I'll tell you some of my experiences with the Japanese people when we get a chance to talk."

"I'll look forward to it. So where will you be sailing to next?"

"Skagway, Alaska."

Flora gasped and gripped his arm with a gloved hand, pulling him to a halt. "Jack, your company doesn't send ships to Alaska."

He cleared his throat. "I know that, Mama. You see, this morning I told the ship captain that I was quitting my sailor job because I'm going up to the Klondike and dig for gold."

Flora closed her eyes and bit her lower lip, then opened them again. "Jack, I thought you had that fool notion out of your head by now. The newspapers report that only a small minority of the gold seekers in Yukon Territory ever hit it big."

"I know, but I've got a strong feeling that I can be in that small minority. I've just *got* to go up there and try it. I have enough money to pay for the trip all the way to Dawson City, according to articles I've read in the newspapers."

"Oh, Jack, how could you do this? Your job has paid you so well. And now, you're going off to Canada with no guarantee that you'll find any gold. I have very little money. If you do this foolish thing, what will happen to me?"

Tears filled Flora's eyes, and she quickly dashed them away with her gloved hands.

"Well, Mama, until I make it big in the gold fields of the Klondike, you'll need to find some extra work. With me gone from home, maybe you could take in some elderly widow as a lodger. That would bring in some money. And maybe one of the hotels or restaurants in Oakland would hire you. You're only forty-one. I'm sure you can make it."

They started walking again.

When Jack realized his mother was not going to comment on his last statement, he said, "Mama, it would only be for a little while. I'll make it big up there in the Klondike within a few months, I just know it. I'll come home with loads of money. You'll never have to work another day in your life, then."

Flora had been so stunned by what she was hearing from her son that she was unable to reply.

Jack laid a hand on her shoulder as they made their way along the dock. "Mama, I haven't meant to upset you, but I've just got to make lots of money so I can take care of you for the rest of your life…and I'll stand a much better chance of getting a good woman for a wife if I'm well-fixed financially."

Flora let a few more seconds go by, then looked up into his eyes and said, "What's happened to your big dream of becoming a novelist? Have you given up on that? Need I remind you that your English teachers told you that because you have such a special way with words, you should pursue a writing career?"

"I haven't forgotten that, Mama, and no, I haven't given up on it. I've given it a lot of thought lately. I feel that I could make it big writing novels, but I need some inspiration. I just can't seem to come up with any good story ideas. I figure up in Yukon Territory I just might come up with some. You know…arduous snow country…wild bears, wolves, and maybe even wild dogs. I plan to take some writing materials along with me. If any good novel ideas pop into my head, I'll write them down. Then when I come back a rich man from mining gold, I can concentrate on my writing career. How does that sound?"

Flora let a few seconds of silence hang in the air, then said, "Son, you'd probably become wealthy a lot sooner if you would just remain a sailor and concentrate on story ideas while you're at sea. They would come to you, I know. Then you could begin your writing career a lot sooner."

They were drawing up to the ferry that they would ride across the bay. Jack said, "Mama, my mind is made up. I'm going up to the Klondike so I can make my fortune. We'll both be better off for it."

Flora said no more as they boarded the ferry.

An hour later, when Flora London and her son reached the Oakland side of the bay, Jack hired a buggy to take them home. When they got there, Jack paid the driver and Flora headed toward the front porch of their weatherworn frame house. The light blue paint was peeling in places. A few scraggly bushes decorated the barren front yard. Flora gazed at the small two-story house, took a deep breath, and squared her slender shoulders. "Well, little house," she said in a low, thin voice, "you've been my home and sheltered me for many years. At least you're paid for, and even though the furniture may be shabby, at least you're clean and neat."

Jack moved swiftly past her, carrying his canvas bag. He dashed up the porch steps, opened the door, and held it open for her. She managed a faint smile as she moved past him and started unbuttoning her coat.

While Flora was hanging her coat on a peg, Jack set the canvas bag down and headed for the kitchen.

A moment later, Flora entered the kitchen and saw her son standing at the cupboard, holding the door open, a puzzled look on his face. "Where are my whiskey bottles?"

"I threw them out right after you left for Japan. You know I don't want liquor in this house."

Jack felt a surge of temper well up inside him, but suppressed it. He closed the cupboard door softly and said, "I'll take my bag up to my room and clean it out."

That evening, when mother and son were finishing their supper, Jack wiped his mouth with a napkin and said, "Mama, I'm going to the Gun Barrel Saloon for a few drinks."

Flora sighed and looked at him across the table. "Son, I'm warning you—as I have many times before—if you go on like this, you'll become an alcoholic."

Jack laughed as he dropped the napkin on the tabletop. "Mama, you needn't worry yourself over my drinking. I can handle my liquor."

With that, he shoved his chair back and headed for the hall door. "I'll be back in a couple of hours."

Flora did not comment. Jack hurried away, and Flora began carrying dishes to the counter, which had a washbowl. While she washed and dried the dishes, tears streamed down her cheeks.

Flora London sat in the small parlor of her home, reading a book by lantern light, when she heard her son's uneven footsteps on the front porch, and the door came open. She looked up at the clock on the wall and noted that it was nearly midnight.

When Jack staggered into the parlor, Flora laid her book down and rose to her feet. "You were only going to be gone a couple of hours," she said, her voice tight. "What happened?"

Jack's eyelids drooped and his head moved unsteadily as he said with slurred tongue, "I met some other guys who're going to the gold fields in the Klondike. We had a good time talking about it." He hiccupped and had to take hold of the back of a straight-backed wooden chair to steady himself.

Flora shook her head. "Shame on you. You're drunk as a skunk. Jack, I'm telling you, if you don't quit drinking, you're going to become a senseless alcoholic."

Jack laughed, looked at his mother through hazy, drooped eyes, and said, "I've told you before, Mama. I c'n handle my liquor." With that, he staggered into the hall, saying he was going up to his bedroom.

She stepped into the hall and observed as he slowly made his way up the narrow staircase, stumbling and falling on almost every step.

When Jack finally reached the top of the stairs, he held onto the wall as he made his way down the hall toward his room. He had to stop every few steps, but finally made it to his bedroom.

He opened the door, closed it behind him, and staggered to the bed by the dim light that came through his window from a street-lamp across the street. Leaning against the foot of the bed, he tried to take off his jacket, but his fumbling fingers wouldn't cooperate. He shuffled around the foot of the bed, dropped on it facedown, and immediately passed out.

Flora ascended the stairs carrying a lantern, and headed down the hall toward her bedroom. When she reached her door, she paused and glanced across the hall at Jack's door. She took a deep breath, crossed the hall, and slowly opened the door. She saw Jack lying fully clothed on the bed.

She could barely breathe. Both hands curled into such hard fists that her fingernails pressed into her palms. With a shaky sigh, she entered the room, moved slowly up to the side of the bed, and looked down at her drunken son for a long moment. She placed the lantern on the small table beside the bed, then leaned over and caressed his flushed face with the back of her hand. Then, with tears running down her cheeks, she went to the closet, picked up a quilt, and covered Jack with it, tucking it around his neck.

She looked down at him for a moment, then picked up the lantern and left the room, closing the door softly behind her.

When Flora doused the lantern in her own room and slid beneath the covers, she broke into sobs and, after a while, finally cried herself to sleep.

The next morning, when Flora had dressed and left her bedroom, she looked across the hall toward Jack's room, noting that the door was open. She moved to the door quickly, and when she looked in, the crumpled quilt lay on the bed.

When she went downstairs to the kitchen, Jack was not there

either, but she found a note on the table. She picked it up and read it:

> Mama, sorry about last night. I'm on my way to the San Francisco Bay docks to buy a ticket to Alaska. Be home soon.
>
> Love, Jack

It was almost noon when Jack London entered the house and went to the kitchen where his mother was cooking soup for lunch.

"Soup's about ready," she said. "I made enough for both of us just in case you came home in time. Ah…did you get your ticket?"

Jack reached into his shirt pocket. "Sure did," he said as he pulled out an envelope and removed the ticket.

Flora glanced at it. "So tell me."

Jack made a weak smile. "Well, I bought a ticket for Skagway, Alaska, on the steamship *Alaska* for March 20."

She nodded, biting her lower lip. "March 20. That's just a little over a month away. You'll be gone before I know it."

He took hold of her shoulders. "But Mama, look at it this way. The sooner I go, the sooner I'll strike gold and make my fortune. Actually, I'll be back before you know it!"

Tears welled up in her eyes and spilled down her cheeks as she hugged him. "I'll miss you, son, but I do hope you strike it big in the Yukon gold fields."

Jack wrapped his arms around her and kissed her tear-stained cheek.

"Mama, I'll come home a rich man, I promise. You'll never have to want for anything again."

Flora looked up into her son's dark brown eyes. "I hope so, son. I sure hope so. Now, you go wash your hands, and I'll get lunch on the table."

On Friday afternoon, February 18, at a rundown house on a small farm just outside of San Leandro, California, ten miles from the west bank of San Francisco Bay, a wagon turned into the yard from the dusty road that ran past the place and drew up at the front porch.

Five men were in the wagon. At the reins was forty-eight-year-old Hank Osborne. Seated next to him was his oldest son, Russell, who had recently turned twenty-seven. In the bed of the wagon were his other sons, T. J., who was twenty-five; Lou, who was twenty-two; and Vernon, who was twenty.

The younger men all had solemn looks on their faces as they followed their weeping father into the house.

Hank led them into the parlor and said, "Sit down, boys."

As the Osborne brothers were choosing chairs to sit on, Hank went to the mantel and picked up a framed photograph of his wife Elsie, whose funeral they had just attended at San Leandro's cemetery. He looked at the smiling woman in the picture, kissed it, then replaced it on the mantel.

Hank went and sat in his favorite chair and ran his gaze over the somber faces of his sons. "Well, boys, now that your ailing mother is gone, and there's no need for us to be here any longer, we need to make our plans to go to Yukon Territory and get in on the gold strike."

"Nothing to stop us now," Lou said.

Hank and his sons discussed the newspaper articles they had read lately, which had declared the cost of ship tickets to Dyea, Alaska, plus the food, clothing, and equipment the Canadian government insisted they have with them before they would be allowed in to dig for gold. There would also be the cost of getting to Dawson City from Dyea. When they totaled it up, it came to about twelve hundred dollars per man.

Russell sighed and looked at his father. "We've gotta come up with six thousand dollars, Pa. How are we gonna do that?"

"I've been giving it a lot of thought, boys, and I've got the solution worked out."

T. J. moved to the edge of his chair. "Well, tell us, Pa!"

"Since the Wells Fargo company is now using armored wagons to transfer money between banks all over the bay area, we'll hold up one of those wagons and take all the cash they're carrying. Certainly there'll be more than six thousand dollars on any armored wagon. I'm sure we'll have more than enough cash to get us to Dawson City."

Vernon playfully punched Ernie on the shoulder. "Hey, Ernie, we're gonna get rich in the Klondike!"

Lou and T. J. laughed and shook hands, with T.J saying, "We'll all be millionaires!"

All five men whooped it up for a few minutes. When they settled down, Russell said to the others, "You guys know my friend Billy Hawkins, who works on the docks. Well, I ran into Billy when I was in San Francisco on Wednesday. Right after Ma had died. I told him about Ma, and about our plans to go to Yukon Territory. He told me that all Alaska-bound ships out of San Francisco are booked up through March 18. He said the *Alaska*, which sails March 20, was only about a third booked. That was Wednesday. There's probably still room for more passengers."

"We need to pull our holdup right away so we can buy tickets on the *Alaska*," Hank said. "I've had this holdup on my mind a lot lately. Let me tell you how we're gonna do it."

FIVE

As darkness fell on Tuesday evening, February 22, Hank Osborne and his four sons were in their wagon, moving along a country road through a wooded area some five miles south of San Francisco.

Russell and his father were sitting on the seat with Russell handling the reins. Hank pointed up ahead to an opening in the thick stand of trees several yards from the road. "Pull in there, Russell. We'll camp in that open area for the night."

Some twenty minutes later, the five men sat around a fire while their food cooked and the coffee was heating in the pot.

The darkness deepened as they began to eat, and the campfire blazed brighter. Hank said, "When we've finished eating, we'll go over our plan for tomorrow one more time. I want to be sure you boys have everything locked into your minds so we pull off this robbery without a hitch."

Night was on them completely by the time they had finished their meal. Hank laid his tin plate aside, drained his coffee cup, and noted that the stars were twinkling in the black sky overhead. There was no moon.

"Well, boys," Hank said, "since we have carefully checked

out the daily schedule of the armored wagon we're gonna hit, we know it will arrive at the Pacific Bank in downtown San Francisco right around one thirty tomorrow afternoon. They'll load it up with moneybags at the Pacific Bank, then go to the California State Bank a few blocks south. Then it'll head south out of San Francisco for the ten-mile jaunt to San Bruno, where it'll stop at the American Bank there." Hank chuckled. "But we're gonna be right here to stop that armored wagon and rob 'em of every moneybag they've got."

Hank and his sons had a good laugh, then Hank said, "We'll go into San Francisco in time to make dead sure the wagon arrives at the Pacific Bank on schedule. Once we see it there, we'll head back out here. When we pulled in, I noticed a large dead tree over there. When we know the armored wagon is coming this way, we'll drag that dead tree out onto the road and block their path. We'll hide in the brush close to the road, wearing our masks and robes. When they stop, we'll get the drop on 'em, and the money will be ours."

"So what'll we do so they can't follow us, Pa?" Lou said.

"We'll turn their horse team loose and tie the driver and the guards up inside the wagon. We'll be long gone before someone comes along to let 'em out."

"Good plan, Pa," said Vernon. "We hadn't talked about that part, yet."

"So then, Pa, we'll drive the wagon straight home and count the money, right?" Russell said.

"We most certainly will!"

Vernon's eyes sparkled with the firelight reflected in them. "Then we'll go to the docks and buy our tickets for Alaska!"

Russell laughed. "We're gonna get rich in those gold fields up in the Klondike!"

Hank took a deep breath. "Right now, we'd better get these

dishes washed and put out the fire so we can get us a good night's sleep. Big day tomorrow!"

The next day, under a bright sun that shone down from a partly cloudy sky, Hank Osborne and his sons drove into downtown San Francisco and parked their wagon at the hitch rail across the street from the Pacific Bank. It was just after one o'clock.

Hank pointed to a spot between two buildings a few steps away. "Let's go over there, boys. We can watch and nobody will notice us."

The Osbornes made their way to the shaded spot and quietly watched the street as vehicles and pedestrians passed by.

At one thirty, they saw the Wells Fargo armored wagon appear a block away, moving slowly toward the bank.

When the wagon drew up in front of the Pacific Bank, the driver and one armed guard climbed down from the driver's seat, and another armed guard hopped out through the door at the rear of the wagon. Each man wore a uniform with Wells Fargo written on the back of his jacket.

The Osbornes watched the scene as the two armed guards entered the bank while the driver carried a bucket from the wagon to a water trough a few yards away, then returned to the two horses that were hitched to the wagon and gave each of them a drink.

Moments later, the two Wells Fargo guards emerged from the bank, carrying canvas moneybags toward the armored wagon, accompanied by a bank guard, who kept his hand on the handle of his holstered revolver, his eyes sweeping the area cautiously.

Lou Osborne chuckled and said, "They're really careful, ain't they, Pa?"

"Sure are," Hank said, "but we won't have that bank guard to deal with when we rob the wagon. We'll be out in the country."

They watched as the Wells Fargo men placed the moneybags in the rear of the enclosed wagon, and the bank guard said something to them, then headed back inside the bank.

Suddenly, three men who had seemed to be casually standing on the boardwalk dashed up to them, guns drawn, and one of them barked, "We want those moneybags!"

The Wells Fargo guard who was about to climb into the rear of the wagon stiffened when he saw two of the robbers holding guns on the driver and the guard with him. The third robber pointed his gun at the guard at the rear of the wagon, stepped toward him, and snapped, "You heard what I said, mister! We want those moneybags!" He then turned to his accomplices and said, "Ralph, let Todd keep his gun on those two! Come here and help me get the bags out of the wagon!"

Ralph drew up and said to the guard, "Gimme your gun!"

The guard pulled his revolver from its holster and handed it to the robber.

"Now, open that door and stand back!" Ralph said.

The guard opened the door, and suddenly a third Wells Fargo guard who had been in the rear of the wagon all along had a double-barreled shotgun aimed at the two robbers. Before they could react, two shots were fired, one right after the other, and the two robbers went down.

The robber named Todd started to turn and run, but another shot rang out, and he dropped to the dusty street with a bullet in the center of his back. He didn't move. His open eyes stared sightlessly at the sky. The bank guard stood just outside the bank door, his gun smoking.

People on the street closed in on the scene when they saw that the robbers were all dead, and a man hollered that he would run and get the sheriff.

Across the street, a dry-mouthed Hank Osborne spoke in a low voice. "If that wagon goes ahead on its route, boys, we'll still get our loot. Let's see what happens."

The Osbornes stayed in the shadowed area between the two buildings and watched as the sheriff and two deputies arrived and were told the story by the Wells Fargo men and the bank guard. The bodies of the dead robbers were picked up and placed in a nearby wagon, and the man who owned the wagon told the sheriff he would take the bodies to the nearest undertaker.

The lawmen talked with the Wells Fargo men for a few minutes, then the Osbornes heard one of them say they would go ahead and resume their route.

"All right, boys, let's go," Hank said. "Just walk slow to the wagon so we don't draw attention to ourselves. Pretty soon, that loot will be in our hands."

Russell untied the reins from the hitching post while his father and brothers climbed into the wagon, then made his way up onto the driver's seat next to Hank and slowly drove the wagon away.

Soon they reached the spot along the road where they had spent the night. They pulled into the woods, and when they were out of sight from the road, they hopped out of the wagon. Each man reached into a box in the bed of the wagon and took out a black robe and a hooded mask. When they were in their robes and wearing the hoods with only their eyes showing, they went to the side of the road and hunkered down in the brush next to a ditch.

The only traffic on the road was a farm wagon that came along a few minutes later, heading toward San Francisco. When it was almost out of sight, Hank said, "Okay, boys. Let's get the dead tree laid across the road. That armored wagon will be here soon, for sure."

Moments later, just as they had returned to the brush, they saw the Wells Fargo armored wagon coming down the road.

The wagon drew near the place where the tree blocked its path, and Hank and his sons could hear the conversation between the driver and the guard next to him. The guard said something the Osbornes couldn't make out, but they understood the driver as he said, "We can't go around it because of those ditches on both sides of the road. I don't like the looks of this."

Even as the driver was saying that, he and the guard were suddenly facing five men wearing hooded masks and black robes and holding guns on them. One of five commanded them to throw their guns down and raise their hands in the air. They immediately obeyed.

Russell Osborne, who had made the command, stepped up close on one side, as did Lou on the other side, and they pointed cocked revolvers at the two men on the driver's seat. Russell said, "One move and you're dead. Understand?"

When Hank, T. J., and Vernon reached the rear, Hank shouted, "Hey, you two inside! We know you're both in there! Come out with your hands up, or we'll kill those two on the driver's seat! We've got 'em covered!"

Inside, the two guards peered through the curtained windows on the sides of the enclosed section, then the rear door came unlatched, and the two solemn-faced guards came out with their empty hands held above their heads.

Their guns were removed from their holsters, and they were forced to move to the front of the wagon, where Russell and Lou now had the other two men standing on the ground.

While Russell and Lou held the guards and driver at gunpoint, Hank, T. J., and Vernon took all the moneybags out of the armored wagon and placed them in the bushes alongside the road.

T. J. and Vernon then unhitched the horses from the wagon and shouted and slapped them on the rumps, sending them galloping away, dragging the reins behind them. The guards and driver were then tied up inside the wagon so they could not see out the windows, and the door was closed.

As Hank and his sons moved toward the bushes to pick up the moneybags, Russell looked both ways on the road and said, "Worked perfectly, Pa. I'm sure glad no one came along while we were pulling this job."

They picked up the moneybags and dashed to their team and wagon. They tossed the moneybags into the rear of the wagon, stuffed the robes and masks back into the box, hopped in the wagon, and with Hank at the reins, drove away hurriedly.

When the Osbornes reached their farm, they put the horses and wagon inside the barn, then went to a spot in an open area and burned the robes and masks. Once the fire was reduced to ashes, they went into the house and counted the money. There was just over twenty thousand dollars…more than enough to get them to Dawson City.

The next day, the San Francisco newspapers reported the robbery of the Wells Fargo armored wagon, telling how much money was stolen. The reports included the fact that the five robbers wore black hooded masks and robes, that they made a clean getaway, and that there were no leads as to who the robbers might be.

Hank and his sons had a good laugh, then Russell and T. J. went to the docks on the San Francisco side of the bay and purchased five tickets, making reservations on the ship *Alaska* for March 20.

On Friday, February 25, at the Canadian Northwest Mounted Police post one mile south of Dawson City, Yukon Territory, it was snowing hard and a stiff wind was blowing. There were already eight inches of snow on the ground.

A young man rode up in front of the Mountie post and dismounted. As he started toward the door of the log building, he noticed two dogsleds rushing by and paused to look at them.

One of the dog teams was made up of Siberian huskies with a mixture of colors. The other was solid black Newfoundlands.

The men driving the sleds waved as they blinked against the snow that pelted their faces. The young man smiled and waved back, then crossed the porch and entered the building. The wind blew snow in around him, and he quickly closed the door.

Seated at a desk just inside the door was a man in a Mountie uniform. He looked up at the young man and said, "May I help you?"

"Sir, my name is Virgil Woodring. I live in Dawson City."

The Mountie rose to his feet and extended his right hand across the desk. "Glad to meet you. I'm Corporal Harold Mickelsen. What can I do for you, Mr. Woodring?"

"I know that applicants who want to join the Northwest Mounted Police must be between twenty-two and forty years of age."

"That's right."

"Well, sir, I just turned twenty-two on February 19, and I'd like to join up."

Mickelsen nodded. "All right. I'll take you to the post's chief officer, Captain Lee Jensen. Come with me."

They stepped into a narrow hallway, and on the door of the first office on their right, painted letters told Virgil this was the office of Captain Lee Jensen, the post's chief officer.

Corporal Mickelsen tapped on the door, and a deep male voice inside said, "Yes?"

The corporal said loud enough to be heard, "Sir, I have a

young man here who wants to join the Mounties."

"Well, bring him in!"

Mickelsen opened the door, ushered Virgil Woodring into the office, and introduced him to the captain. Jensen rose to his feet, gave the young man a warm handshake across his desk, and told him to sit down. Corporal Mickelsen excused himself and left the office, closing the door behind him.

The captain sat down behind his desk and said, "Well, Virgil, let me point out first that applicants who want to become Mounties must be at least twenty-two years of age. I assume Corporal Mickelsen told you this."

"He did, sir, but I already knew that. I turned twenty-two on February 19."

"All right. Let me point out next that, to be a Mountie, a man must be able-bodied, of thoroughly sound constitution, and must produce certificates of exemplary character and sobriety."

Virgil smiled. "I can do that, Captain. There are responsible citizens in Dawson City besides my parents who know me well."

"Good. Next, applicants must understand the care and management of horses and be able to ride well."

"I am also aware of that, sir. All of my life, my father has had horses. As I grew up, Dad taught me everything I would need to know about them. I've been riding them since I was just a boy."

Jensen smiled. "Well, so far, so good. Are you aware that the term of engagement for a Mountie is five years?"

"Yes, sir. I've talked to Mounties since I turned fifteen, asking questions, and they've always been kind enough to answer them for me."

Jensen opened a desk drawer and drew out a brochure. "This brochure gives the history of the Northwest Mounted Police, Virgil. I suggest you read it as soon as possible. In order to become a Mountie, you must make your formal application at the Northwest Mounted Police Yukon Territory office at Fort Selkirk. Do you know where that's located?"

"Yes, sir. I've been in that area a few times."

"Good. You'll need to meet with the superintendent, Lieutenant Colonel Sam Steele."

"I've heard his name. I wasn't aware that he was superintendent in Yukon Territory. Isn't he rather famous as a Mountie?"

"That he is. In fact, I'll say that Lieutenant Colonel Steele is the *most* famous member of the Northwest Mounted Police. He's been a member of the force since it was formed in 1873, twenty-five years ago. During all these years, Colonel Steele built himself a reputation in gun battles with outlaws and in tracking down fugitives from the law. Because of his record, he played a big part in establishing the Mounties' motto that they "*always get their man.*"

"I hadn't heard that," Virgil said.

"Well, you have now. You see, when the Northwest Mounted Police force in the Yukon needed a new superintendent just three weeks ago, the authorities at the main office in Winnipeg, Manitoba, quickly appointed Lieutenant Colonel Steele to the position. In his short tenure as superintendent, he's already shown himself worthy of the position. He's a fine man."

"Sounds like it, sir. I'll look forward to meeting him." Virgil rose from the chair. "Thank you so much for your help. I'll make the trip to Fort Selkirk as soon as this snowstorm is over."

Captain Jensen stood up and once again extended his right hand across the desk. As Virgil met his grip, Jensen said, "You've impressed me, young man. I have no doubt you'll become a Mountie. In fact, I'd like to have you serving right here at the post."

"Well, sir, we'll see how it works out. I certainly would like to work under your command."

Virgil stepped out of the captain's office, and when he entered the area where Corporal Mickelsen's desk was, he stopped and said, "Thank you, Corporal Mickelsen, for helping me."

The corporal stood up. "My pleasure. So I assume you still want to become a Mountie?"

"I sure do. As I told Captain Jensen, as soon as this snow-storm is over, I'll be going to Fort Selkirk to talk to Lieutenant Colonel Steele."

"Well, I hope it works out for you. I believe you'd make a good one."

The telegraph ticker on a small table behind Mickelsen's desk began to click. The corporal turned to it, then glanced over his shoulder at the young hopeful.

"I'll see you later," Virgil said, and went out the door into the storm.

SIX

Corporal Harold Mickelsen smiled to himself as he watched Virgil Woodring move out the door, then turned back and picked up a pencil. He translated the Morse code and carefully wrote down the message. When it was complete, he stood up, paper in hand. He hurried to the chief officer's office and tapped on the door. "Captain, I have a telegram for you from Lieutenant Colonel Sam Steele at Fort Selkirk."

"Come in!"

The corporal opened the door and moved up to Captain Lee Jensen's desk. Handing him the sheet of paper, he said, "It's about a missing man the lieutenant colonel wants us to try to find."

Mickelsen sat down in the chair that faced the desk and waited for Jensen to read it.

Jensen learned that Colonel Steele had just received a wire from Sheriff Lance Beckett of San Francisco County, California. A woman in San Francisco named Martha Bray had come into Beckett's office to report that her husband, Weldon Bray, left home on October 14 last year to go to Dawson City and the gold fields. She has not heard from him since.

The American Shipping Company, whose ship he was on, told her that Weldon Bray definitely arrived in Dyea, Alaska, with the other passengers.

Jensen read on and learned that Mrs. Bray had a nineteen-year-old daughter, and both of them were upset that they have not heard from Weldon. They feared he might be dead. Sheriff Beckett was asking for help from the Northwest Mounted Police. Colonel Steele wanted Captain Jensen to have his men investigate and see if anyone in Dawson City or in the gold fields knew Weldon Bray.

The captain laid the paper on the desk before him and looked up at Corporal Mickelsen. "Wire Lieutenant Colonel Steele back, Harold, and tell him I'll get right on it."

"Yes, sir. I'll do it right now."

"Before you do, will you go to the barracks and tell Cam Shields and Seth Murray to come see me right away?"

"Certainly, sir. You're going to give them this assignment?"

"Yes."

As Mickelsen hurried away, Captain Lee Jensen picked up the written message and read it through again, carefully. He had just finished and was laying the paper down when there was a knock on his door. A voice said, "Captain, it's Shields and Murray."

"Come on in!" Jensen smiled as Sergeant Cam Shields and Corporal Seth Murray entered the office. "Sit down, gentlemen. I've got an important assignment for you. Did Corporal Mickelsen tell you about the telegram I just received from Lieutenant Colonel Steele at Fort Selkirk?"

"No, sir," Shields said. "He just said you have an assignment for us, and that you would explain it."

"All right. Let me read this telegram to you, then I'll explain what I want you to do."

When both Mounties had heard the message, Captain Jensen

assigned them to search for Weldon Bray. "First thing," said the captain, "is to go to the Dawson City Bank. Just about every gold seeker in town has an account at the bank."

Shields nodded. "Good idea, sir. If the bank doesn't know him, we'll visit all the stores and shops in town. Maybe they will."

"Then if you still don't find anyone who knows Bray, you'll have to go to the gold fields and ask around there. If he's out there, somebody will know him. And…when you find him, bring him to me right away."

In Dawson City, the bank president shook his head after searching through the files. "Sorry, gentlemen. We have no account for a Weldon Bray."

Shields and Murray thanked him, then stepped back outside into the biting wind and swirling snow. They went from store to store, asking the owners if they knew Weldon Bray.

After inquiring in thirteen stores, Shields and Bray had found no one who knew a man by that name. They entered the hardware store, and threading their way among customers, stepped up to the counter where the proprietor, silver-haired William Donaldson, was doing some paperwork between customers.

Donaldson greeted the Mounties with a smile. "Some particular item you're looking for?"

"Not this time, Mr. Donaldson," Shields said. "This time we're looking for a man."

"In here?"

Corporal Murray chuckled. "Well, not exactly. We just need to know if you're acquainted with a gold seeker from California who's been here since last October."

A few feet from the counter, a male customer in dusty clothing was looking at shovels. His ears perked up when he heard the

Mounties say they were looking for a man who was a gold seeker from California.

When the customer heard William Donaldson ask the name of the man the Mounties were seeking, he stiffened as the sergeant replied, "Man's name is Weldon Bray."

The man took a sharp breath, coughed, and almost dropped the shovel he was examining. He saw William look at him.

"Hey, Roger…?" William said.

"Yes, William?" Roger Whitson said, gripping the shovel handle to keep his hands from shaking.

"You've been working in the gold fields for a while. You know a fella named Weldon Bray?"

Roger shook his head. "Nope. Never heard of him."

So Martha and Livia have the Mounties looking for me. Well, they'll never be able to find Weldon Bray, not with this heavy beard to help disguise my face. When the Mounties report that they didn't find me, my wife and daughter will think I'm dead. I'm free of them, and I plan to keep it that way. I'm not sharing my gold with them or anybody else!

Roger Whitson went back to looking at shovels, but his ears were open to what was being said at the counter. He heard the Mounties tell the store owner about the wire from San Francisco County's Sheriff Lance Beckett.

William Donaldson said, "Maybe something happened to Bray on his way north from Dyea."

"Maybe, maybe not," said Sergeant Cam Shields. "We've still got to ask around town, and if no one here knows him, Corporal Murray and I will have to do a search in the gold fields." He then looked at the man who was still examining shovels. "Ah…Roger…?"

Roger Whitson met his gaze. "Yes?"

"If you should happen to meet this Weldon Bray, would you

come to the Mountie post outside of town and let Captain Lee Jensen know? It's very important."

"Sure will, Sergeant."

"Thanks." Then Shields turned back to the proprietor. "And I ask the same of you, William."

"You can count on it, Sergeant."

"Good. Well, Corporal Murray, you and I need to continue our search."

Roger Whitson waited till the Mounties were gone, then bought a new shovel and a new pick for his gold mining. Outside in the icy wind, Roger walked up to his wagon, laid the new tools in the wagon bed, and climbed up onto the seat. As he put the team into motion and headed out of town, he was sweating in spite of the cold.

He thought back to last October when he left Martha and Livia and sailed north to Alaska, intending to go to the Yukon gold fields. His wife and daughter didn't know it as they waved to him from the docks when the ship pulled away, but he was not coming back. He was tired of being a husband and father, and was going to build a new life for himself. Upon arriving at Dawson City, Weldon Bray registered for his claim site as Roger Whitson. After his first good strike, he opened an account at the bank in Dawson City in his new name.

While driving the wagon eastward on the winding snow-laden road, Roger assured himself that once the Northwest Mounted Police informed Martha that her husband could not be found, she would give up on ever seeing him again. She would figure that he had died and his body was never found. He had left Martha and Livia enough money in the bank to last them a year or so. By that time, Livia would be married to Nate Clark, and the two of them would take care of Martha.

Roger arrived at his claim site in just over an hour. He put the new tools in his small tool shed, unhitched the team, and placed them in his minuscule corral, then went inside the cabin he had built.

The fire in the stove was still burning a little. Roger tossed in a couple more logs, then removed his coat and hat. The day before, he had taken a load of gold nuggets to the assayer's office in Dawson City and had ordered the gold made into coins. Before going to the hardware store on this day, he had taken the coins to the bank and made a deposit.

He took the bank deposit receipt out of his shirt pocket and smiled at the amount: $20,200.00.

"Weldon, ol' boy, you're doing all right. You now have over sixty thousand dollars in the bank." He chuckled. "Well…Roger Whitson now has over sixty thousand in the bank. You'll soon be a rich man. And best of all, you'll have it all to yourself!"

In San Francisco on Saturday morning, February 26, Livia Bray was mopping the kitchen floor of their two-story frame house while her mother was upstairs putting clean linen on the beds.

As Livia was wringing out the mop for the last time, she happened to glance at the calendar on the kitchen wall. All twelve months of 1898 were in view. She moved up closer to the calendar, focused on Saturday, April 9, and made a happy sigh. She looked down at the engagement ring on her left hand, then closed her eyes and said, "Oh, Nate, only six weeks and I'll be *Mrs. Nate Clark!*"

Suddenly there was a knock at the front door. Livia set the mop down, leaned the handle against the wall, and hurried up the hall to answer it.

When she opened the door, she found her close friend, Nadine Ryerson, standing on the porch. The two of them had graduated from high school together the previous year.

Livia could tell by the look in Nadine's eyes that something was troubling her. Smiling, she said, "Hello, Nadine! Come in."

When Nadine stepped through the door, Livia closed it, then hugged her. With her arms around Nadine, she could feel her body trembling. Easing back, Livia gripped her friend's shoulders and looked into her eyes. "What's wrong?"

Nadine bit her lower lip. "I...I need to talk to you, Livia. It...it's very important."

"Take off your coat and scarf. Let's go into the kitchen. Mom's working upstairs. There's a fire in the stove, and I'll make some tea. We can sit down, have some tea, and talk."

The floor of the kitchen was dry now, and the two young women moved toward the round oak table.

"Sit down, honey," Livia said. Nadine pulled out a chair and eased onto it, and Livia placed the teakettle on the stove. When she turned around and looked at Nadine, she saw tears running down her cheeks.

Livia sat down next to her friend, took both of Nadine's hands in her own, and said, "What is it?"

Nadine took a deep, shaky breath, brushed away the tears from her cheeks, and her voice was filled with anguish as she said, "I wish I didn't have to bring this to you, but I'm your friend, and you need to know what's going on."

"Going on with whom?"

Nadine sniffed and swallowed hard. "Nate."

"Nate? What about Nate?"

"Three weeks ago, I saw him with his old high school sweetheart, Matilda Hornbeck, in a restaurant in Daly City, eating together. Neither of them saw me."

Livia's face lost color. She forced herself to take deep, even breaths.

Nadine wiped a palm across her eyes. "I tried not to let it bother me. I told myself that Nate and Matilda are just friends from their high school days. But a few days after I saw them in Daly City, I ran into Sally Denton in downtown San Francisco. Sally told me that one night quite recently, she happened to be looking out the parlor window and saw Nate and Matilda arrive at the Hornbeck house in Nate's buggy. Sally watched as Nate walked Matilda to the door and kissed her good-night. She told me how shocked she was, knowing that Nate is engaged to marry *you*."

Livia stared at Nadine. Cold, white fury was in her eyes. Her lips were pressed into a thin line.

Nadine shook her head. "I didn't want to be the one to tell you this and see your heart break. But…last night I saw Nate and Matilda on Fulton Street, walking together, holding hands. That was all I could take. I had to come and tell you what Nate is doing."

Livia sat wringing her hands, which were now clasped in her lap. All at once, her features turned red.

"No! No, it can't be! Nadine, how could you make up such a story about the man I love? You know it isn't true! Nate would never do this to me!"

Nadine reached out and grasped her arms. "Livia, I'm not making this up. Why would I do that? I know you're upset, but please believe me. I'm telling you the truth! Go talk to Sally. She'll tell you what she saw. Oh, honey, I didn't want to hurt you this way, but I couldn't let it go on without your knowing about it."

Livia laid her head on her folded arms atop the table and broke into uncontrollable sobs

Nadine bent over her and put an arm around her shoulders. "I know how much this hurts you, Livia. I would rather take a beating than to have been the one to tell you, but I couldn't just stand by and let you go on blindly in this horrible situation. I don't know what's in Nate's mind, but I couldn't let you marry a man who is already unfaithful to you. I'm so sorry, Livia."

Slowly the sobbing ceased, and Livia raised her head. Through her tears, she looked deeply into her friend's compassionate eyes. Her cheeks were still shiny from weeping, and her lips were trembling. In a barely audible voice, she said, "I'm sorry I accused you of lying to me, Nadine. Please forgive me. I know you would never do that to me. I…I just can't understand how Nate could be so two-faced. But thank you for being honest with me, though it hurt you to do it. I'd rather know now than after I'd married him."

A fresh rush of sobs convulsed her again. "How could he do this to me?" she wailed, and jumped up from her chair, clenching her fists. "How? He told me he was over Matilda! Our wedding date is just six weeks away!"

Nadine gathered her weeping friend into her arms. "Go ahead and let it all out, honey. I'm here for you, and together we'll get you through this."

At that moment, Martha came into the kitchen, looked at her daughter, then at Nadine. "What has her so upset?"

Nadine started to reply, but Livia took a trembling breath and looked at her mother. "I'll tell you, Mama."

While Martha listened, Livia told her every detail of what she had just learned from Nadine. Martha could only stare at Livia with a blank look on her face.

"Every word of it is true, Mrs. Bray," Nadine said.

The veins stood out sharply on Martha's temples. "That lowdown skunk! How could he do this to my daughter? Somebody ought to beat him to a pulp!"

Livia wiped tears from her eyes. "Mama, you remember that Nate and I are supposed to have Sunday dinner tomorrow with his parents. When he comes to pick me up, I'm going to confront him and break the engagement."

The next morning, after spending a restless night with more weeping, Livia threw the covers back and sat up on the edge of the bed. Her face was drawn and gray and her eyes were puffy, but a fierce determination had taken control of her. "I don't need the likes of Nate Clark in my life. I'd rather be an old maid than marry a two-timer like him."

As Livia thought about the beautiful wedding they had planned, and all the plans they had made for a happy life together, tears once again cascaded down her cheeks, splashing onto her tightly clasped hands resting in her lap.

Her bedroom door opened, and Livia looked up through her tears as her mother stepped in and said, "Did you get any sleep at all, honey?"

Livia sniffed, palmed tears from her cheeks, and nodded. "A little bit, Mama."

Martha went to her, wrapped her arms around her, and said, "I'm so sorry you've been hurt like this."

Livia hugged her in return. "I'll get over it, Mama."

Martha eased back and looked into her eyes. "You want some breakfast? I have some pancakes on the stove."

Livia stood to her feet. "I really don't have any appetite, but I know I need some food in my stomach. I'll wash my face and come to the kitchen in my robe."

"All right, honey. I'll get the table set."

When it was almost noon, Livia was sitting in the parlor, waiting for Nate to arrive. She had asked her mother to let her handle the situation on her own, so Martha was down the hall in the sewing room.

Livia was on the verge of tears again when she looked out the parlor window and saw Nate drive up in his buggy. She took a couple of deep breaths, rose to her feet, and said, "Well, this is it."

She heard Nate's footsteps on the porch stairs as she headed into the hall with her shoulders back and her head held high. The knock came, and steeling herself, Livia opened the door.

With a smile on his face, Nate Clark stepped through the door and started to fold Livia into his arms. Her face turned stonelike as she jumped back and snapped, "Don't you touch me, you two-timing snake!"

Nate's eyes bulged. "W-what are you talking about?"

"Don't put on that innocent look for me, Nate! I know about you and Matilda!"

Nate licked his lips and shook his head. "There's nothing between me and Matilda."

Livia's eyes flashed. "Oh, no? Well, friends of mine have seen the two of you together several times, and one friend even saw you kissing!"

A guilty look came into Nate's eyes. He cleared his throat nervously. "Livia, I was only seeing her because of what we were to each other in the past. I wanted to know for sure how I felt about her. I wanted to make sure I was in love with *you*. And now I know I am absolutely in love with you. I want to marry you now more than ever."

Livia pulled off her engagement ring, threw it into his face, and screamed, "Well, it's too late now!"

The ring had struck his cheek and fallen to the floor. He looked down where it lay on the carpet, then met her fiery gaze again. He started to say something, but she cut him off. "Get out!

Get out of this house and out of my life! If I never see you again, it'll be too soon!"

Nate wheeled and passed through the door, which still stood open. As he reached the porch steps, he flinched when he heard the door slam.

SEVEN

In the sewing room, Martha Bray heard her daughter's angry voice as she spoke to Nate Clark at the front door of the house. She could not distinguish the words, but Livia was definitely holding nothing back. Martha shoved her chair back from the sewing table, stepped to the door of the room, and opened it. She heard Livia snap, "Get out! Get out of this house and out of my life! If I never see you again, it'll be too soon!"

Biting her lips, Martha stepped into the hall just as she heard the front door slam. She saw Livia turn around, lean her back against the door, her head lowered and her eyes closed.

Martha headed toward her.

Livia felt a sob come from somewhere deep inside her, and the heart that she had so willingly given to Nate Clark broke into a million pieces. The sob came out and turned into a wail. Livia was surprised when she felt her mother's arms wrap around her. Through her tears, she looked into Martha's eyes and another wail came out.

Martha held her tight and said, "Livia, honey, don't let this tear you up. It'll be all right, you'll see."

But Livia wailed again and broke into sobs.

Martha held her tight. "Go ahead, honey. Cry it out. All of it."

In a few more minutes, the sobbing eased and the tears were coming slower. Martha guided Livia into the parlor and eased her onto a settee. She sat down beside her, taking Livia's trembling hands into her own. "Sweetheart, I know this hurts, but it's not the end of the world. Believe me, you'll get over this hurt eventually."

Livia nodded and took a deep breath.

Letting go with one hand, Martha reached into her dress pocket, took out a handkerchief, and wiped the last of the tears from her daughter's face. "One day, honey, that right young man will come into your life."

Livia brushed a lock of blond hair from her forehead, stared off into space, and half whispered, "That right young man." She then looked at her mother. "Yes, Mama. That right young man. It's best that I found out what kind of man Nate is before I married him. The *right* young man will love me as he ought to. He will treat me good, and he'll be true to me."

"Let's go into the kitchen, dear. A nice cup of hot tea will help calm your nerves."

Livia managed a slight smile. "All right."

Together, mother and daughter entered the warm, sunny kitchen. Martha told Livia to sit down at the table, and busied herself making the tea. When it was done, and each of them was sipping from a steaming cup, they looked at each other across the table.

Livia said, "You know, Mama, you may be right. This tea does make a person feel better. It's doing that for me, as well as dissolving the cold lump in my heart."

Martha smiled and reached toward Livia. "I've told you so all along, haven't I?" she said, patting her daughter's hand.

c√ɔ

A few days passed.

On the cold, windy Wednesday afternoon of March 2, Martha Bray was using a feather duster on the furniture and the mantel in the parlor when there was a knock at the front door. Laying the duster on a small table, she hurried into the hall, and the knock was repeated as she stepped up to the door.

Martha pulled the door open and her eyes widened. "Well, hello, Sheriff Beckett. Please come in."

Sheriff Lance Beckett stepped into the foyer, took off his hat, and hung it on a wall peg. As he was removing his coat, he looked around. "Is Livia here?"

"No, sir. She's cleaning a house a few blocks away at the moment."

"I was hoping to get to talk to both of you."

Martha's eyes brightened. "Do you have some good news from the Klondike about Weldon?"

He reached inside his coat pocket and took out a yellow envelope. "Not really *good* news, but I need to tell you what's in this telegram."

"Let's go into the parlor and sit down."

Martha led him into the parlor, and they sat down only a few feet apart, facing each other.

Beckett held up the yellow envelope. "This came from Northwest Mounted Police superintendent, Lieutenant Colonel Sam Steele, at Fort Silkirk. He says in the telegram that he contacted Captain Lee Jensen at the Dawson City Northwest Mounted Police post, as I told you he would."

"Yes."

"Colonel Steele told Captain Jensen about your concern for your husband's whereabouts, so the captain sent two Mounties in search of Weldon. They started in Dawson City, but found no one who knew Weldon Bray, or had ever heard of him. They then went to the gold fields, but again could find no one who knew your husband, nor anyone who had ever heard of him."

A look of despair was on Martha's face.

The sheriff leaned forward in the chair. "But Colonel Steele also says in here that there are now some six thousand gold seekers in the gold fields east of Dawson City, with more arriving almost every day. He said there is no way the Mounties could talk to everyone, and they may have simply missed your husband."

"You mean there's still hope that my husband is in the gold fields," Martha said.

Beckett nodded and smiled. "Yes, ma'am. There is still hope. When I said I didn't really have *good* news, I meant that I couldn't say he had been found…but it's still not *bad* news because he could very well be there."

She formed a thin smile. "I understand."

"Mrs. Bray, I could wire Colonel Steele back and ask if he would keep some Mounties looking for Weldon, but I know the Mountie force is already short on men. It would be asking too much."

Martha wiped tears from her eyes, and a new determination welled up in her heart. "Tell you what, Sheriff. I know my chances may not be real good, but I'm going to take Livia up there to Yukon Territory. I've got to find out whether Weldon is dead or alive."

The sheriff scratched at an ear. "Are you aware of the cost of getting from San Francisco all the way to Dawson City?"

"I am. I know approximately how much money Weldon was going to put out to get there, and I've read the figures in the newspapers. Livia and I have enough money to make the trip.

We've *got* to do it, Sheriff, since there is a chance we can find him alive and well."

Beckett noted the gleam of hope in the woman's eyes. He rose from the chair and said, "Well, I wish you the very best in your search, ma'am."

Martha stood up. "Thank you."

Beckett shook her hand. "You're some woman, I'll tell you that! Most women would never make that trip."

"Well, I can tell you right now that Livia is that kind of woman, too."

He smiled. "Again, I wish you the very best in your endeavor to find your husband, ma'am. If there's anything else I can do for you, please let me know."

"Of course."

"So you and your daughter will be going to Canada soon, I assume."

"As soon as possible, Sheriff."

"All right. Tell you what. I'll wire Mountie Captain Lee Jensen in Dawson City and tell him you'll be coming. When you arrive in Dawson City, go to the Mountie post and check in with Captain Jensen for any news he might have about your husband."

"We'll do that. Thank you, Sheriff Beckett. You've been most kind, and I appreciate all that you've done for us."

Martha walked Beckett to the door, thanked him once more, and watched him as he stepped off the porch and headed toward his buggy at the curb. She closed the door against the cold air, then went to the kitchen. Taking paper and pencil from a cabinet drawer, she sat down at the table and began making a list of the provisions she and Livia would need for their journey to Dawson City.

Martha was still making out the list when she heard the back door open and looked up to see her daughter enter the kitchen, rubbing her gloved hands together. "Hello, Mama. I left the meat you asked me to buy at the grocery store on the back-porch table."

"Thank you, dear. It'll keep much better out there."

Shivering from the cold, Livia slipped her gloves from her hands, took off her knitted hat, and removed her coat. "Br-r-r-r! It's cold out there, Mama."

Martha snickered. "Most people in this country don't believe it gets cold in California."

"Well, it does in San Francisco," Livia said. "Remember that quote from Mark Twain that was in the newspaper a couple of years ago?"

"I'll never forget it. Mr. Twain said, 'The coldest winter I ever lived was the summer I spent in San Francisco!'"

Mother and daughter laughed together, then Livia looked down at the piece of paper her mother had been writing on.

"What's this list you're making?"

"Go hang up your coat and hat, then hurry back. I've got something to tell you."

In less than a minute, Livia returned to the kitchen. Martha looked up at her. "Come sit down, honey."

Livia pulled out a chair and sat down at the table.

"A couple of hours ago, Sheriff Beckett came here with a telegram he had received from the superintendent of Canada's Northwest Mounted Police at Fort Selkirk."

"Is the telegram about Papa?"

"Mm-hmm. Let me explain what was in it, and what Sheriff Beckett said about it."

When Martha had told her daughter the whole story, Livia caught the excitement she heard in her mother's voice, and said, "Mama, we *must* go to Dawson City and the gold fields! Certainly Papa is there! Let's go to the docks and get tickets on the next ship that has room for us."

"I know it will be an arduous trek," Martha said, "but we're both strong and healthy. I can't just sit around the house hoping to hear from your father. I have to know whether he's dead or alive. My life has been in limbo for months."

"I know what you mean, Mama. I have to know about Papa, too. I can't go on like this. Besides…I think the trip will be good for both of us."

Martha and Livia Bray arrived at the docks on San Francisco Bay in a hired buggy. They entered the office of the American Shipping Company and purchased tickets to sail for Dyea, Alaska, on March 20 aboard the *Alaska*.

They were given a brochure by the ticket agent, and when they arrived back home, they sat down and read it together. The brochure described the equipment and food they would need to take aboard the ship for the journey beyond Dyea.

It also told about the "Golden Stairs" they would have to climb to get over Chilkoot Pass, and about the raft ride they would take northward on the Yukon River to Dawson City. The brochure cautioned that if the Yukon River was still frozen when the travelers arrived there, they would have to go by dogsled—for a price.

Early the next morning—Thursday, March 3—Jess Colgan was talking excitedly to his cell mate, Fred Matthis, about how good it was going to be when he walked through the prison gate of San Quentin to freedom. They were sitting together on the bottom bunk.

"I'm sure just smelling that freedom air is going to be great, Jess," Fred said.

"I'm sure it will be," Jess said. "But there's something ahead that's even greater."

"The Yukon gold fields?"

"You've' got it! Freddie, my friend, I am absolutely sure I'm gonna strike it rich up there! I'm gonna become a millionaire!"

Footsteps were heard in the corridor, and both men looked up to see a guard draw up at their cell door and insert his key into the lock.

"Colgan, your parents are waiting for you in Warden Hardesty's office," the guard said, peering between the bars.

Jess and Fred both stood up from the bunk at the same time. Jess looked at Fred. "Well, the time has come."

Fred gripped Jess's hand. "I'll sure miss you, Jess. I wish you every success up there in the gold fields. But…but…"

"But what?"

Fred gripped his hand harder. "Jess, I wish you had opened your heart to Jesus like I did."

"That 'get saved' stuff is fine for you, Fred, but not for me. My mind is on one thing right now…to get rich in Canada!"

"Let's go, Colgan," the guard said.

Jess let go of Fred's hand and patted him on the shoulder. "Take care, pal."

As the guard escorted Jess Colgan toward Warden Duane Hardesty's office, he said, "I hope you do well up there in the Yukon, Colgan, because I sure don't want to see you in here again."

Jess grinned at him as they drew up to the warden's door. "Don't fret about that. I won't be back."

"Well, about half of them end up back here again," the guard said, and opened the office door.

"I assure you, I'll remain in the other half."

The warden's assistant sat at a desk just inside the door. He greeted Jess, saying his parents were with the warden in the inner office, and led him there.

Lawrence and Maybelle Colgan were seated in front of the warden's desk. Both looked up and greeted their son as he entered. As the assistant left, closing the door behind him, Warden Hardesty gestured toward a third chair and told Jess to sit down.

The warden set his eyes on Jess. "Colgan, I'm warning you that if you ever commit another robbery, your next sentence will be a whole lot longer than seven years."

Jess met his gaze head-on. "I assure you, sir, I will never do such a foolish thing again. I'm going to Yukon Territory in Canada and get rich by honest labor in the gold fields."

Moments later, with his parents flanking him, Jess Colgan passed through the prison gate, drew a deep breath, and said, "Freedom! Boy, does it smell good!"

Lawrence and Maybelle smiled at each other. When they reached their wagon in the prison's parking lot, Jess helped his mother up onto the seat while his father climbed up on the other side. Jess sat down beside his mother. Lawrence put the team in motion, and soon they were moving along the road to the sound of the horses' clopping hooves and the wagon's squeaking wheels.

Maybelle took hold of her son's hand. "I'm so glad you're out, honey."

Jess smiled back. "Me too, Mom."

Lawrence leaned forward and looked past Maybelle so he could see into his son's eyes. "Jess, I really wish you would forget this Yukon adventure and just let me help you find a good job here in the San Francisco area."

"Dad, I appreciate your offer, but nothing can change my mind. I'm going to the Klondike and get rich."

Jess looked up ahead at a buggy coming toward them and recognized the lone man driving the buggy. "Hold it, Dad! Stop! That fellow is a friend of mine, Bernie Brodak. I told you and Mom about him."

"Oh, the convict whose life you saved," Maybelle said.

"Yes, Mom."

Lawrence pulled the wagon to the side of the road. Jess waved at the oncoming driver, who waved back and guided the buggy across the road, drawing up with the horses facing each other.

Bernie Brodak jumped out of the buggy with a large brown envelope in his hand and walked quickly to the Colgan wagon as Jess hopped down to meet him.

"Jess!" said Bernie, extending his hand. As the two shook hands, he said, "I didn't think the warden would let you out so early today!"

Jess laughed. "I guess he wanted to get rid of me as soon as he could! Dad and Mom helped by being at the prison so early."

Jess introduced Bernie to his parents, then Bernie extended the brown envelope to his friend. "This is for you, Jess. It's the money I promised you."

Jess took the envelope, felt the weight of it, and said, "Is there something in here besides the money?"

"No. Remember I said I'd give you twice as much as the newspapers are estimating that it takes to go from San Francisco to Dawson City? Well, there's *three times as much* in that envelope. I want to make sure you get there with some money left over."

Jess shook his head, glanced at his smiling parents, then looked back at his friend. "Bernie, you didn't have to do that."

"Oh yes, I did. You saved my life when Nolan Waters tried to kill me. Without you, I'd be dead. You didn't even hesitate to put your own life in danger to save mine. The least I can do is see to it that you get to Yukon Territory with some cash left in your pocket."

Jess laid a hand on Bernie's shoulder, and there was moisture in his eyes as he said, "Thank you."

He then turned to his father. "Dad, will you take me to the docks right now so I can buy my ticket on the first ship that has room for me?"

Lawrence looked at his son in hesitation.

"Mr. Colgan," Bernie said, "if you don't have time to take Jess to the docks, I'll take him for you."

Lawrence and Maybelle exchanged glances, then Lawrence looked at Bernie. "Thank you, but Maybelle and I will take him."

Bernie nodded. "All right, sir. I'll come with you if you don't mind, so I'll know when Jess is leaving."

"Of course I don't mind, Bernie. You can ride with us."

"I appreciate the offer, Mr. Colgan, but I'll drive my buggy so I can go back to work at my uncle's company right there on the docks."

When they reached the ticket office of the American Shipping Company, Lawrence and Maybelle stayed in the wagon while the two young men went inside.

Lawrence reached over and grasped Maybelle's hand. She turned to face him, and he saw the worry and heartache in her eyes. "Sweetheart, we've done all we can for our boy. We brought him up the best way we knew how. I know we've been poor, but Jess has always had plenty of love and care from both of us. All we can do now is hope for the best."

"I guess so, dear," she said, brushing at a tear that had formed in one eye. "It...it's just so hard to reconcile his selfish, greedy behavior with the way we raised him."

"You're right about that, but he isn't a child anymore. We can't make his choices for him. I only hope he's ready to pay the consequences for his choices."

Lawrence took a handkerchief from his hip pocket and gently wiped the tears from Maybelle's eyes. She smiled up at him, nodding her head.

Some twenty minutes later, Jess and Bernie came out of the office, with Jess smiling and waving a ticket at his parents.

As they drew up to the wagon, Jess said, "I'm all set. I got a ticket on a ship called the *Alaska*. I'll be leaving on March 20."

"Well, I'd best get on to work," Bernie said. "Jess, I'll come and see you before you leave."

"I'll look forward to it, my friend. And thank you, again, for your generosity."

Bernie jumped in his buggy, waved to the Colgans, and drove away. Jess once again climbed up and sat next to his mother.

As Lawrence drove the Colgan wagon toward the place where they would board a ferry and cross to the other side of San Francisco Bay, Jess's mind went to his prison days. He thought of guard Howard Ziegler, who had beaten him unmercifully, leaving him scarred for the rest of his life.

Ziegler, it's a good thing for you that I'm leaving this country, because if I ever saw you again, I'd kill you!

EIGHT

On Monday, March 14, there was a clear sky overhead when the American Shipping Company vessel *Excelsior* pulled into the harbor at Skagway, Alaska.

The temperature was twenty-two degrees below zero, with a brisk wind that made it feel even colder. The passengers preparing to leave the ship when it docked stood on the deck in the biting cold, the breath puffing out before their faces.

The water in the harbor was a deep blue in the brilliant sunlight, with shining waves and white foam alongside the hull of the ship. Gleaming chips of ice could be seen in the water along the edges of the harbor, and there were three feet of snow on the ground.

From the ship's two smokestacks, black, greasy smoke curled skyward.

Inside the pilothouse, Captain Cecil Warren was talking to Abe Snelling, a friend who was heading for Skagway, rather than Dyea, which was eight miles farther north.

"So how many of us will be getting off at Skagway, Cecil?" Abe asked.

"Sixty-seven of you. All the others will be going on up to

Dyea. I suppose you've chosen to make your trek to Dawson City and the gold fields over White Pass Trail because it's not as high nor as steep as the trail over Chilkoot Pass."

Snelling nodded. "My friends and I agreed that even though we were told that White Pass Trail is more difficult, we'd go that way since it's not as steep."

The captain smiled. "But the majority—by far—choose Chilkoot Pass because the Golden Stairs make the climb so much easier. It's the same every time I bring gold seekers up here on this ship."

Snelling shrugged his shoulders. "My friends and I are happy with our decision. We'll do fine, Cecil."

The captain grinned. "I'm sure you will."

At that moment, the engines were cut and the pilot steered the ship close to the dock, which had been shoveled free of snow.

Just over two hours later, the *Excelsior* pulled into the harbor at Dyea. The snow depth was the same as at Skagway, and the thermometer outside the pilothouse door showed it was now twenty degrees below zero.

The 249 passengers moved in a long line down the gangplank. Among them were Cleve Holden, who was forty-four years of age; his wife, Maudie, who was forty-three; and their son, Matt, who was twenty-three.

When they reached the dock, Cleve and Matt placed the baggage they were carrying at Maudie's feet, and moved back up the gangplank to carry more of their bags of supplies down to the dock. Like the rest of the passengers who were headed for the Yukon Territory gold fields, they had to make several trips to collect all their supplies.

As the last of the bags was finally deposited on the dock, a dock official came out of the office nearby, carrying a megaphone. All eyes turned to him as he made his way to a small platform, placed the megaphone to his mouth, and said so all could hear, "Ladies and gentlemen, welcome to Dyea! All of you boys and girls, too! I know you're all eager to get moving toward Chilkoot Pass, climb those Golden Stairs, and head for Dawson City. As you might suspect, the Taiya River, which is used in the summer months to transport people to the base of the pass, is still frozen."

He pointed toward a large number of dogsleds near the north edge of the pier. "See all those dogs? They're hitched to their sleds and ready to go. And that group of men clustered there beside them are the sled drivers. They're waiting for you to hire them to take you to the base of Chilkoot Pass."

Matt Holden turned to his parents and said, "I'll hurry over there and ask one of the drivers to come and look at our luggage so we can hire him."

"Do it!" Cleve said.

He and Maudie watched as their son dashed toward the sled drivers.

Drawing up to the group, Matt chose the one that was smiling at him and said, "My name is Matt Holden, sir. I'd like to hire you to take my parents and me to the base of Chilkoot Pass."

The man was still smiling. "That's what I'm here for, Mr. Holden. My name is Hank Johnson. So there are three of you in the party?"

"Yes."

"All right. With three of you…if you have the luggage required by the Northwest Mounted Police, it'll take two sleds."

"We do, and that's fine."

Johnson turned to another driver standing close by. "Kenny, I believe you heard our conversation."

"Sure did," he said, stepping up to Matt. "Mr. Johnson, I'm

Kenny Hoagland. Between Hank and me, we'll get you, your parents, and your luggage to the pass."

Matt smiled. "Let's go."

Johnson and Hoagland followed Matt to where his parents were waiting next to the luggage. Matt introduced the drivers to them, then asked their price, which he found reasonable. The dogsleds were hired, and within twenty minutes the drivers and the Holden men were placing the last of the luggage on the two sleds.

Within a few minutes, all the passengers and the sled drivers were bundled up for their trip to Chilkoot Pass. The only thing visible of the drivers and passengers were their eyes. Their mouths and noses were covered by knitted scarves, with hats or caps pulled down over their foreheads and ears.

The travelers eagerly climbed aboard their dogsleds. The children, especially, showed their excitement.

The sleds lined up in one long row, with lead driver Spence Gellet's sled out front. The drivers stood on small platforms at the rear of their sleds, each bearing a leather whip.

Gellet snapped his whip in the air above the sled and cried, "Mush!"

The other drivers did the same, and soon the dogsleds were making their way swiftly up the east bank of the frozen Taiya River, singlefile, weaving among snow-laden boulders and low spots.

Cleve and Maudie Holden rode together on Hank Johnson's sled in the long line with Matt on Kenny Hoagland's sled right behind them.

The trail alongside the frozen river was beautiful, with several long, slender glacial lakes in snow-covered fields off to their right, and forests of spruce, mountain ash, lodgepole pine, and balsam fir to their left.

Matt's squinted eyes were smiling as he took in the glorious scenery around him.

The dogsleds moved at a steady, rapid pace. They had been on the trail for a little over an hour when Spence Gellet spotted a large spruce tree lying directly across his path, with no way to go around it.

He waved his gloved hand over his head to signal the drivers behind him, and drew the dog team to a halt. The long line of sleds came to a stop, and the passengers looked on as Spence and the other drivers trudged through the deep snow up to the tree. Matt Holden and his father and several other men on the sleds moved up to the group as some of the drivers were commenting on the massive size of the tree.

Hank Johnson shook his head and said, "Spence, look at this. The tree is completely broken loose from its base."

"I noticed this tree leaning precariously the last few days," one of the other drivers said. "It apparently had rotted inside and finally collapsed."

Spence nodded. "I'd say so. Well, we've got to move it, and it's not going to be easy. There's only room for a few men to have sufficient footing to get hold of it." Spence looked around at the group. "I think we'll only be able to have four men on each side. I need the strongest seven men to help me."

Cleve Holden spoke up. "Mr. Gellet, my son is exceptionally strong. You should definitely use Matt."

Matt looked at Spence shyly. "Dad may have me overrated, but I'll sure be glad to help."

Spence noted the wide span of Matt's shoulders and grinned. "You're hired!"

Spence ran his gaze over the group, then chose three other drivers and three husky men from among the passengers. Everyone watched while the eight men took their positions.

"All right, men," Spence said. "Find something on the tree to get a grip on. I'll count to three. On three, give it all you've got. We'll move it in the direction of the rest of the trees on this side of the trail. Ready? One! Two! Three-e-e!"

Struggling and grunting, the eight men began inching the huge tree off the trail. The going was slow.

They had been at the task for about five minutes when the tree suddenly started to roll to one side on the slanting terrain, threatening to crush the four men on that side, including Matt Holden. The men looking on hollered, and there were shrieks from the women and children.

Matt braced himself and managed to find solid footing in the deep snow. He amazed everyone as he was able to keep the spruce from falling on the other three men.

Quickly, the men on the other side came around to help, and soon the tree was left in the snow a few feet off the trail.

Spence Gellet, still puffing from the effort, said, "Matt Holden…if you hadn't done what you did…your three partners would have been…seriously injured! Good going!"

Everyone cheered, and Matt felt his face flush with embarrassment.

"Any one of you would've done the same thing if you'd had the footing I had," he said.

Some of them laughed, and one of the men who had been on the side of the tree with Matt said, "Tell you what, Matt…even if I'd had those rocks to stand on that you did, that tree would've crushed me. I don't have anywhere near the strength that you do!"

A rousing cheer went up from everyone in the crowd. Again, Matt felt his face flush.

Spence stepped up close and looked into Matt's dark-brown eyes. "How did you get to be so strong?"

Matt shrugged, took off his hat, and ran his fingers through his thick black hair. "Just by working hard. Doing physical labor."

Cleve Holden was standing next to his son. "Matt, should I tell them what kind of physical labor?"

Matt placed his hat back on his head. "That's not necessary, Dad. Besides, we need to get moving toward Chilkoot Pass."

"You're right, Matt," Spence said, "but maybe sometime you can tell all of us what kind of labor your Dad's talking about."

Matt shrugged again. "Maybe."

It was almost one o'clock in the afternoon when the dogsleds from Dyea drew up to what the drivers called Tent City at the base of Chilkoot Pass.

The drivers explained to their passengers that many gold prospectors had purchased tents from the Mounties to be used for the rest of the trip to Dawson City. The tents were necessary to protect them from the cold weather, especially when they bedded down for the night. The tents had been pitched the day before, and stood in a long single row in the snow.

Several cabins stood nearby, which the drivers said were quarters for the Mounties that worked at the base of the pass.

A number of Mounties were checking the bags of the prospectors to make sure they had the required amount of food and supplies to last until they got to Dawson City. When Matt Holden stepped off of Kenny Hoagland's sled, he heard a Mountie telling a few people they did not have adequate supplies and would have to hire sleds to take them back to Dyea.

As the people who just came in were getting off the sleds, the drivers told them to look up toward the top of Chilkoot Pass. They all stood in awe at the sight. They could barely see the top for the thick forest between where they stood and the peak of the pass, but they were able to make out the line of gold prospectors climbing the Golden Stairs.

A Mountie in his bright-red uniform was walking by, and one of the men in the newly arrived group said, "Pardon me, sir. Do you know how many steps there are on the Golden Stairs?"

"Fifteen hundred. They're kept chipped and smooth by Randall Evans and Wayne Philbrick, the two men who first made them just over a year ago."

"Do they get anything for all that work?"

"Yes. They charge ten cents a step for each person who climbs them."

Most of the group who had just arrived were now gathered around the Mountie. One man pointed up to the Golden Stairs and said, "Sir, I read that several Chilkoot Indian men carry baggage to the top of the pass for prospectors."

"That's right," said the Mountie. "It's difficult from this distance to pick out the Indians from the prospectors and their families, but those Chilkoots are up there right now, carrying baggage."

"And they charge for their services, right?"

The Mountie smiled. "Oh, yes. But they're reasonable about it, as you'll see if you hire them to help get your baggage and equipment to the top. Believe me, it's worth the cost."

Soon the Mounties who had finished with the crowd that had been there since the day before went to the new people and began checking their bags on the sleds and asking questions. The Mounties explained that it would be the next morning before they could move on up the trail.

Cleve and Matt Holden purchased a tent and began scooping snow from the spot where they were going to pitch it. They were glad for the heavy bedrolls the Canadian government insisted they carry. The Mounties told them it would get down around forty below zero when night fell.

Maudie stood a few yards away, stamping her feet, and a woman who had been in the same dogsled train stopped and said, "I was sure proud of your son for what he did back there on the trail, Mrs. Holden. My name is Effie Connor."

Maudie smiled. "Glad to meet you, Mrs. Connor."

"Pardon my nosiness, but is Matt your stepson?"

"No. I gave birth to him."

Effie smiled and shook her head in wonderment. "You just look too young to be Matt's mother."

"Well, thank you, Mrs. Connor, but I'm forty-three. Matt is twenty-three."

"Hard to believe. You're a very beautiful young woman, I'll say that for you."

Maudie smiled again. "You're so kind. Thank you."

Effie patted Maudie's arm and walked away.

Maudie watched the older woman walk away, unaware that while Cleve and Matt drove tent stakes into the hard-crusted snow, two men who had been in Tent City since the day before had come out of their nearby tent and were moving her direction.

Each man carried a half-full bottle of whiskey, and they were having a difficult time staying on their feet in the slippery snow.

Maudie heard footsteps in the snow behind her and turned to see who was coming. The two men drew up, and one of them said with slurred tongue, "Hello, there s-sweetheart. What's-s-s your name? You're lookin' mighty good."

Maudie stiffened. "My name is none of your business, and I'm not your sweetheart!"

The other one hiccupped and stepped closer to her. "Now, no need to get huffy, honey." As he spoke, he laid a hand on her shoulder.

Maudie quickly stepped back, her eyes blazing. "You stay away from me!"

Cleve and Matt looked up to see the two men with the whiskey bottles standing in front of her.

Anger reddened Cleve's features. "I'm gonna put a stop to this, son. You keep on driving stakes."

"No, Dad. I'm going with you."

Cleve rushed away. "I'll handle it. You stay here."

Matt watched as his father approached the two men.

"Hey!" Cleve shouted. "Get away from my wife!"

"We didn' mean no harm!" one of them snapped back, his eyes wide.

"Move on, right now!"

Matt heard both men curse his father. He dropped the hammer in his hand and dashed toward the scene.

NINE

As Matt Holden plowed through the deep snow toward his father and the whiskey-controlled men who had dared to bother his mother, he saw a third man heading that way. The man stopped long enough to pick up a thick, four-foot-long broken tree limb off the snow. His eyes were fixed on Cleve Holden, who was yelling at the two intruders, his back toward the man with the tree limb.

When Matt saw the man hurry up behind his father, the tree limb raised to strike him, he shouted, "Dad! Look out behind you!"

Cleve whirled around, but the man cracked him with the limb on the right side of his neck and shoulder. Cleve fell to the ground as Maudie cried out and hurried to him.

Matt rushed up, and the men who had accosted Maudie called out a warning to their friend, who wheeled around and swung the limb at Matt's head.

Matt dodged the weapon and slammed the man on the jaw with a powerful blow. The sound of the blow echoed over the Tent City as the man went down, unconscious.

The other two rushed toward Matt, cursing and swinging their bottles at him.

Matt dodged both bottles, and one of the men slipped and went down to one knee. The other one was about to swing his bottle at Matt again, but Matt lifted him off his feet with two quick punches. He fell on his back in the snow, out cold.

The one who had gone down on one knee smashed his whiskey bottle against an ice-crusted rock, leaving it with sharp, jagged edges. He jumped to his feet, let out a wild yell, and went at Matt again.

Matt sidestepped him, the bottle just missing his face, then seized the wrist of the hand that held the bottle and gave it a violent twist. The man howled as his fingers went limp and the bottle fell into the snow.

He glared at Matt and doubled up both fists.

Matt shook his head. "You don't want to do this."

The man came at Matt with his right fist swinging. Matt used his left forearm to block the blow and followed with a right to the jaw. The man staggered back a few steps, growled like a wild animal, and came at him again.

Matt avoided the man's fists, landing a right to the ribs and a left that popped the man's head back, dropping him to the snow-covered ground in a heap. He groaned, then rolled on his side and went unconscious.

By this time, three Mounties and a crowd of travelers had gathered.

Matt explained to the Mounties what had happened, and one of them said, "Wow, mister! We saw you handling all three of them while we were hurrying to get over here. You're really good with your fists, I'll say that for you!"

"Yeah, well, I wish I'd gotten to them sooner. I need to go see how my dad's doing."

Matt moved toward his parents, and the Mounties began throwing snow in the faces of the three men to revive them.

Maudie was on her knees beside Cleve when Matt hunkered down beside her. She looked at her son and said softly, "He's hurt pretty bad."

Matt looked down at his father's face, which was twisted with pain. "You hurting a lot, Dad?"

Teeth clenched in pain, Cleve nodded slowly.

Matt patted his father's arm. "I'll be back shortly."

The Mounties now had the three men sitting up in the snow, and when Matt drew up, he heard one of the Mounties giving them a tongue lashing for drinking liquor on the Chilkoot Trail, which they knew was not allowed. He also railed at the two who had pushed themselves on Mrs. Holden, then told all three they would be put on a dogsled immediately and sent back to Dyea to catch a ship for Seattle or San Francisco.

With that, the Mounties ordered the three troublemakers to their feet and ushered them away. Not one of them would even look at Matt Holden.

Matt was once again kneeling over his injured father. One of the men in the crowd that had gathered said, "Mr. Holden, where did you learn to fight like that?"

Matt rose to his feet, but before he could reply, another man in the group said, "Hey, I know you! You're that professional fighter, Matt Holden. I saw you fight Merl Dupler in Chicago in November of '96. In the sixth round, you put him down for the count! You really *are* a puncher!"

The men in the crowd began to talk among themselves, being acquainted with the names Matt Holden and Merl Dupler.

One of them stepped up to Matt and said, "Mr. Holden, Merl Dupler fought Bob Fitzsimmons in New York City before Fitzsimmons was heavyweight champion. I'm from New York, and I saw the fight. Fitzsimmons couldn't whip Dupler. The fight ended in a twenty-four-round draw. You know about that fight?"

Matt nodded. "Yes. I read all about it."

"Well, since you knocked Dupler out, you should demand a bout with Fitzsimmons. You'd probably whip him and become the heavyweight champ!"

Matt shook his head. "Not now, sir. I'm through with boxing. I could never whip Bob Fitzsimmons now."

The man frowned and cocked his head. "The way I just saw you put those three big, husky guys out? Sure you could!"

Another man stepped up. "I agree with him, Mr. Holden. What do you mean you're through with boxing?"

"Yeah," put in another man. "With your fighting ability, you could be champ. I know it!"

Matt ran his gaze over the inquisitive faces of the men gathered around him. "I started fighting when I was nineteen years of age, but something happened to me about three years later that changed my whole life. My parents and I are from Chicago, and a friend invited me to a revival meeting where the famous evangelist, Dwight Moody, was preaching."

Some of the men exchanged glances.

"Well," Matt went on, "the sermon Mr. Moody preached went to my heart. It was all about how God's only begotten Son, the Lord Jesus Christ, came into this world to shed His blood and die on the cross of Calvary. This was so He could save sinners who would believe on Him from going to hell and take them to heaven when they died. When the sermon was finished and the invitation was given, I walked down the aisle and received the Lord Jesus Christ into my heart as my personal Saviour. I took my parents to hear Mr. Moody the next night, and they also went forward at the close of the sermon and received Christ."

"Okay, Matt, so you became a Christian," one man in the

crowd said. "Boxing is an honest profession. Why couldn't you go on with your career?"

Matt smiled. "Well, in order for a fighter to make it to the top, he must have the 'killer instinct.' I had that 'killer instinct' before I became a Christian, but now it just isn't in me to pound a man until he drops, just to make money."

The same man said, "You just pounded three men into unconsciousness. Seems to me that 'killer instinct' is still in you."

Matt shook his head. "Sir, what I did to those men was to protect my father and mother. It wasn't to make money. I can still punch a man, if needed, to protect someone else, or even to protect myself, but not in a prize fight." He then said to everyone gathered, "Please excuse me, folks, but my father is injured. I must see to him."

Matt hunkered down once again beside his mother and saw that she had unbuttoned his father's coat.

"Look at this, son," she said, pulling Cleve's shirt open at the neck. "Tell me what you think."

Matt examined the swollen red spot on the right side of his father's neck and shoulder, which was turning purple. Cleve's eyes were glazed over in pain. Gingerly, Matt tried to move his father's right arm.

Cleve stiffened and emitted a loud groan.

Matt placed the arm as it was before and patted it gently.

He looked at his mother. "Mom, I think Dad's got a broken collar bone."

Maudie nodded. "That's what I thought."

"We've got to take him to the nearest doctor."

Both Hank Johnson and Kenny Hoagland were close by. Hank stepped up with Kenny on his heels and said, "Matt, the closest doctor is in Dyea. I'll be glad to take him there on my sled. Your mother can ride with him. That'll be the fastest and most comfortable way for him. And there will be no charge."

"There won't be room for all three of you on Hank's sled," Kenny said, "but I'll take you to Dyea if you want to go. And I won't charge you, either."

Matt let a grin curve his lips. "Yes, I do want to go, Kenny. Thank you." He turned to one of the men who had come from Dyea in the same train of dogsleds that day. "Will you tell the Mounties what we're doing, and that we'll be back as soon as we can to go over the pass?"

"Sure will, Matt."

"Son, we need to make a sling for your father's arm before we head for Dyea," Maudie said.

"I have a long scarf in my tent," one of the men in the crowd said. "It'll work well as a sling. Be right back."

The man was back quickly and handed the scarf to Maudie. She thanked him and carefully put her husband's arm in the makeshift sling.

Once the sling was in place, Matt and Hank carried Cleve to the sled as Kenny helped Maudie make her way through the deep snow.

When Cleve was in a comfortable position on the sled, Maudie made a snowball and held it to Cleve's mouth. "Here, darling, I want you to eat this snow. You need some liquid."

Cleve held the snowball in his left hand and started sucking on it as Maudie covered him with warm blankets.

Matt helped his mother onto the sled. He gave her an encouraging smile, patted her hand, and climbed onto Kenny Hoagland's sled.

Both drivers shouted "Mush!," and while the crowd looked on, the sleds hurried away over the snow-laden ground.

Hank's sled was in the lead, and as Kenny's dog team followed close behind, Matt sat alone and spoke in a whisper, "Lord, please give us safety on this trip and help the doctor in Dyea to properly treat Dad's injury. Please give Mom Your grace through all of this, and thank You for always caring and keeping Your hand on Your children. I love You, Lord Jesus."

On the other sled, Maudie too was praying to the Great Physician as she caressed her husband's right arm beneath the blankets.

When Cleve looked up at her, she said, "You'll be all right, sweetheart. The Lord will take care of you."

Cleve's face was gray, and he grimaced with every bump of the speeding sled. But he managed a thin smile for his wife.

As the sleds glided southward toward Dyea, Kenny Hoagland said, "Matt, are you and your parents going after Klondike gold because your boxing career is over?"

"Yes, we are. My parents had run into financial difficulties that I was planning to take care of, but then I left the ring because I had become a Christian. So we decided to take up the challenge of the Yukon Territory gold fields we had read so much about in the newspapers. We agreed that if the Lord blessed us with enough gold, we would also give money to needy churches and to people we know who need help."

"Well, I commend you for that," Kenny said. "May I ask you something else?"

"Sure." Matt turned halfway around to look up at him.

The sled hit a bump, and Kenny had to grasp the handles tightly to stay aboard. When it was running smoothly again, he said, "Just curious, but is there a young lady in your life?"

Matt's features took on a grim look. "There was, but when I became a Christian, it made her angry, and she walked out of my life."

"Too bad."

"Well, Kenny, I know that the Lord has a young lady for me,

and He'll bring her into my life when He's ready to do so."

Kenny thought about that for a moment, then said, "Before you ended your boxing career, did you use gloves?"

"All of my fights were with gloves. I started boxing in '94, and the bare-knuckle fights ended in this country in early '89. All professional fighters in the United States since that time have had to wear four-ounce gloves."

"And I guess the gloves are for double protection…the fighters' hands when they punch, and their faces when they get punched."

Matt smiled. "You got it."

"Something else…how long has Bob Fitzsimmons been the world's heavyweight champion?"

"Well, since he knocked out James J. Corbett in fourteen rounds on March 17, 1897, at Carson City, Nevada."

"And you knocked out Merl Dupler, whom Fitzsimmons couldn't even whip. Won't it haunt you, never knowing if you might have whipped Fitzsimmons if you fought him, and become heavyweight champion of the world?"

"I've thought about it a lot, Kenny, but when Jesus comes into a man's heart, He changes his outlook on life. The new man in Christ sees people as souls needing to be saved. Unless he's forced to fight to protect someone else or to defend himself, the desire to pound somebody senseless just isn't there."

Kenny smiled. "Mr. Holden, you're amazing."

Matt shook his head. "No, Kenny, my Lord Jesus is the one who's amazing."

TEN

When the two sleds reached Dyea, both drivers had heard the gospel of Jesus Christ. Matt Holden had witnessed to Kenny Hoagland, and Maudie had done the same with Hank Johnson.

Soon the sleds hauled up in front of a log building on Main Street, where a sign above the door declared it was the office of William Slater, M.D.

As the drivers and Matt Holden hopped off the sleds, Matt said, "Hank…Kenny…could you wait till the doctor has seen Dad before you go? I'd like to talk to both of you."

Hank and Kenny looked at each other, then Kenny said, "We need to head back, Matt."

"We really do," Hank said. "What do you want to talk to us about?"

"I overheard Mom telling you about your need to be saved, Hank, even as I was talking with Kenny about the same thing. I'd like to see both of you open your hearts to Jesus. Right now, I've got to get Dad in there to the doctor, but if you'd just give me a little time with both of you, I—"

"We really do have to get going, Matt," Kenny said. "But I

promise I'll give what you told me some serious thought."

Hank swung his gaze to Maudie, who was holding Cleve's hand while listening to the conversation. "Mrs. Holden, I'll make the same promise to you. I certainly will think about the things you said to me on our way here."

Maudie smiled. "Please do. Your eternal destiny depends on it."

"How about Hank and I carry Mr. Holden into the doctor's office before we go?" Kenny asked.

"I appreciate the offer," Matt said, "but I can carry him in."

"How about I help you, then? Hank can stay out here with the dogs."

"Okay. If you insist."

Maudie started to get off the sled, and Hank helped her to her feet in the snow, then Matt and Kenny moved up to the sled.

Pain was etched into Cleve Holden's features as he looked up at them.

"We'll do our best not to hurt you, Dad," Matt said.

Cleve nodded and tried to smile.

Matt and Kenny gingerly lifted Cleve from the sled, and making a chair with their hands and arms, carried him toward the doctor's office, with Maudie going ahead to open doors.

Two middle-aged men who were walking along the board-walk stopped, and one of them opened the door. "Here you go, ma'am."

Maudie smiled. "Thank you, sir."

Matt and Kenny followed Maudie inside with Cleve still riding the "chair." There was a wood-burning stove in the corner of the waiting room, and several people were sitting on wooden chairs, waiting to see the doctor. The room was comfortably warm.

Matt and Kenny seated Cleve on a chair, then Matt said,

"Thanks for the help Kenny. And don't forget your promise."

Kenny looked at him quizzically.

"The 'serious thought' promise."

"Oh! I'll do it, Matt." Kenny patted Matt's arm and hurried out the door.

The other people in the room put their attention on Cleve, and a young woman who was holding a little girl on her lap in the chair next to Matt said, "He seems to be hurting quite a bit."

Matt nodded. "Yes, he is."

"Did he break his arm?"

"It's his collarbone. I'm sure it's broken."

An inner door opened, and an older man with a bandage around his head emerged. Behind him came a short, stocky man in his late forties, clad in a white physician's frock.

The older man's wife stepped up to him and began helping him into his coat.

Dr. William Slater, scrubbing a hand over his well-trimmed beard, said in a kind voice, "Who's next?"

Everyone looked toward Cleve Holden as a redheaded man said, "Doctor, we were all here before those three came in, but this man with the scarf for a sling seems to need your help right away. No one else here is suffering like he is."

The others spoke their agreement.

The doctor looked at the Holdens. "Bring him in, please."

Matt rose to his feet and ran his gaze over the faces of the others. "Thank you all. Thank you very much."

Matt helped his father off the chair and half carried him through the inner door. Maudie followed.

When they entered the examining and surgical room, Dr. Slater told Matt to take off the injured man's hat and coat and lay him down on the examination table.

As Matt was doing so, he said, "Doctor, these people are my

parents. I think Dad has a broken collarbone. His name is Cleve Holden, Mom is Maudie, and I'm Matt. We're from Chicago and are headed for the Yukon Territory gold fields. We were up at Tent City at the base of Chilkoot Pass, with plans to climb the Golden Stairs tomorrow. Two drunken men were bothering my mother, and Dad went after them. But a companion of the two men came up behind him and struck him with a tree limb."

Dr. Slater shook his head as he began unbuttoning Cleve's shirt. "So did they get away with it?"

"Not exactly," Maudie said. "My son knocked all three of them out cold. When they came to, the Mounties told them to go back where they came from...that they wouldn't be allowed into Canada."

"Good. Now let's see what we've got here."

After a careful examination, Dr. Slater looked at Maudie and said, "Your husband indeed has a broken collarbone." Then he said to Cleve, "Mr. Holden, I can see that you're in extreme pain. I'm going to give you a good dose of laudanum to ease your suffering. I'll give it a little while to take hold while I take care of a couple other patients, then I'll set the bone, wrap your shoulder up tightly, and put your arm in a real sling."

Cleve nodded while grimacing. "Sounds good to me, Doctor."

After administering the laudanum, Dr. Slater took care of two other patients behind curtains on the other side of the examining room while Maudie and Matt sat next to the examining table and watched Cleve slip under the influence of the drug.

Soon the doctor returned, set the broken collarbone, wrapped the shoulder in thick cloth, and put a sling on Cleve's arm. When he was finished, he looked at Matt and Maudie and said, "I'll have to keep a close watch on the injury for a few days to make sure the bone is set correctly."

"We understand, Doctor," Matt said. "For sure, we want it to be right. We'll get a room at the Dyea Hotel as long as needed. I can carry Dad there, since it's only four doors down."

Cleve was barely conscious. "Fine, son," he said thickly.

When the Holdens entered the waiting room again, Matt was carrying his father in his arms. He and his mother repeated their thanks to the people who had allowed Cleve to see the doctor ahead of them.

The redheaded man said, "I hope he heals up real good."

As Matt and his mother stepped out into the cold air, they noticed that the sky had grown cloudy and soft flakes were falling, spotting their coats and hats.

A few snowflakes touched Cleve's face as he rested in his son's arms. He opened his eyes and blinked. "Snowing," he said with a thick tongue.

"Sure is, Dad. It's only a few steps to the hotel."

Seconds later, Matt used his shoulder to push the lobby door open, allowed his mother to enter first, then stepped in with his father in his arms.

The desk clerk looked up and said, "May I help you?"

"Yes, sir," Matt said. "My parents and I need two rooms. One for them and one for me."

The desk clerk smiled, showing several gaps where teeth used to be. "We can take care of you, sir. Is your father all right?"

"We just had him at Dr. Slater's office. He has a broken collarbone, but he'll be all right in a few days. Right now, we're not sure just how long we'll be here."

"No problem, sir. You can stay as long as you like."

The clerk worked rapidly to register the Holdens, then handed Maudie the keys to both rooms, saying they were next door to each other.

The Holdens climbed the stairs to the second floor, and

when Maudie stepped into the room she and Cleve would occupy, she was pleasantly surprised. A welcoming fire burned in the small fireplace, and the sight of the bed pleased her with its colorful spread and pillows. She fluffed up the pillows while Matt sat his father in an overstuffed chair long enough to remove his hat and coat.

"Son, I'll undress him later," Maudie said. "Go ahead and put him on the bed."

Matt did so, and while his mother covered his father with a thick, soft woolen quilt, Matt stoked up the fire and tossed in another log.

Cleve was still under the influence of the laudanum, and within a minute or so, was fast asleep. Maudie sat on the edge of the bed and stroked his hair.

"Mom, I'll go check my room," Matt said, "then head down the street to the café on the corner and get us something to eat."

Maudie looked up at him with admiring eyes. "Thank you, son. I am a bit hungry. This has been quite an ordeal."

On Sunday morning, March 20, at San Francisco Bay, Pastor Wayne Dukart and four men from the church arrived in two wagons carrying Missionaries Tom and Peggy Varner, their young children, Johnny and Rebecca, and their luggage.

They pulled up at the wharf where the American Shipping Lines vessel, the *Alaska*, was docked. The ship was due to pull out at 11:30, and it was now only 8:45.

When everyone was out of the wagons, Tom said, "Pastor, I wish the ship's departure had been on a weekday, or even on Sunday afternoon, so the church members could have come to see us off. So many had expressed their desire to do so."

Pastor Dukart smiled and nodded. "I wish the time of departure was different too, but you had no control over when the *Alaska* was scheduled to head out to sea."

Two dock workers drew up pulling a cart and began to load the Varners' luggage to take it aboard the ship.

"Let's all join hands," Pastor Dukart said. "I want to pray for Tom, Peggy, and these precious children before they board the ship."

As he prayed, little Rebecca, who stood between her parents, was trying her best to be still and reverent, but the excitement as they were about to board the ship and head for Alaska was just too much for her. She couldn't keep her hands or her feet still. She felt the pressure of her father's hand on her own small hand, and she kept her head bowed and her eyes closed. But what she really wanted to do was look up and take in the smokestacks and the fascinating structure of the huge ship.

Soon the pastor finished his prayer, and he bent down and gave Rebecca a firm hug. She wrapped her arms around his neck and said, "I'm sure gonna miss you, Pastor." Tears misted her eyes. "I've known you all of my life."

"I'll miss you, too, sweetheart, but tell you what. You write to me and draw pictures of some of the things you see up there in Alaska and Canada. You're already quite the little artist. You've drawn me pictures of things around San Francisco, and I really like them. Will you do that for me?"

A bright smile replaced the tears. "I will, Pastor!" She hugged his neck again, then took her mother's hand.

As the Varner family headed for the gangplank, Rebecca looked over her shoulder and saw the pastor wiping tears from his eyes. Facing forward again, she walked at her mother's side as they mounted the gangplank, her little heart not knowing whether to be happy or sad.

Tom handed their tickets to a white-uniformed crew member, resplendent with gold braid and insignia. He welcomed them aboard, then Tom led his family to the rail, where they waved to the five men on the dock.

Later, when the Varners were in their cabin alone, Johnny jumped up and down, saying, "We're about to leave for Yukon Territory! I can't wait to see some Mounties!"

Rebecca jumped up and down and just as excitedly said, "And I can't wait to see some Eskimos!"

About nine-thirty that morning, passengers booked on the *Alaska* began to arrive by the dozens. Among them were Hank Osborne and his sons, Russell, T. J., Lou, and Vernon. After the dock workers transported the Osbornes' luggage to their cabin, the brothers began to talk about what it was going to be like to be millionaires. They had read in a newspaper that very week that three more prospectors in the gold fields east of Dawson City had struck it rich.

Hank said, "Boys, most prospectors in the Klondike will never become millionaires, and you know it. But I really like your positive attitude. Just keep thinking that way!"

At twenty minutes till ten, Dale and Elaine Burke arrived at the docks with their children, Susan and Ernie, along with Norman and Margo Fleming. Dale went ahead of the others, pushing Norman in the wheelchair up the gangplank. Other passengers stepped aside, allowing Dale to keep the wheelchair moving.

When the Burkes and the Flemings were on deck together, they handed their tickets to a white-uniformed crew member, then another crewman guided them to their cabins, which were only a few doors apart.

They arrived at the Fleming cabin first, and just before the Burkes were led on to their cabin, Margo saw a troubled look in Elaine's eyes.

After Dale wheeled Norman inside the cabin, he said, "I'll go help my family get settled. If either of you need me, just let me know."

Norman smiled up at him. "Thank you so much for your kindness."

When Dale had gone, Margo stood over Norman, her brow furrowed.

He looked up at her and cocked his head to one side. "Honey, what's the matter?"

"I'm worried about Elaine. She's just not happy. Do you mind if I go talk to her?"

"Of course not. But how are you going to get her alone?"

"I'll just ask her to take a walk on the deck with me."

Some forty minutes later, Margo entered the cabin and found Norman almost asleep in his wheelchair. His head bobbed, his eyes came open, and he looked up at Margo. "You get to talk to her alone?"

"Yes."

"She all right?"

"She is now. Elaine is just having a hard time being uprooted. She misses their home in Omaha, their family and friends back there. I tried to encourage her and get her to make the best of this situation and be optimistic about their future."

"So it helped her, I take it."

Margo nodded. "She just needed some encouragement from a woman older than herself. I think she'll be all right now.

Before she headed back to her cabin, she thanked me tearfully for caring about her and gave me a hug."

Norman smiled and took hold of Margo's hand. "Sweetheart, I'm proud of you for showing so much kindness and understanding to Elaine…both that day at the hotel when the Burkes checked in, and today."

"Thank you. Lots of women have a hard time leaving their homes to go on a venture like this. I can understand that, even though it's different for me than it is for Elaine. You and I are going to Dawson City to establish a hotel—which is pretty much a sure thing. I have it easier than those women whose husbands are hoping to make a good strike in the gold fields, when they know that few men really do."

Norman squeezed Margo's hand. "I'm so glad my wife has such an understanding and tender heart toward others."

Shortly after the Burkes and the Flemings had boarded the steamship *Alaska*, a hired buggy drew up next to the ship. In the buggy, Jack London embraced his mother, who was beside him on the seat, and kissed her cheek.

"I love you, Mama," he said, and stepped out of the buggy.

"I love you too," Flora said softly. "And Jack…remember, you promised to write me often."

"I remember, Mama."

She looked deep into his eyes. "And what about the other promise?"

"Mama, I know I can't carry liquor up White Pass into Canada. The Mounties would be on my back in a hurry."

"Well, I'm sure you won't take a chance on getting into trouble with the Mounties, but you promised me you would quit drinking altogether."

Jack leaned back into the buggy, kissed her cheek again, and said, "Okay. I promise I'll never touch another drop."

Flora kissed her son's forehead. "Thank you. I'll hang onto that."

He smiled. "Love you, Mama."

"I love you, too."

Jack turned his luggage over to a dock worker to take aboard the ship, waved at his mother, and slipped into the crowd climbing the gangplank. When he reached the deck, he gave his ticket to a crew member and was assigned his cabin. He quickly moved across the deck to the railing, saw his mother in the buggy, and waved to her again.

With tears in her eyes, Flora waved back as the driver put the buggy in motion.

ELEVEN

At five minutes before ten, the Colgan buggy pulled up to the edge of the dock in front of the *Alaska*. Passengers, some with children, were slowly climbing the gangplank, while others made their way toward the ship across the dock, and others on the dock were still saying their good-byes to friends and family.

Two dock workers pulling a cart stepped up to the Colgan buggy and offered to carry their luggage aboard.

Jess hopped down and said, "I'm the only one traveling, but you're welcome to carry my luggage onto the ship. Everything here in the rear of the buggy goes."

Lawrence helped Maybelle down from the seat, and she stood gazing up at Jess's face, her hands clasping and unclasping nervously. *This is the only child we were ever blessed with,* she thought as Jess's eyes shone with excitement, darting from bow to stern as his father commented on the ship's size and beauty.

I hardly know my boy anymore. He wasn't raised to be greedy or think only of himself.

Tears welled up in her eyes. She blinked them back and looked down at her hands, which were now clasped together. *I know we've always been poor, but there's no disgrace in that. Lawrence and I are hardworking people. I just don't understand how our son turned out to be so selfish and self-serving.*

Maybelle's mind flashed back to Jess's childhood days, and she recalled what a sweet, unselfish boy he had been. No longer able to hold the tears at bay, she wrapped her arms around her son and held him close to her heart. "Oh, Jess, I will miss you terribly. When you were locked up in prison, at least your father and I could come see you. But with you way up there in the Yukon, we—"

She broke into sobs.

Jess hugged her tight. "Please, Mom, don't cry."

Lawrence also put an arm around her, and after a minute or so, she stopped sobbing.

"How long are you planning to stay in Canada, son?" Lawrence asked.

Before Jess could answer, one of the luggage handlers stepped up. "Sir, we'll go ahead and take your luggage aboard. We'll watch for you so we can take you to the cabin you're assigned to. You won't make us wait very long, will you?"

"No, I won't be long. Thank you."

As the two men wheeled the cart toward the gangplank, Jess turned back to his father. "Dad, how long I stay in Canada depends on how quickly I make my fortune. It may take several months or a few years. There's no way to know. But I want you and Mom both to understand that I'll stay there until I'm a very rich man." Jess looked toward the gangplank, and saw that the cart bearing his luggage was almost halfway up to the deck. "I've got to go," he said.

Lawrence grabbed his son and patted his back while he hugged him. Easing back, he looked into Jess's eyes. "Son, your mother and I will always be here for you. If things don't work out as you've planned, you'll always have a home to come back to. Okay?"

Jess grinned. "Sure, Dad." He quickly hugged his mother, then dashed to the gangplank.

Lawrence placed his arm around Maybelle, and she laid her head on his shoulder. Tears streamed down her cheeks and dripped off her chin. Lawrence took a handkerchief from his hip pocket, kissed her forehead, and began tenderly wiping the tears away.

Up on deck, Jess stepped off the gangplank and handed his ticket to one of the uniformed crewmen. The crewman welcomed him aboard and matched the ticket number to a list he held on a clipboard. "Mr. Colgan," he said, "you'll be in cabin nineteen on the main deck. There are already two other men in the cabin."

Jess frowned. "I don't want to be in a cabin with someone else. I made that clear when I bought the ticket at your company's office."

"I'm sorry, sir, but we no longer have enough room on the ship to give you a private cabin. We're filling up quickly, and we're going to be at capacity."

"Look, I bought a ticket for a private cabin, and I insist you give me a private cabin!"

Another crewman, who had silver hair beneath his white cap, stepped up. "What's the problem here?"

"Mr. Colgan was under the impression that he was going to have a private cabin," the younger crewman said, "and he became upset when I told him he would be in a cabin with two other men."

The older man stepped in front of Jess. "I'm sorry, Mr. Colgan, but there are no more private cabins available. With the ship filling up as it is, you'll have to share the cabin with those other two men."

"I paid for a private cabin, and *I want a private cabin!*"

The silver-haired man noted the other passengers looking on. Brow furrowed, he said levelly, "Mr. Colgan, get a grip on your temper, or I will have you put off the ship!"

Jess gritted his teeth, breathing hard. "All right. All right." He moved to the two dock workers who had his luggage on their cart and said, "Let's go. I'm in cabin nineteen here on the main deck."

Jess followed the cart to the other side of the deck, not bothering to give a final wave to his parents.

Down on the dock, Maybelle shook her head and looked up at her husband.

Lawrence shrugged his shoulders. "I guess that's it. He's gone. We've done all we could do, and he knows we're here for him. Our son is a grown man, now, and has to make his own choices."

"You're right, of course," she said, tears once again very close to the surface.

"Let's go home, sweetheart," Lawrence said quietly.

She nodded. "Yes, love. Let's go home."

At 10:45, passengers were still arriving to board the *Alaska*.

A hired buggy pulled up, and Martha and Livia Bray stepped out. Martha paid the driver while two dock workers took their luggage out of the buggy and placed it on a cart. As mother and daughter stood together, waiting for the dock workers to move the cart toward the gangplank, they ran their eyes over the ship.

"This is really something, Mama," Livia said. "Do you realize I've never been this close to an ocean-going vessel before?"

Martha giggled. "Well, I haven't either."

"Really?"

She nodded. "Really."

The *Alaska's* pristine white hull loomed like a giant building before them. Its trio of red smokestacks, protruding from black towers over the deck, were already giving off thin wisps of smoke as the engines were being warmed up.

As the cart was being pushed up the gangplank, Martha and Livia followed.

When they reached the deck, a crew member greeted them, asking for their tickets. "You ladies will be in cabin number twenty-two on B deck, which is on the starboard side. That's the next deck up." He pointed behind him. "The closest stairs are right over there. Just follow these men with the cart."

Martha and Livia followed the men with the cart that carried their luggage. They were met by a smiling steward at the foot of the staircase that led to the second deck.

"Welcome aboard, ladies. What is your cabin number?"

"Twenty-two B, sir," Martha said.

"Follow me. We'll go ahead of the cart."

He led them up the stairs and to the door of cabin twenty-two. He opened the door for them, then said, "Well, ladies, I have to get back to my post. Hope you enjoy the trip."

Martha and Livia thanked him, then stepped into the cabin and asked the two dock workers to place their luggage on the floor next to the door.

There were two single beds, each with a royal blue spread embossed with the insignia of the American Shipping Lines. The curtains that adorned the cabin's two portholes were matching royal blue with gold flecks. A large dark blue braided rug covered much of the floor. A small table with two chairs stood against one wall, and a white painted wash stand with three drawers stood against another wall, with a dark blue pitcher and bowl atop it.

They gladly noted that there was ample drawer space for the two of them in a small dresser.

"Well, Livia, this is our home away from home. What do you think?" Martha said with a pleased look on her face.

"It's lovely, Mama, and not nearly as small as I figured it might be. I just hope we have a smooth voyage because I don't think either of us will fare well if the seas get choppy."

Martha patted Livia's hand and smiled. "Let's just hope we don't have to find out, honey." She took a deep breath. "Well, I guess we'd better get unpacked."

They had hardly begun when Martha heard Livia sniffling. Martha stepped to her daughter and laid a hand on her shoulder. "Honey, why are you crying?"

Livia stood up straight, wiped her tears, and said, "No matter how hard I tried, Mama, it still hurt when Nadine came to the house this morning to tell us that Nate and Matilda had gotten married yesterday."

Martha put her arms around her, speaking soft, comforting words. Livia sobbed for several minutes, then dabbing at her tears with a handkerchief drawn from her dress pocket, she drew a shaky breath and said, "Thank you, Mama, for being such a comfort to me." Her eyes narrowed and her jaw jutted. "This is enough. I'll never cry over Nate again. He isn't worth it."

Martha stroked Livia's cheek. "Good for you. Now, let's go outside and get some fresh air."

Mother and daughter stepped out onto the deck, moved to the railing, and watched the passengers swarming on the lower deck. The last few passengers were just coming up the gangplank.

A few minutes later, Martha and Livia noticed a slender man in his late fifties, clad in a captain's cap and an immaculate white uniform with fancy gold braid trimming, appear on the lower deck. His mouth was curved in a smile underneath an impeccably groomed mustache. He raised a megaphone to his mouth and said, "Ladies and gentlemen! I am Captain Eric Fillmore! I want to have a brief meeting with all passengers here on the main deck. Please gather around quickly!"

As mother and daughter moved toward the metal staircase, they noticed crew members tapping on cabin doors to make sure all passengers were aware that the captain wanted to meet with them on the main deck.

When the crowd of passengers was gathered in front of him, with the crewmen lined up behind him, the captain took out his pocket watch, looked at it, and said into the megaphone, "To those of you who have just come from your cabins, I am Captain Eric Fillmore. It is now eleven fifteen. We will be shoving off in fifteen minutes. Listen carefully."

Fillmore announced that there were 504 passengers on board, then gave a ten-minute speech regarding rules of conduct aboard ship, and usage of the lifeboats should the *Alaska* be damaged and begin to sink.

He warned them that it was very possible they would run into a storm or two as they sailed for Alaska's ports at Skagway and Dyea, and if so, everyone must obey any orders given by him or his crew.

"If any of you have questions, you are free to ask me or any of the uniformed men aboard. Let me say that I wish all of you a pleasant cruise, and that I hope you all become wealthy in the gold fields of Yukon Territory."

All over the main deck, passengers smiled at each other.

"One final suggestion, folks. Since we're running full in the passenger department on this journey, if you don't want to stand in line at the dining hall waiting for a table at mealtime, I strongly suggest that you make your reservations early."

At that instant, the ship's bell resounded across the sunlit bay, and crewmen at the bow began weighing anchor.

Moments later, Livia Bray felt the great power of the ship's engines throb through the floor of the deck.

Martha saw the expression on her daughter's face and leaned close. "Honey, are you all right?"

"I'm fine, Mama. When the vibration from the engines made my feet tingle, it frightened me just a little."

The ship pulled away from the dock, and many of the passengers stood at the handrails and waved to family and friends.

Greasy black smoke lifted in billows from the three smokestacks and curled skyward.

Livia took a deep breath and looked at her mother. "Well, Mama, we're on our way. Papa's in for a big surprise, isn't he?"

Martha bit her lower lip and nodded. "That is, *if* he's still alive."

Livia took hold of her mother's hand. "Papa *has* to still be alive, Mama. He just *has* to be."

The *Alaska* steamed its way past the United States military prison on Alcatraz Island, then turned left toward the great Pacific Ocean. Soon the ship was on the sapphire blue Pacific, with the propellers at the rear of the ship churning the water white.

The green hills and sandy beaches of California's coast slowly shrank from sight above the whitened wake on the ocean's surface. After a short time, the ship made a right turn and headed north toward Alaska…and Canada.

Martha turned to Livia. "We should take the captain's suggestion and go sign up for early seating for dinner this evening."

Livia smiled. "Good idea."

TWELVE

As the afternoon passed, the sky stayed clear, and in spite of a slight breeze, the surface of the ocean remained smooth. The sun shone brightly on the happy, excited passengers aboard the *Alaska*.

Many moved about the decks, getting acquainted with other passengers, while others sat in deck chairs and on benches, in lighthearted conversation. Still others chose to remain in their cabins.

Martha and Livia Bray chose to stay in their cabin for some time, then finally stepped out on B deck and sat on an unoccupied bench a few steps from their door.

While the ocean breeze toyed with her long blond locks, Livia let her eyes sweep over the beautiful blue Pacific. After a while, she turned to her mother, her brow furrowed. "Mama, I've been thinking about your comment earlier when I said Papa is in for a big surprise when we get to Yukon Territory."

"You mean when I said *if* he's still alive?"

"Mm-hmm. You don't really think he could be dead, do you?"

"Well, honey, it just seems so strange that we haven't heard from him in all these months, especially since we know there's mail service up there." Martha's eyes filled with tears. "So why haven't we heard from him? And why couldn't the Mounties find him?"

Livia bit her lower lip. "I...I don't know, Mama. But we can't give up. I really believe he's alive. Something may have happened to the letters he sent us."

Martha sighed and thumbed the tears from her eyes. "I hope you're right, honey, but I just don't have a good feeling about him."

"All we can do, Mama, is move forward with our plan to find him."

Martha nodded. "You're right. All we can do is go up there and see if we can find him, or find someone who knows him and will tell us whether he is dead or alive."

Martha let out a deep moan and broke into sobs. Livia put her arms around her, and they wept together.

In late afternoon, the sun dropped down in the western sky with magnificent splendor, and when it reached the waves it was like a red fire on them for a few minutes, then it sank away, leaving a crimson flame.

That evening in the dining room, Norman and Margo Fleming sat at a table next to the Burke family. Dale Burke had pushed Norman's wheelchair all the way from the Fleming cabin to the dining room.

During the meal, Dale leaned close to his wife and whispered, "When we're having dessert, I'll go over to the Flemings' table and talk to Norman so I can get to know him better. How about you invite Margo to come over here?"

Elaine whispered back, "Sure. The more time I have with her, the better."

Elaine then looked over at Margo and said, "How about coming over here to our table to eat dessert? Dale says he wants to spend some time with Norman, and they can eat their dessert together."

Norman smiled and spoke before Margo could reply. "Come on over, Dale. Our wives can do their women-talk while you and I do some men-talk."

The desserts were brought on a small cart, and Margo and Dale changed tables.

Dale and Norman started talking about Dawson City and the hotel the Flemings planned to build there.

The three Burke children were discussing what it was going to be like in Canada as Margo leaned close to Elaine and asked in a low voice, "How are you doing, honey, with this Yukon adventure, now that we're on our way?"

Keeping her own voice low, Elaine said, "I'm still a bit jittery, but I'm slowly getting adjusted to the idea. I'm sure I'll be all right."

Margo smiled. "If you ever need me while we're still on this ship, please let me know."

Elaine's eyes showed a bit of extra moisture. "Thank you. I will." She paused, then added, "I sure wish our family was going to Dyea instead of Skagway."

Margo patted her hand. "Well, both White Pass Trail and Chilkoot Trail lead to Dawson City."

"I know, but I'd like to have you close to me at that time, too. And I've read so much about those Golden Stairs on Chilkoot Pass. I'd sure like to see them!"

Margo chuckled. "I'm looking forward to seeing them myself. Climbing them, too. We're going to hire a Chilkoot Indian—two if needed—to move Norman up those Golden Stairs in his wheelchair."

Elaine's features took on a wistful look. "I know it's too late to change our traveling schedule, but it sure would be great for Dale, the children, and me to be with you and Norman while we're climbing to the Canadian border."

Margo patted Elaine's hand again. "Well, at least you and I will spend lots of time together in Dawson City while your husband is in the gold fields."

"Oh yes! It'll be wonderful to have a friend nearby. You may get tired of me pestering you. From what I can pick up about the men working in the gold fields, even those with families in Dawson City sometimes stay out there for days at a time. Being alone with my active children will take some doing, but they're good kids, and they mind well. It's just that since Dale and I have been married, I've never spent a night without him. It will definitely take some getting used to."

"I'm sure it will, dear," said Margo. "But don't you ever for a minute think that you're pestering me. I'll love every minute of it."

Elaine smiled. "Thank you. But I'll still try not to be a pest."

Margo gave her a mock scowl. "You could never be a pest, Elaine."

"Of course, I *will* be quite busy helping Barry and Susan with their schoolwork, and a good part of each day, I'll have housework to do. I'll stay occupied most of the time, come to think of it."

Margo nodded. "See there, honey, you're already doing much better about this Yukon challenge. Just think what an adventure it will be. Not only for Dale and you, but also for your children." A twinkle flashed in her eye. "Just think! You'll have lots of stories about the Yukon to tell your grandchildren!"

"Oh, right! But for now, I'll just be thankful to get these three raised!"

∾

A few tables away from the Burkes and the Flemings, two tables were vacated by passengers who had finished their meals. When both tables had been cleaned by a busboy, a waiter led Hank Osborne and his four sons to one of them, and another waiter guided Tom and Peggy Varner, along with Johnny and Rebecca, to the empty table beside them.

The Varner family discussed the new life before them as missionaries in Dawson City while the Osbornes discussed how rich they were going to become in the Klondike gold fields.

Occasionally, one of the Osbornes used profanity, and they were speaking loud enough that the Varners could hear every word.

Johnny and Rebecca stared at the foulmouthed men. Tom said in a low voice, "Don't listen to that bad language, children. Just ignore it."

When Russell Osborne used an especially foul word, Johnny and Rebecca looked at each other, eyes wide. Johnny was about to say something when his father said, "I'm going over there and ask those men not to use that kind of language in front of my wife and children."

Just as Tom shoved his chair back, the waiters arrived with carts bearing the meals for both tables. Tom scooted his chair back up to the table as their waiter placed full plates in front of him and his family.

Peggy leaned toward her husband and whispered, "Those men look pretty rough, Tom. Maybe it would be best to remain peaceable. Let's just make sure we don't sit close to them on the rest of this trip."

Tom met her gaze. "I'll try to remain peaceable, sweetheart, but I don't like for you and these children to have to listen to that filthy language."

The Varners joined hands, bowed their heads, and closed their eyes. Tom led them in prayer, thanking the Lord for the food and asking for a safe journey all the way to Dyea.

While they were praying, Hank Osborne and his sons gawked at them, and T. J. said loudly, "Well, lookie there, Pa! We got us some religious fanatics on board!"

Tom closed his prayer and forced himself not to look at the men at the next table.

"Peace, peace," Peggy whispered.

Tom picked up his fork. "I'll do my best."

"I'm praying in my heart for you."

"Thank you, dear."

When Tom heard the five men chuckling together, he stiffened, but kept his attention on his wife.

On the other side of the dining room, Jack London was eating with two other men about his age that he had met on board; Laird Thompson and Heath Caldwell. Like London, they were native Californians.

As the meal progressed, Laird said, "I wish I knew more about the wildlife in Yukon Territory. I did a study on wolves not long ago, and for sure, they're up there. But I know very little about other animals in that area. How about you two? Do you know much about it?"

"I've read quite a bit on the subject," Jack said.

Heath nodded. "I've read a little about it."

Laird ran his gaze between them. "Are there any cougars up there?"

"I don't know about cougars," Heath said with a shrug.

Jack took a sip of coffee. "Just recently I read that there are cougars in Canada, but only in southern British Columbia. We won't be seeing any cougars where we're going."

"I know there are lots of bears in Yukon Territory," Heath said. "Brown, black, Kodiak, grizzly, and polar bears."

The three men talked about other wildlife in Yukon Territory, then Jack said, "Laird, you mentioned your study on wolves. I have to tell you…my favorite animal is the wolf. I read that Yukon Territory is loaded with them. I have long been interested in wolves, and I hope someday I can learn more about them."

"Well, they are magnificent animals," Laird said. "And the most important thing I learned about wolves is that most people have the wrong idea about them. They're not 'man's natural enemy' as so many believe. Wolves don't attack human beings like bears and cougars do. The only time a wolf will attack a human is when the wolf believes that person represents a threat, especially to its pups. There have been a few cases where wolves attacked humans when the wolves were starving, but all in all, they're not enemies of man."

"That's good to hear," Jack said. "Aren't wolves highly intelligent? I mean, compared to other animals?"

"Wolves are near the top of the list when it comes to animal intelligence. One of the authors I read told how in the heyday of the buffalo hunters in America, some thirty and forty years ago, wolves learned to head toward the sound of gunfire. They would come upon the scene where buffalo were being shot down, then hide close by and watch while the hunters skinned out their buffalo. When the hunters had gone away with the skins, the wolves would feast on the abandoned carcasses.

"Of course, wolves are excellent hunters themselves and exceptionally strong for their size. The average adult male weighs ninety-five to a hundred pounds. Some have been known to weigh as much as a hundred and twenty pounds, but that's still small compared to what deer, cattle, and other animals they hunt weigh."

"I read that wolves are also known for their speed," Jack said.

Laird nodded. "One of those physical traits I spoke of. There isn't an animal they choose as prey that can outrun them."

After they had finished their meal, the three men left the dining room and stepped out on the deck. Lanterns burned at various spots to give light for both crew and passengers to move about the ship at night. They noticed Captain Eric Fillmore move past a lantern in his white uniform, coming their direction. As the captain drew up, the three introduced themselves, and the captain warmly welcomed them aboard.

"Captain," Jack said, "I've been thinking about what you said about the possibility of us running into a storm or two. Do you anticipate them being bad storms?"

"Well, Mr. London, there have been some pretty bad ones between here and Skagway of late, and it's quite possible there will be some of the same ahead of us."

Laird Thompson's brow furrowed. "Captain, if we do run into a couple of bad storms, will they delay our getting to Skagway and Dyea as scheduled?"

"They could. The ship travels an average of sixteen knots per hour in good weather. It's just over two thousand miles from San Francisco to Skagway, which is eight miles south of Dyea. In good weather, the journey will take approximately five days. If we have bad weather, we could be two or three days late. But let's hope for the best. Goodnight, gentlemen. I'm off to my quarters."

When Jack entered his cabin, he lit a lantern, sat in his overstuffed chair, and went over in his mind what Laird had told him at dinner about wolves. "Tell you what, Jack London," he said aloud, rubbing his chin. "Maybe when you start your writing career, you ought to write a novel with wolves in the story."

THIRTEEN

As Captain Eric Fillmore was nearing the door of his quarters, he heard a familiar voice call from behind him, "Captain! I need to see you!"

Fillmore turned around to face one of the stewards, a silver-haired man named Alfred Stutz, as he came rushing up."

"What is it, Alfred?"

"Sir, we've got trouble on A deck in cabin nineteen."

"What kind of trouble?"

"A passenger named Jess Colgan started a fight with his two roommates."

"Over what?"

"Well, this morning I had an encounter with Mr. Colgan when he boarded the ship. He had expected to have a private cabin, and when Benny, who was taking tickets, told him he would be in a cabin with two other men, he became very angry. He was demanding to have a private cabin when I stepped up and asked what the problem was. Benny explained the situation to me, and I told Mr. Colgan there were no more private cabins available. With the ship filling up as it was, he'd have to share a cabin with two other men."

"And what was his reaction?"

"Well, Captain, he said he had paid for a private cabin, and he demanded a private cabin. I told him to get a grip on his temper or I'd have him thrown off the ship. He quieted down then, and grudgingly headed for cabin nineteen."

Fillmore scrubbed a hand over his mouth. "But apparently this Jess Colgan is still unhappy with his situation."

"Yes, sir. A few minutes ago, Colgan started a fistfight in the cabin, and two of our crewmen, Arnold Michener and Roger Fulton, heard the sounds coming from the cabin and rushed to the scene. Arnold and Roger asked a passenger who was passing by to tell me to get to cabin nineteen.

"When I got there, Arnold and Roger had Colgan subdued, and they had his two roommates, Gordon Glover and Everett Maxwell, tell me the story. They said Colgan had been giving them trouble ever since he joined them this morning. Finally, this evening an argument broke out and Colgan punched Glover. Maxwell jumped in and Colgan punched him, too. Fists were flying when Arnold and Roger showed up and stopped the fight. They're waiting for you to come and decide what to do with him."

Fillmore shook his head in disgust. "All right, let's go."

Moments later, the captain entered the cabin with Alfred Stutz at his side. They found the two husky crewmen standing over Jess Colgan, who was sitting on a chair, looking sullen. Gordon Glover and Everett Maxwell were sitting on their bunks.

The captain stepped up to Jess and said, "Mr. Colgan, I understand you had a confrontation with Mr. Stutz, here, when you boarded the ship this morning."

Jess shrugged. "I guess you could call it that."

"Mr. Stutz told me how upset you got when you found out you would be sharing a cabin with Mr. Glover and Mr. Maxwell."

Jess met the captain's level gaze but did not reply.

"It was explained to you that there were no more private cabins available on the ship. Right?"

"Yeah."

"And you agreed to go to this cabin."

"Yeah."

"Then why have you been giving Mr. Glover and Mr. Maxwell trouble? It's not their fault that the ship has a full load and you had to share this cabin with them."

Jess squared his jaw. "I wasn't giving them trouble. They lied to these two stewards! They started the fight, not me!"

Everett Maxwell jumped to his feet, his features livid. "*You're* the liar, Colgan!"

Gordon Glover turned to Fillmore. "Captain, this…snake showed up here at the cabin this morning while Everett and I were out on deck. When we came back, we found him lying on this bunk by the porthole. It was Everett's bunk. He had taken Everett's things and tossed them on that bunk over there in the corner. Everett and this lying snake argued about it for a while, as you might imagine, but Everett finally gave in and took the other bunk."

"Shortly after that, Captain," Everett said, "Colgan shoved Gordon's clothes and mine to the rear of the closet and hung his clothes right in front."

Captain Fillmore set steady eyes on Colgan. "Why did you do that?"

Colgan met his gaze head-on. "I just hung my clothes in the closet. I didn't pay any particular attention to where I put 'em."

"Well, you *should* have," Fillmore said. "Seems to me you're purposely hard to live with."

"Captain Fillmore," Glover said, "Colgan has been mean and malicious ever since we found him here in the cabin. Finally, when I'd had my fill, I told him to go talk to one of the stewards and ask to be put in a cabin with someone else. He called me some choice names, then punched me. Everett stepped between us, telling Colgan to get out of the cabin, and he punched him, too. We both went after him just as these two stewards showed up and put a stop to it."

Fillmore leaned down and gave Jess a cold stare. "Mr. Colgan, I'm sure these gentlemen would rather I put you in another cabin, and I can't blame them, but I'm going to leave you right here."

Jess started to get off the chair, and four strong hands gripped his shoulders and pushed him back down.

"Don't even think about it, mister," Roger Fulton said. "Believe me, if you try anything with us, you'll be sorry."

"I'm warning you, Mr. Colgan," Fillmore said. "If you cause any more trouble, you will be *very* sorry. Do you understand that anyone who causes trouble aboard a passenger ship is breaking international law?"

Jess looked into the captain's eyes. "International law?"

"That's what I said. I have the authority by law to lock up troublemakers aboard my ship in one of the dark rooms down in the hold next to the engine room, to keep them there for the rest of the journey, then to put them in the hands of the local authorities wherever the ship docks next. Being a troublemaker at sea, Mr. Colgan, is considered a felony, and the troublemaker will be punished to the full extent of the law. Do you understand what I'm telling you?"

Jess nodded slowly.

"Then are you going to cooperate with us?"

Jess held his gaze and grunted, "I'll cooperate."

The captain made a thin smile. "Thank you." Then he turned to his stewards. "We can go, gentlemen."

When the door went shut, Jess Colgan rose from the chair. Gordon Glover gave him a cold glance, then turned to his friend and said, "I need to take a walk and get some fresh air. Did you notice how brightly the moon is shining? I want to see the ocean in the moonlight."

"I need some fresh air, too," Everett said. "I'll walk with you."

When they were about to step out onto the deck, Glover looked back at Jess and said, "We expect you to keep your word to the captain, Colgan. If you don't, we'll see to it that you get locked up in one of those dark rooms down in the hold. Understand?"

Jess stared at them without expression. "Yeah, I understand."

When the door clicked shut, Jess Colgan picked up Glover and Maxwell's canvas travel bags, then gathered up some of their possessions and stuffed them into the bags. When the bags were nearly full, Jess carried them out onto the deck. By the light of the ship's lanterns, he saw that no one was on the deck at the stern of the ship. Jess made his way to the stern and moved up to the railing and balanced both bags on it.

Glover and Maxwell happened to be walking along the railing on the ship's port side, heading toward the stern.

"I tell you, Gordon, it isn't gonna work," Everett said. "That hot-tempered idiot will give us more trouble, no matter how sternly he's been warned."

"Yeah, I agree. Maybe we oughtta go have a private talk with Fillmore and flat tell him we don't want Colgan in our cabin."

"I'd like to think it would work, but since Colgan promised him he'd cooperate, it could make us look like the bad guys."

Gordon was taking in the beauty of the moonlight on the surface of the ocean. "Yeah, I suppose you're right. I just don't know what to—" He pointed toward a spot on the port side of the stern. "Look, it's Colgan! He's got our canvas bags!"

Both men bolted toward Jess Colgan just as he let both bags fall overboard. Jess leaned against the railing and watched the bags strike the water, chuckling to himself.

Gordon and Everett ran up behind Jess and grabbed hold of him. Jess tried to fight them off, but they picked him up, hoisted him above the railing, and threw him overboard.

They watched him splash into the water, then looked around to make sure no one was in sight.

"Let's get back to the cabin, Everett," Gordon said. "Fast!"

Down in the cold, choppy water, Jess Colgan bobbed up and down, gasping and coughing each time his head went below the surface and came back up. He barely knew how to swim, and realized that even if he were a good swimmer, he was too far from land to ever make it to safety.

His heart pounded savagely.

Struggling and splashing about, Jess thought of what Chaplain William Glaxner had told him about dying in his sins without Jesus Christ and spending eternity in hell. He also remembered Fred Matthis urging him to open his heart to the Saviour.

Suddenly, in the expanding distance between himself and the ship, Jess saw a man standing at the rear of the second deck, just behind the pilot's cabin.

Jess waved his arms wildly and cried out, "Hel-l-l-lp! Hel-l-l-lp!"

Tom Varner heard the cry for help from out on the ocean's surface, and because of the bright moonlight, he was able to quickly focus on the terrified figure splashing and waving his arms.

Tom ran to the pilot's cabin, stuck his head in the open doorway, and said to the man at the wheel, "There's a man overboard! He's behind the ship! I'm going in after him!"

The pilot's eyes were wide. "Go! I'll turn the ship around and alert Captain Fillmore!"

As Tom ran toward the staircase, he felt the ship's speed ease back as the pilot cut the engines. He nearly flew down the stairs to the main deck and dashed to the railing. He could still see the struggling man in the foamy water of the ship's wake in the distance. He kicked off his shoes, climbed over the railing, stood on the lip of the deck for a second or two, then dove into the ocean.

Tom swam with every ounce of his strength, praying that the Lord would help him. In a matter of minutes, he drew up to the bobbing, floundering man and was able to make out the stark panic in his face as he grabbed him by the shoulders and said, "Hold onto me!"

Jess Colgan was gasping for breath. His strength was almost gone. He feebly wrapped his arms around his rescuer's neck and felt a great surge of relief as two strong arms tightened around his chest.

Tom held the man's head out of the water and looked back toward the ship. It was heading toward them. "It's all right, my friend," he said. "They'll pick us up real soon, now." Tom saw the relief on the man's face and said, "I'm Tom Varner. What's your name?"

"Jess…Colgan. Thank you for…for coming in after me."

"Glad I could get to you in time. I don't think you would've lasted much longer."

Jess took a shallow breath and said, "I…I know I wouldn't."

Soon the ship coasted up close to the two men in the water. A lifeboat was lowered, and within minutes, two crewmen had pulled Jess and his rescuer safely into the lifeboat. When the boat was raised up to the main deck of the ship by thick ropes, Captain Eric Fillmore and several crewmen were there.

Tom Varner stepped out of the lifeboat and said, "Captain,

I'm sure glad I was taking a walk on the upper deck and happened to hear this man crying for help out there in the water."

"I am, too, sir. And your name?"

"Varner, sir. Tom Varner."

"Well, Tom, risking your life to save Mr. Colgan's life was a mighty brave thing to do." Captain Fillmore turned to Jess. "And just how did you happen to fall overboard, Mr. Colgan?"

Jess looked up at him, his eyes bleary and his lids drooping. "I...I think I'm...gonna...pass out."

Fillmore turned to two crewmen. "Carry him to his cabin. Number nineteen. I'll go tell Dr. Ames to check him over."

Jess was carried to cabin nineteen, and when Gordon Glover and Everett Maxwell responded to the knock on the door, and the two crewmen told them that Colgan somehow had fallen overboard but had been rescued, they were stunned.

Gordon looked at the bleary-eyed Colgan and said to the crewmen, "That's his bunk back there in the corner."

Everett followed the crewmen as they placed Jess on the bunk and said to them, "Gordon and I were wondering if he was going to walk on the deck much longer. We were about to go look for him."

At that moment, the ship's physician, Dr. Roy Ames, appeared at the door, carrying his black medical bag.

One of the crewmen said, "Come in, Doctor. He's about to pass out on us, but maybe he will stay awake long enough for you to check him over."

The crewmen left, and the doctor moved up to the bunk where Jess lay. He bent down and laid a palm on his forehead. "How did you fall overboard, Mr. Colgan?"

"I...I don't remember," Jess mumbled.

The doctor listened to his lungs with a stethoscope, then told Glover and Maxwell that Jess had water in his lungs. He turned

Jess over on his stomach and pumped firmly on his back. Jess coughed and choked as water came from his nose and mouth. Dr. Ames kept it up until he was satisfied he had gotten enough water out of his lungs.

He placed the stethoscope back in his bag, bent over his bleary-eyed patient, and said, "You'll be fine, Mr. Colgan. You get some rest now."

When the doctor had gone, Glover and Maxwell stood over Jess until, in curiosity, he opened his eyes and looked up at them.

Glover elbowed Maxwell. "Look at those eyes. He's not groggy. He was pretending."

"Just as I thought," Maxwell said. "Quite a show you put on, Colgan."

Jess sat up. "If I had drowned, you two would be guilty of murder."

"You brought that dip in the ocean on yourself," Glover said.

Jess's face reddened and his eyes became slits. "I could tell the captain you threw me overboard, intending to kill me! How would you like that?"

Glover leaned down, looked Jess in the eye, and said, "We could tell the captain that you stole our property, and we saw you throw it in the ocean! How would you like *that*?"

Jess ran his tongue over his lips and said nothing.

"Seems to me we're at an impasse," Maxwell said. "I'd say we'd better agree to keep the truth from Captain Fillmore and the crew, and just get along with each other for the rest of the trip."

Glover looked at Maxwell, nodded, then looked back down at Jess. "What about you? You willing to do as Everett just suggested?"

Jess swallowed with difficulty, then nodded. "Seems the only sensible thing to do. I'll just tell the captain or anyone else who asks that I was leaning over the railing, lost my balance, and fell in."

Glover extended his right hand. "Shake on it?"

Jess reached up and gripped his hand, then shook Maxwell's hand, too.

The next morning, word spread quickly aboard the *Alaska* about Jess Colgan falling overboard and of his rescue by Tom Varner.

Jess was resting on a deck chair outside of cabin nineteen, and many passengers came by to tell him they were glad the brave missionary had rescued him. Jess was amazed to learn that the man who saved his life was a missionary, but did not let on.

As a group of passengers was walking away from Jess, he saw Tom Varner coming toward him with a young woman and two children at his side.

When they drew up, Tom smiled and said, "Jess, I want you to meet my wife, Peggy, and our children, Johnny and Rebecca."

Jess stood and shook Peggy's and the children's hands.

"I'm sure glad my husband was able to hear your cries for help last night," Peggy said, "and that he was able to see you in the moonlight."

"How did you fall off the boat, Mr. Colgan?" Johnny asked.

Jess told his lie, as he already had several times that morning.

Rebecca looked up at him. "Were you ascared, Mr. Colgan?"

"Boy, I sure was ascared, honey! That's an awfully big, black ocean out there at night."

Rebecca grinned at Jess, her upper two front teeth missing. "I'm sure glad my papa rescued you."

"Me too. I was all alone out there. If your daddy hadn't heard my cry for help, I wouldn't be standing here today."

Rebecca grinned again. "You know what, Mr. Colgan?"

"What, honey?"

"If it had been me out there in the ocean last night, I wouldn't have been alone."

Jess's eyebrows arched. "You wouldn't?"

"Huh-uh. 'Cause I have Jesus in my heart, so He's always with me!"

"W-well, good for you, Rebecca. Good for you."

Peggy took her daughter's hand and looked at Jess, smiling. "I'm happy that you're still with us, Mr. Colgan." Then to her son, "Let's go, Johnny, and let Papa and Mr. Colgan have some time together."

As Peggy walked away holding both children by the hand, she whispered softly, "*Out of the mouths of babes,* Lord. Please help Tom to lead Jess Colgan to You."

Tom and Jess watched Peggy and the children move across the deck, then Jess turned to Tom and saw him take a small Bible from his inside coat pocket.

"I just learned this morning that you're a missionary," Jess said. "Are you a missionary to Alaska or Canada?"

"To Canada. Dawson City. I haven't been there yet, but I'm going up there to establish a church."

Jess nodded. "Oh."

"I'd like to ask you something, Jess." Tom looked at him levelly. "If you had drowned last night, where would you be now?"

Jess grinned. "At the bottom of the ocean."

"I mean *you.* Your soul."

"No offense, Mr. Varner, but the subject is not one I wish to talk about."

"It's the most important subject in the world, Jess. Jesus said, 'Except a man be born again, he cannot see the kingdom of God.' If you've never been born again, according to the Word of God, here, you would be in hell right now."

Jess pondered the thoughts that had raced through his mind

when he had been in danger of drowning. But now that the danger was over, he hardened his heart toward the Lord. Meeting Tom's searching gaze, he said, "Again, Mr. Varner, I mean no offense, but I'm really not interested in hearing anything from the Bible. I want to thank you once more for rescuing me at the risk of your own life, but I'm just not interested in hearing what the Bible has to say."

Tom opened his Bible. "Let me just show you what Jesus Himself said about hell."

Jess shook his head. "I...I need to be going, Mr. Varner. I don't mean to be rude, but I really need to get back to the cabin."

Jess dashed to the cabin door and hurried inside.

When the door clicked shut, Tom walked away with a heavy heart.

FOURTEEN

On Tuesday morning, March 22, the sky was heavy with dark clouds over Dyea, Alaska, and it was snowing. Matt Holden stood at the window of his second-story room in the Dyea Hotel, buttoning the last three buttons at the top of his shirt while looking down at the few buggies, wagons, and riders on horseback as they moved along the street.

The wind was blowing the snow horizontally past the front of the hotel, then suddenly it changed direction, sending the snow spattering against the window.

Matt walked to the door and opened it, then stepped across the hall and tapped on the door of his parents' room.

Maudie opened the door and smiled. "Good morning, son."

They hugged each other, then Matt looked past her to where his fully dressed father sat on the edge of the bed. "How's he doing, Mom?"

Maudie closed the door and sighed. "He didn't sleep well because of the pain in his collarbone and shoulder."

"You feel like going down for breakfast, Dad," Matt said, "or would you like for me to have your meal sent up to the room?"

"I can make it down there if you'll help me."

"Okay. Let's go."

Matt kept a solid grip on his father as the three of them walked down the hall toward the staircase. Carefully, with his mother at his side, Matt guided his father down the stairs, and Cleve groaned a few times before they reached the floor.

"Even though Dr. Slater set your next appointment for tomorrow, I'm going to take you over to his office right after we eat breakfast," Matt said as they moved through the lobby toward the dining room. "He needs to know you had a bad night. There has to be something he can do to ease your pain."

When breakfast was over, Matt kept a strong hold on his father as they made their way along the snow-laden boardwalk toward Dr. William Slater's office. The cold air was like a knife blade, slicing through their coats and slipping in around their necks and cuffs. The wind howled at them, driving snow into their eyes.

"I'm sure glad it's such a short distance to the doctor's office," said Cleve, his breath coming in gusts of steam while he used his left hand to wipe snow from his eyes.

Matt wiped snow from his own eyes. "Me too, Dad. We'll be there in another minute."

When they entered the doctor's office, no one was in the waiting room. Matt guided his father to a chair, and at that instant, the examining room door came open and a father came out beside his young son who had a brand-new cast on his left arm. Behind them was the short, stocky Dr. Slater in his white frock.

The doctor told the boy not to be playing with his sled while his arm was in the cast, then stepped up to the two men in the waiting room and said, "I believe your appointment was for tomorrow morning, Mr. Holden. Is something wrong?"

"Dad had a real bad time last night, Doctor," Matt said. "His shoulder and collarbone were hurting him a lot."

Dr. Slater put a hand to his bearded jaw. "I'll look at your collarbone first. I want to make sure it's set properly."

The doctor guided father and son to the examining room, and after having Cleve lie down, he checked the collarbone. "Everything's all right here. The collarbone is set properly. It seems I just didn't make your medicine strong enough."

Dr. Slater went to the medicine cabinet and came back with several small packets of laudanum powder. He handed them to Matt. "I had hoped the dosage I'd set for him would be enough, but I'm going to double it."

"Will it make me sleepy, Doctor?" Cleve asked.

"Yes, but you need plenty of rest anyhow. Sleep is a great healer, so take twice as much laudanum each time as you did before."

Cleve nodded. "Okay, Doctor. I don't relish another night like last night. I'm sure Maudie will be glad if I sleep well, 'cause when I don't sleep, she doesn't either."

Dr. Slater smiled. "I'm sure that's true, especially when you're in a hotel room." He looked at Matt. "Let me know if he has any further problems. Let's go to the office and set an appointment for day after tomorrow so I can make sure the double dose isn't too much. I want to keep a close eye on him, anyhow, so I'll be able to tell you when he's ready to make the trip over the Golden Stairs. If we can get his pain under control, and he can get his rest, I don't think it'll be very long."

"All right," Matt said. "Thanks for your help."

Slater grinned, his brown eyes tired but twinkling. "That's what I'm here for, son."

❧

Maudie was sitting at the window in the hotel room's rocking chair, watching the storm, when she heard the door open. She rose from the chair and hurried to father and son. "So what did Dr. Slater say?"

Cleve sat down on one of the room's overstuffed chairs, and Matt filled her in on what the doctor had said and told her of the new appointment, then handed her the packets of laudanum powder.

She smiled at her husband. "I figured he would increase your dosage, but I sure didn't think he'd double it. Well, at least you'll get lots of sleep, like the doctor said."

Maudie paused in thought, then looked at her son. "Since your father needs this much laudanum to keep the pain in check, maybe we had better forget going to the gold fields. It might be too much for him. Especially climbing those Golden Stairs. Perhaps we should just go back home."

"I'll be fine, dear," Cleve said. "It's only a broken collarbone, not life and death. Don't fret about me."

"Dad'll be fine, Mom," said Matt, moving up beside the chair where his father sat. "With a little more time to rest up, he'll be good as new. You'll see." Matt patted his father's shoulder. "He's a tough old codger."

Cleve looked up at his son with a wry grin. "Watch that 'old codger' stuff, Matthew. I can still put you over my knee and spank you."

"Okay, but I definitely want the doctor's approval before we head back for Chilkoot Pass," Maudie said. "I certainly want to go on to the gold fields if the Lord makes it possible. We need the money, and the Lord knows there are many of our Christian friends back home we want to help if we strike it rich."

"I want Dr. Slater's approval first, too, sweetheart," Cleve said. "Now, if you don't mind, I think I'll lie down for a while. Maybe I can make up for some of that sleep I missed last night."

"Sounds like a good idea."

"Well, I'll go on back to my room so you two can get some rest," Matt said.

Nearly two hours later, Matt crossed the hall to his parent's room and quietly opened the door a few inches. When he looked inside, both of them were sound asleep. His father lay on the bed, covered to the chin with a quilt, and his mother was asleep in the rocking chair by the window.

Aboard the steamship *Alaska* on the afternoon of March 22, Martha and Livia Bray sat on deck chairs in the bright sunlight, taking in the beauty of the vast blue ocean around them.

After a while, Livia's mind went once again to her father. "Mama, I just can't imagine how Papa could go off to Yukon Territory and never write to us. Why would he do such a thing?"

Martha moved her head slowly back and forth. "It's a mystery to me, Livia. I always thought your father and I had a good marriage." She paused. "Oh...sometimes he would get restless and a bit irritable. You've seen that in him. But I think all men do that at times in their lives. If your father didn't love us anymore, or want us to be a part of his life, he certainly didn't let on.

"Maybe the gold has taken over his mind and made him forget his wife and daughter. I've heard that gold does strange things to otherwise normal people. I guess we'll know the answer to all of this when we find him. If he's alive."

Livia noticed a woman pushing a man in a wheelchair toward them. "Look, Mama, it's that man in the wheelchair."

When they drew near, the woman stopped and said, "If you don't mind, darling, I'm going to rest for a few minutes."

He smiled up at her. "Of course I don't mind, sweetheart."

Margo Fleming smiled at Martha and Livia and said hello.

"Nice day, isn't it?" Livia said.

"Sure is. I'm Margo Fleming, and this is my husband, Norman. We're from San Francisco."

"Oh? Well, we're from San Francisco, too. I'm Martha Bray and this is my daughter, Livia."

Norman nodded and said, "You probably know where the Victorian Hotel is in downtown San Francisco."

"Oh yes, we sure do," Martha said.

"My wife was assistant manager of the hotel until she resigned so we could go to Dawson City to start up a hotel there. From what we've learned about Dawson City's need for a hotel, and with Margo's experience, we believe we'll be successful in our venture."

"Sounds like you folks should do quite well there," Martha said.

"So are you, your husband, and your daughter going to Yukon Territory to get in on the gold strike?" Margo said.

Martha shook her head. "No. Livia and I are going to Dawson City to see if we can find my husband, Weldon. He left home last October to go to the gold fields, but...well, we haven't heard from him since."

Margo's eyes widened. "Oh, my. I hope something hasn't happened to him."

"He was on a ship owned by this same company, and they confirmed to me that he arrived in Dyea with the other passengers. We've had the Canadian Mounted Police looking for him for almost a month now, but so far they haven't been successful."

Norman's brow furrowed. "Ladies, I'm amazed that you're

making this trip alone. I'm glad the Mounties have been called in, but if he's up there in the Dawson City area, shouldn't they have found him by now?"

"Well, not necessarily," Martha said. "Those gold fields cover a lot of territory, and it's impossible for them to look everywhere. There are hundreds of people swarming into Yukon Territory, wanting to get in on the gold strike, and there just aren't that many Mounties."

"Mama and I will find a place to live in Dawson City and try to find Papa," Livia said. "We know full well that it sounds like an impossible task, but we have to do something. We couldn't just sit at home, not knowing whether he's dead or alive."

"I can certainly understand," Margo said. "If it was Norman who had gone up there, and I had heard nothing from him, I'd be doing exactly what you two are doing. When we get to Dawson City, if there's any way I might be of help to you, please let me know."

Martha gave Margo a warm smile. "Thank you for caring."

"If I were in your situation, I sure would appreciate it if someone cared. Norman and I hope you find your husband alive and well."

Livia's eyes seemed brighter than before. "Thank you both. Your kindness means more than Mama and I could ever tell you."

That night, when most of the passengers were in their cabins, Jack London stepped out of his cabin and sniffed the sea air. The breeze was calm as he moved to the railing on the starboard side of the ship and gazed over the gently rolling Pacific Ocean painted ivory by the moonlight.

London moved slowly along the railing, and as he drew near

the pilot's cabin, situated on the bridge above him, he saw Captain Eric Fillmore come out and head down the stairs to the main deck.

London smiled as he drew up. "Good evening, Captain."

"Good evening, Mr. London. Out for a moonlight walk, are you?"

"Yes, sir."

"Well, it's a nice night for it."

Jack's brow furrowed. "Are you still expecting us to run into a storm or two?"

"It's quite possible."

"Not tonight, though. The ocean is so calm and smooth."

The captain chuckled. "At sea, Mr. London, a storm can come up quickly. It can be like this, then all of a sudden, the wind can come up, and the ship will be bobbing like a cork in a bathtub with a three-year-old boy!"

The two men chatted another minute or so, then Jack returned to his cabin and read a few pages in a Robert Louis Stevenson novel before putting out the lantern.

The next morning, a few minutes before dawn, Tom Varner rose from the double bed in the cabin while Peggy was still asleep.

She stirred, made a moaning sound, and opened her eyes. She was able to make out her husband's form in the near darkness, and said, "Honey, are you all right?"

"I'm fine," Tom whispered. "I just want to go out on deck and talk to the Lord about the new work we're going to start in Dawson City."

Tom dressed warmly, and Peggy was already back to sleep as he stepped out of the cabin and walked to the starboard side of the ship. Tom gripped the railing and gazed at the eastern horizon and saw the dawn glimmer. As he moved along the railing toward the stern, he asked God for wisdom and spiritual power for planting a church in Dawson City and to let him see many souls come to Jesus.

A deep, abiding peace filled Tom's heart as he prayed, and he thanked the Lord for allowing him and his family to be missionaries to Yukon Territory.

"I know, Lord," he said, "that it's a wild and troubled place up there, but wherever we are, I know You are there with us, and I thank You for giving me the privilege of preaching Your Word. I know in my heart that we're going to see souls snatched from Satan's clutches and brought into Your family."

Tom prayed for Peggy and their children, asking the Lord to help them adjust to the new life ahead of them.

When he finished praying, he was standing at the ship's stern. The sky was growing brighter. He breathed deeply, inhaling the brisk sea air. The water was an enchanting deep blue, and he marveled at the beauty of the white foam churned up by the propellers. He told himself that since they were only some three days or so from Skagway and Dyea, maybe the captain's prediction of a storm or two was wrong.

At noon, when most of the ship's passengers were in the dining room, Captain Eric Fillmore stood next to the pilot's cabin on the bridge, looking eastward. A strong wind had come up in the last few minutes. The captain let his gaze sweep to the north at the darkening horizon and the overcast sky.

He stepped inside the pilot's cabin and said to the pilot on duty, Dave Lasiter, "There's a storm coming for sure, Dave."

"Appears that way to me, sir." Lasiter pointed to the compass in front of him. "Look here. The wind is going counterclockwise around the compass. You know that always means bad weather is coming."

"I've got to get the message to the passengers and get the crew prepared."

Hastily, the captain made his way down to the deck, which was already swaying and pitching on the roughened sea, and went to the dining room. He stood where everyone at the tables could see him and said loudly, "Ladies and gentlemen, may I have your attention?"

As soon as everyone was looking his way, he said, "All of you can tell that the ocean is getting very choppy. We have a storm coming. By every indication, it's going to be a rough one. I want you to finish your meals quickly and get to your cabins. Please stay there till further notice."

The Burkes and the Flemings were eating lunch together, and Dale offered to wheel Norman to their cabin. The two families left together with Elaine and Margo holding onto the hands of Barry, Susan, and Ernie as they made their way across the lurching, heaving deck with Dale pushing the wheelchair ahead of them. Once Norman and Margo were safe in their cabin, Dale took Elaine and their frightened children to their own cabin.

Captain Fillmore met with his crewmen, telling them to follow protocol in preparing for the oncoming storm. He assigned a number of them to see that every passenger who had not heard his warning in the dining room received the same message. The rest of the crew tightened down the anchor fastenings and secured every hatch and watertight door on the ship. They checked the hatches on the lazarette, where the steering mechanism was housed, making sure they were secure. They double-lashed the fuel barrels that were stored in a room next to the engine room and tied down anything in the engine room that could break loose and cause damage.

Tom and Peggy Varner were in their cabin sitting on their bed. Tom held Rebecca on his lap, and Peggy held Johnny. As the ship tossed on the stormy sea, Rebecca's eyes bulged with fright. She kept trying to look through the water-speckled porthole, but found it impossible to see out.

"Let's pray," Tom said.

They bowed their heads and Tom asked the Lord to keep the ship from sinking or even being damaged.

Rebecca felt the seriousness in her father's words and huddled close to his chest. He felt her little body trembling even as Peggy and Johnny moved closer to his side.

As the wind howled and the sea roared, Jess Colgan and his roommates sat on their bunks and tried to find something to hang on to.

Jess thought about his talks with Chaplain William Glaxner, Fred Matthis, and more recently, Tom Varner about heaven and hell. But he told himself the ship was not going to sink. They would make it through the storm, and he would be just fine.

FIFTEEN

The *Alaska* plowed her way through the violent storm as the day wore on. When the larger swells came, she plunged into the crests, stalled, and launched out the far side, spray streaming off her bridge and the pilot's cabin where Dave Lasiter was battling a twisting wheel.

On the stairs that led up to the bridge, Captain Eric Fillmore was in a battle himself. The sway of the ship and its constant rise and fall made it extremely difficult to climb the slick, wet steps. The decks were awash, the ship was heaving and rolling, and spray was hitting the struggling captain like grapeshot.

Finally, Fillmore made it to the bridge and stumbled his way to the pilot's cabin, where he yanked the door open, teetered inside, and closed the door. He was dripping wet.

"Bad one, isn't it, sir?" Dave said.

"I'd say the wind is up to at least seventy knots."

"I was thinking more like eighty to eighty-five knots, sir."

"You may very well be right."

"How's it going down in the ship, sir?"

"All of the crewmen have done their jobs to prepare for this storm, and I sent them to their stations to ride it out. As for the passengers, I looked in on a few and already a number of them are suffering seasickness."

Dave was fighting the wheel with all his might, doing what he could to steady the ship, when suddenly he pointed forward, through the wet windshield. "Captain, look!"

Fillmore's body stiffened when he saw it. A massive wave rose up straight ahead of them. It stretched away in a straight line as far as they could see in either direction. Seconds later, it rocked the ship sideways, then pitched it up and down.

Above the moans and cries from inside the vessel were the thunderous sounds of waves pounding the sides of the *Alaska*, and the howling of the wind as it surged over the decks and whipped around the smokestacks.

The sky had gone black. Thick white foam blew over the surface of the sea in long streaks, often flying whiplike into the air. Lightning illuminated the somber black clouds, and the thunder that followed hammered the decks and walls of the *Alaska*. The bow plunged into the rolling sea, the deck heaving and falling away sharply. Waves exploded high into the air, leaving salt spray to mix with the driving rain.

Hours passed as the *Alaska* was tossed to and fro on the wild Pacific Ocean. In their cabins, the crew and passengers listened to the wind and the waves and to the water hissing across the decks.

Darkness fell, and the storm continued into the night.

In their cabin, Martha and Livia Bray sat together on one bed, holding on to each other. A single lantern burned, firmly attached to the bed stand. Yet the storm that raged outside was minor compared to the storm raging in Martha's heart.

Livia could read the torment in her mother's eyes. "Are you frightened from the storm, Mama?"

"I am, honey, but this nagging anguish over your father has me upset even more."

Livia squeezed her mother harder.

"Your papa and I have been married twenty-five years. We waited so long for you to come into our lives, and your papa was so happy when he learned that we were going to have a baby. He was even happier the day you were born.

"I thought we had a good marriage. There was hardly ever even a cross word between us. Sure, we had to struggle some to make ends meet, but I never saw that as a problem as far as our marriage was concerned. It was just *life*. I—I must have done something wrong. Somehow, this must be my fault. It's not like your papa to just go away and never even write a letter."

Tears spilled down Martha's cheeks.

Livia wrapped her arms around her mother and held her close.

"No, Mama, don't say that. It's not your fault. I've lived with you and Papa for nineteen years, and I never saw you do him wrong in any way. Let's not borrow trouble. We'll just find Papa up there in those gold fields, and when we do, we'll work everything out. Please don't let this tear you apart. We've got to conserve our strength for whatever lies ahead."

Livia took a clean handkerchief from her dress pocket and dabbed at her mother's tears. "Don't cry now, Mama. No matter what happens, you and I still have each other."

A quivering smile formed on Martha's lips as she looked into her daughter's eyes. "All we can do on this mission of ours is try, honey. If we fail, and don't find your father, we'll go back home. Hopefully, Mr. Ames will give me a job at the hotel." She caressed Livia's face. "We'll make it, honey."

"Mama, our lives seem to be like those waves out there…up and down, up and down," Livia said.

Martha nodded. "I guess most people's lives are pretty much like that—sometimes a valley and sometimes a mountain top."

After several moments of silence between them, Martha saw anguish in her daughter's eyes. "Honey, are you all right?"

Tears welled up. "Not exactly. Something is bothering me."

"What?"

"Oh…what happened between Nate and me."

Martha's brow furrowed. "I thought you were over him."

"I am, Mama, but…did I do the wrong thing by breaking my engagement with him when he told me he still loved me? Should I have given him another chance? Should I have listened to his excuses as to why he was seeing Matilda?"

Martha took Livia's hands in her own and looked into her unhappy eyes. "Honey, you did the right thing. Nate's motives for seeing his old flame were totally wrong. If he had to do that in order to determine that he loved you, then something in his heart was amiss. I doubt he would have been a faithful husband to you. His unfaithfulness would have been so much worse if you were married to him. Don't try to second guess yourself. You did the right thing."

Livia managed a thin smile. "Thank you, Mama. I guess I just needed some reassurance."

"Let me remind you of what you said after the way Nate treated you. You said he wasn't worth crying over. Remember?"

Livia took a deep breath and nodded. "Yes. And I was right. I will shed no more tears over him. I have the hopeful expectation that somewhere in my future there is a nice, earnest young man I will fall in love with. He will fall in love with me, too, and he'll be faithful to me and treat me right. We will marry and live happily ever after."

Martha hugged her. "You just hang onto that hope."

"I will, Mama. With all my might."

❧

Hank Osborne and his sons were all sitting on their individual bunks as the ship pitched and rolled.

"I wish we'd never boarded this stupid ship," Lou said. "I wish we'd stayed home."

"Aw, cheer up," T. J. said. "Sooner or later we'll make it to the Klondike, stake our claim, and start digging gold out of the ground. It'll be worth having suffered through this storm when we become millionaires."

Lou scowled. "Well, I sure hope you're right. Right now I'm miserable."

Russell chuckled. "You'll get over it when you're holding all that money in your hands."

"Listen to your brothers, Lou," Hank said. "This storm will vanish from your memory once you're depositing huge amounts of money in your bank account."

Alone in his cabin, Jack London clung to the edge of his bunk to keep from being tossed onto the floor. "Sorry, Mama," he said aloud. "I know I promised you I would never imbibe again, but right now I really need a drink."

A gray dawn broke on Thursday morning, March 24, with storm winds blowing as hard as ever. The *Alaska* pitched and rolled in waves whitened by wind and pelted by heavy rain. Thick foam blew across the sea in long streaks.

In the pilot's cabin, Captain Eric Fillmore sat on the seat beside the present pilot, Alex Murdock, who was wearily straining to hold the wheel steady.

"Alex, I'm sure everyone's got to be getting hungry," the captain said. "I suppose most of the passengers brought some food on board, but even that must be running quite low—or even be gone by now. I'd like to put the cooks back to work and open the dining room, but that's just not possible."

"Those who are seasick probably can't stand the thought of food right now anyway, Captain."

"No doubt. I wish it were different, but we'll just have to ride this storm out. When you're on board a ship during a tumult like this, there's no place to seek shelter. No place to 'get off.'"

Alex took his eyes off the wet windshield long enough to look at the captain. "But this storm will wear off soon, I'm sure. My heart really goes out to those passengers who are still seasick. As long as this storm has lasted, sir, it's a good thing you and I and the rest of the crew have developed strong stomachs from our years in this business."

Fillmore grinned and shook his head. "Oh, boy. It sure took me a while to develop my sea-storm stomach, I'll tell you."

When dawn came on Friday morning, the sea was still raging. Captain Fillmore sat beside his tired pilot and looked out the rain-streaked windshield with dreary eyes. "Alex, there's so much water in the air, and so much air in the water, it's impossible to tell where the atmosphere ends and the sea begins."

Alex nodded. "I never heard it put that way before, but it's the truth."

Both men could feel the massive engines pounding in the ship's bowels.

Alex looked at the captain. "I'm sure glad those engines are still running, sir."

"As long as we have coal to fire the boilers, and those big

engines churn the propellers with a full head of steam, we can ride out this storm."

"Yes, sir. But if this storm decided to die right now, I'd sure be one happy pilot."

Dave Lasiter came on duty to relieve Alex Murdock at the wheel at exactly nine o'clock Friday morning. As the day wore on, with the relentless storm continuing to pound and toss the *Alaska*, Captain Fillmore's mind was heavily on his passengers. He knew they understood that he could do nothing about the storm, but he still felt responsible for the care and comfort of the people who had paid good money to ride his ship to Skagway and Dyea.

The stormy hours seemed to drag with unusual slowness.

Finally, darkness began to fall. The captain was in the seat beside his pilot. His eyes were closed and his head was bobbing with the rise and fall of the ship when Alex Murdock entered the pilot's cabin to take over for Dave Lasiter.

Alex took hold of the wheel, looked at the dozing captain, and asked, "Has he been to his quarters for some rest yet?"

Dave shook his head. "He's been right here at my side all day."

Alex looked at the captain, smiled, then turned back to Dave. "He really carries his responsibility valiantly, doesn't he?"

"That he does."

About an hour after darkness had fallen, Fillmore suddenly sat up straight and noted that Alex Murdock was now at the wheel. "Oh. You back already?"

Alex nodded and smiled at him. "Yes, sir. Don't you think you should go to your quarters, Captain? You could rest better on your bed than you can in that chair."

Fillmore yawned and shook his head. "Can't do it, Alex. It's my job to see that this ship keeps operating, even in the storm. I'll just close my eyes for a while yet."

"You do that, sir. I'll let you know if anything changes."

Less than twenty minutes had passed when Captain Fillmore was snapped from his dozing by his pilot's loud, excited voice. "Captain! Captain, wake up!"

The captain opened his eyes, and saw Alex Murdock pointing through the windshield. "Look, sir! Look! After three days, we're finally at the edge of the storm!"

Fillmore rubbed his eyes and focused on the wind-driven clouds that were parting in the sky overhead, revealing twinkling stars. "Oh yes! Yes!"

When dawn broke on Saturday morning, March 26, the sky was clear. The wind had stopped, and though the ship was still tossing on the churning sea, everyone on board could tell that the rough waters were slowly growing smoother.

Captain Fillmore made his way to the quarters of his crew and told the cooks they could go to the kitchen and start making breakfast for the passengers and the rest of the crew, including themselves.

Crewmen were sent to alert all passengers that the dining room would be open for breakfast in one hour. There was joy on the *Alaska* from bow to stern.

Just under an hour later, happy passengers hung on to each other and fought for footing on the bouncing, water-soaked decks as they hurried to the dining hall.

The cooks had stirred up huge pots of oatmeal, scrambled dozens of eggs, and flipped pancakes as rapidly as possible. Large coffeepots bubbled with the fragrant brew.

When all 504 passengers and all crew members except pilot Alex Murdock were seated in the dining room, Captain Eric Fillmore stood before them and motioned for silence.

"Folks, as you can see, the storm is over! I've been talking with a number of you as you came into the dining hall, and I learned that only a few are still suffering from seasickness. Most of these are children, but they're all here, ready to eat anyway!"

There was joyful, relieved laughter.

"Let me tell you where we are now, folks," the captain went on. "The pilot at the wheel right now is Alex Murdock, and by his estimation, we will be just about four days late getting into Skagway and Dyea. Instead of today, as scheduled, we'll arrive there sometime in the afternoon on Wednesday."

The captain looked at the faces of his passengers and saw no one who seemed upset that they would be late getting to their destinations. He smiled. "Folks, let me say this. We are safe and alive by the grace and mercy of Almighty God. For those of you who do not know our missionary passenger and his family, I want to introduce Tom Varner. He and his family are on their way to do mission work at Dawson City. I'm going to ask Tom to lead us all in prayer, and give thanks to God for bringing us through the storm."

Tom stood up at the Varner table and looked around. "Let's all bow our heads and close our eyes."

While Tom prayed, Rebecca—who was sitting next to her father—heard her stomach growl. She grinned impishly and pushed her hands down on her empty stomach and silently urged her father to hurry his prayer along so they could eat.

Tom poured out praise to the Lord for bringing them safely through the storm. When he finished, his "Amen" was echoed from grateful lips all over the dining room.

SIXTEEN

All 504 passengers aboard the steamship *Alaska* were on the main deck when the ship pulled into the Skagway dock early on Wednesday afternoon, March 30, under a clear blue sky.

Snow covered the land in every direction, and around the town was a frozen landscape of white and shadow. The air was bitterly cold, and the jagged branches of the leafless trees resembled skeletal hands in the bright sunlight.

Nearly two hundred passengers were ready to move down the gangplank, with plans to go to Dawson City and the Klondike gold fields via White Pass Trail. Many were telling those who were staying aboard to go on to Dyea and over Chilkoot Pass that they would meet them at Dawson City or in the gold fields.

Dale and Elaine Burke and their children took a few minutes to talk to Norman and Margo Fleming before leaving the ship. Dale stood next to Norman's wheelchair and looked at Margo. "I sure hope you'll be able to find someone to help you get Norman up the Golden Stairs."

"Well, I've read that the Chilkoot Indians are always ready to help those going over the pass." Margo chuckled. "For a *price*, of course."

"I wish we'd planned to go over Chilkoot Pass rather than White Pass Trail so we could make sure Norman had help getting up the Golden Stairs. But I guess the Indians will do the job."

"I'll be fine, Dale," Norman said, "but I appreciate your concern about me."

"I'd like to have a moment with Elaine," Margo said. "We'll only be a couple of minutes." She took Elaine by the hand, led her a few steps away, and in a soft voice asked, "Are you going to be all right, dear?"

Elaine pressed a weak smile on her lips. "I'm still a bit apprehensive, but I know I can trust my husband to do what's best for the children and me. I think the excitement of the gold and the adventure of going after it is definitely a male thing. Of course, if Dale does make a gold strike, we'll certainly benefit from it. And if he doesn't…well, life will go on, and our family will survive because we love each other."

"Good girl! When I see you in Dawson City, you can catch me up on how your trip went over White Pass Trail."

Elaine gave her new friend a hug, and together they moved back to the others.

Dale smiled at his wife and said, "Well, sweetheart, we'd better be going. Most of the crowd has already gone down the gangplank."

Norman reached toward the children. "I have to have my hugs before you go!"

They all exchanged hugs, then Dale and Elaine led them to the gangplank.

Soon the *Alaska* pulled away from the Skagway dock, with the smokestacks billowing black smoke, and steamed up Chatham Strait toward Dyea.

As Jack London and his two friends, Laird Thompson and Heath Caldwell, walked into Skagway, Jack said, "Fellas, before we go to the foot of White Pass Trail, I want to find a saloon and get myself a good drink."

Heath grinned and looked at Laird. "How about it, Laird? Would you like to belt down a little whiskey, too?"

Laird nodded. "Let's do it."

Moments later, they entered the White Pass Saloon and were surprised to see that the saloon had a telegraph service.

"Well, lookee there," Heath said. "Some of the men who were on the ship must be letting their families know they've arrived in Skagway."

"I'll wait till we get to Dawson City to wire my mother," Jack said.

Heath looked at Laird. "I'm gonna get in line. I told my wife I'd wire her from Skagway, and no doubt she's worried since we're four days late getting here."

"I'll get in line with you and wire my wife, too."

"Tell you what, boys," Jack said. "When you're done here, you can find me over there at the bar."

Over half an hour had passed when Laird Thompson and Heath Caldwell drew up to Jack London at the bar. Holding a shot glass, he looked at them and smiled. "Well, did you get your wires sent?"

"Sure did. And now we're really thirsty," Heath said.

A little later, London, Thompson, and Caldwell moved out onto the snow-laden street. They overheard a group of men talking, and one of them told the others that a Mountie had just come into town from the foot of White Pass Trail. The Mountie told him that so much snow had fallen the past couple of weeks that most people were hiring dogsleds north of town and going on to Dyea to climb Chilkoot Pass.

Jack looked at his friends. "I think we should do the same, guys."

Laird and Heath agreed, and the three of them, carrying their heavy canvas bags, headed toward the north side of Skagway.

They reached the spot where several dogsleds were collected in a large circle and saw other passengers from the *Alaska* there. Among them were Dale and Elaine Burke and their children.

Jack approached Dale and said, "So you're going to sled it to Dyea, eh?"

Dale nodded. "From what I've been hearing about the snow piled up on White Pass Trail, I figure it's best."

Jack threw a thumb over his shoulder, pointing at Thompson and Caldwell. "My friends and I have decided to do the same thing."

Within a few minutes, a good number of the people who had been on the *Alaska* had hired dogsleds. They were whisked away northward at the cry of "Mush!" from the drivers.

Jack and his two friends decided to hire just one sled, so they sat together, each holding his luggage. Since the trip was only eight miles, they decided they could handle it that short distance.

The sleds were in a single line as they sailed over the snow-covered ground toward Dyea.

They were only a couple of miles out of Skagway when they saw a large gray wolf and a small pup the same color at the edge of a forest. Adults and children aboard the sleds were pointing at them. The wolves stood still and watched as the sleds passed by.

"Hey, Laird," Jack said, his eyes shining with excitement, "isn't that large wolf a male?"

"Sure is," Laird said.

"And—correct me if I'm wrong—but isn't the little one a male, too?"

"Yep."

Jack cocked his head. "Why would that big male wolf have a pup with him?"

"Well, male wolves often take their male pups from the den when they're small to teach them about life and survival in the wilderness."

"I've heard about mother wolves training their pups, but I didn't know the fathers got involved too."

"Well, Jack, since you've told Heath and me that maybe you'd like to write a novel someday about wolves in the wild, maybe you ought to write a novel about that male wolf and his son."

Jack laughed. "I just might do that!"

When the steamship *Alaska* docked at Dyea eight miles further up Chatham Strait, there were Mounties waiting to guide the travelers up to the base of Chilkoot Pass, where their luggage would be examined.

Standing on the main deck with his family, Johnny Varner caught sight of the Canadian policemen, and he jumped up and down with elation. "Mama, Papa, look! Mounties! Real Mounties!"

Tom chuckled. "Well, son, I'm glad you finally got to see some real live Mounties."

Rebecca ran her gaze over the Mounties and dock workers. "I want to see some Eskimos."

Tom patted her shoulder. "Be patient, honey. You'll get to see some Eskimos."

She looked up at her father, brow furrowed. "When, Papa?"

"I can't tell you exactly, but there are lots of them up here. I promise."

Soon the entire group was gathered on the dock, and the highest-ranking Mountie stood before them and said, "Ladies and gentlemen, boys and girls, welcome to Alaska. We'll be leading you to the base of Chilkoot Pass, where we will examine your luggage to make sure you are carrying what is necessary to make the trip over the pass and all the way up to Dawson City.

"You will be sold tents at the base of the pass, which will house you until you can make the climb. There has been so much snowfall the past two weeks that Randall Evans and Wayne Philbrick, the two men who created and maintain the Golden Stairs, have told us that it will be a few days before they'll have the pass ready to climb. Some Chilkoot Indians and Eskimos are helping them, and they say that, barring any new snowstorms, the stairs will be ready to climb by next Sunday morning, which is April 3. We'll be heading for the base of the pass in a little while. There are Chilkoot Indians coming here to the docks so you can hire them to help carry your luggage to the base of the pass, and even *over* the pass, if you wish."

Rebecca looked up at her father. "Did you hear that, Papa? He said there are Eskimos up at the pass! I'll get to see them real soon, won't I?"

"You sure will, sweetheart."

The Mounties were moving among the crowd of travelers, answering questions, when a group of dark-skinned men appeared at the end of the dock and headed toward the travelers.

When Rebecca saw them, she grabbed her father's hand and said, "Papa, look! Here come some Eskimos right now!"

A Mountie was passing by, and he stopped and smiled down at her. "Those aren't Eskimos, sweetie. They're Chilkoot Indians. But if it's Eskimos you want to see, when you get to the pass, you'll see some for sure."

Her countenance beamed.

As the Mountie walked on, Peggy leaned close to Tom. "I

guess a tent will protect us some from the elements, but it doesn't exactly sound warm and cozy."

Tom grinned at her. "But if there's any way to make a tent warm and cozy, you're the one who can do it."

Peggy playfully punched his shoulder. "Oh, *you*!" She wrapped her arms around herself and stomped her feet to keep the circulation going.

Tom looked at her tenderly, love and adoration shining in his eyes. "A tent or a cottage, my love. As long as I'm with *you*, it will be home sweet home."

She smiled at him and looked into the dark eyes she loved so much.

In his heart, Tom said, *Thank You, Lord, for this wonderful wife of mine. What would I ever do without her?*

Soon the Indians were carrying luggage, and along with the Mounties, the travelers moved to the edge of town in preparation for the brief walk to the base of the pass. The Mounties had put Norman Fleming's wheelchair on a small sled, but it was large enough for Margo to ride with him as two Mounties pulled it.

Martha and Livia Bray stood in the knee-deep snow, talking to the two Chilkoot Indians they had hired to carry their luggage, when they saw two dogsleds pull up close by. Livia noticed the handsome young man who jumped off the sled he was riding and helped a man and a woman he called Mom and Dad off their sled. The young man's father was wearing his right arm in a sling.

The young man wore a tight-fitting mackinaw, and Livia marveled at the width of his shoulders and his muscular form. There was something vital and compelling about him, a combination of strength and action.

The young man saw Livia and Martha and moved toward them, smiling. "Hello, ladies. My name is Matt Holden, and those are my parents over there. Are you traveling alone?"

Livia gave him a warm smile. "Yes, we are. I'm Livia Bray, and this is my mother, Martha Bray. We're from San Francisco. And the reason we're traveling alone is that we're on our way to Dawson City to find my father. He came to the gold fields almost six months ago, but we haven't heard from him since. The Mounties have looked for him, but so far haven't been able to locate him. Mama and I have come to search for him on our own."

Matt turned and motioned to his parents. They headed toward him, and when they drew up, he introduced Livia and her mother and explained their situation.

"Well, I certainly hope you find him," Maudie said.

Soon the travelers were moving into Tent City at the base of Chilkoot Pass, where they purchased tents in response to the Mounties' warning of cold temperatures. They looked northward in awe at Chilkoot Pass, whose towering snow-covered top they could barely make out because of the thick forest between where they stood and the peak of the pass. They were able to make out the men working on the Golden Stairs.

When Matt Holden and his parents came to the tent they had purchased and occupied over two weeks before, Matt noticed an open space next to it. He turned to his parents. "I'm going to tell Livia and her mother that I'll set up their tent for them right here. Be right back."

"I think our boy is a bit taken with that girl, don't you?" Cleve said as Matt hurried away.

Maudie giggled. "He likes her, that's for sure."

Martha and Livia had purchased a tent, and it lay folded up at their feet as a Mountie inspected their luggage.

Matt drew up, smiling, and said, "Ladies, there's an open

space right next to our tent. I'll be glad to set your tent up for you there if you'd like."

Martha nodded. "We'll take you up on that, Mr. Holden."

Matt grinned. "Great! And, uh, ma'am…?"

"Yes?"

"You can call me Matt."

"All right, *Matt*. Thank you very much. I was just wondering how we were going to manage to put up this tent. We've never had any tent experience."

"Well, you just leave that to me. I'll have it done in a jiffy, and you can move in."

Livia set admiring eyes on him. "Thank you for your kindness, Matt."

"My pleasure, Miss Livia."

"You can drop the *Miss*. Just call me Livia."

"All right, Livia."

"I'll help you, Matt, if you'll tell me what to do."

"All right," he said. "It'll go even faster with your help."

"Well, I'm glad to do it. After all, you're doing Mama and me a big favor. It would probably take us a week to get this heavy thing set up. That is, if we could get it done at all!"

Livia's smile was warm, but Matt noticed it didn't quite reach her blue eyes. She was carrying some kind of sorrow. He told himself people's eyes had such a special way of letting others look inside their hearts.

The Mountie soon finished inspecting Martha and Livia's luggage. Matt picked up the tent and laid it across his shoulders, then managed to carry all of their heavy luggage as well to the spot next to the Holden tent.

Livia helped Matt with the tent while Martha talked to Cleve and Maudie, and soon the tent was up and ready for occupancy.

Martha and Livia thanked Matt for his kindness.

He smiled at them and did a slight bow. "Glad to be of service, ladies. And besides, it would've taken me hours longer if Livia hadn't helped me."

Livia snickered. "I doubt I was that much help."

"Of course you were. If you ladies need anything, I'm right next door."

As Matt plodded through the snow to the Holden tent, Livia said, "He's quite a man, isn't he, Mama."

"Yes, he is," her mother said, a tiny smile playing on her lips.

The gold seekers at the base of Chilkoot Pass were very happy when the Mounties moved among them late Saturday afternoon and said the climb would begin just after sunrise the next morning, as scheduled.

The Mounties explained that because of the heavy snowfall the past two weeks, there could be some minor snow slides as they climbed the pass, but they didn't expect any that could become dangerous avalanches.

Norman and Margo Fleming had hired a couple of Chilkoot Indians to carry their luggage over the pass, but they needed two others to carry Norman in his wheelchair up the Golden Stairs. They couldn't find two who were available, and Margo was frantic about it. Norman said maybe they could hire a couple of the Indians who had been working with Randall Evans and Wayne Philbrick to clear snow and ice from the Golden Stairs.

When the Mounties had finished talking to the travelers, they directed their attention northward, where Randall Evans and Wayne Philbrick were coming toward them, with Eskimos and Chilkoot Indians following behind.

Rebecca Varner and her brother stood between their parents. Suddenly Rebecca pointed and said, "Look, Papa! Look,

Mama! I can tell the difference between the Indians and the Eskimos!"

"How?" Johnny asked.

"Easy," she said, giving her brother a cool look. "The Indians have lots of color in their headgear, but the Eskimos only have white fur on the hoods of their parkas."

Johnny made a mock sneer. "How do you know what they call that stuff they wear on their heads?"

She grinned triumphantly. "Papa has been teaching me!" She turned her eyes up to her mother and said, "Boy, I sure would like to have a warm fur coat like those Eskimos have. Where do you think they got them, Mama?"

Peggy patted the top of Rebecca's head. "I don't know, sweetheart, but I doubt there's a store in Dawson City where we could buy you one."

"Oh, well. I'm just happy I finally get to see some Eskimos!"

SEVENTEEN

Before dark on Saturday evening, Jack London and his two friends, along with the Burke family and the others from the *Alaska* who had chosen to climb Chilkoot Pass instead of White Pass Trail, arrived at Tent City on the dogsleds they had hired at Skagway.

Norman and Margo Fleming were glad to see Dale and Elaine and their children, and a lot of hugging took place in front of the Fleming tent. Dale asked Norman if he had hired anyone to carry him up the Golden Stairs.

"Not yet," Norman said. "We were able to hire two Chilkoot Indians to carry our tent and luggage over the pass, but we need a couple more to carry me and this wheelchair. So far, every Indian or Eskimo I've talked to is already hired for the climb."

Dale smiled and patted his shoulder. "Well, don't worry. You've got me now, and before we got off the dogsleds over there where we pulled in, I was able to hire two Indians to carry our luggage. Between those two Indians and me, we'll get you up those stairs even if we have to carry you piggyback."

Margo's eyes were misty as she said, "Oh, Dale, thank you for being so kind to us."

"I'm kinda concerned those Golden Stairs might be slippery," Norman said.

"Well, we talked to a couple of Mounties about that very thing while we were taking our luggage off the dogsleds. They said Randall Evans and Wayne Philbrick have chipped crisscross grooves on the steps to give good traction for the climb. Of course, they still cautioned us to be careful."

Norman nodded. "That's good to know about the grooves. They'll make the climb a whole lot safer."

Dale Burke pitched the tent he had purchased, and after the Burkes and the Flemings had supper together, they soon were in their tents, ready to retire for the night.

Just after breakfast on Sunday morning, April 3, a small group gathered around Tom Varner and his family. Tom led them in prayer, asking God's protection on them as they made the climb up Chilkoot Pass.

Soon the tents were taken down and placed with the luggage to be carried up the pass. As the Mounties stood before the eager crowd, one of them pointed out that there was a lengthy stretch of steep, snow-covered slope before they would reach the Golden Stairs. But he said they would eventually come to a relatively flat area called the Scales, which was at the base of the Golden Stairs.

Soon the climb was begun, with two Mounties leading the way as the climbers stretched out in a long line. The going was tedious and slow. Dale Burke was carrying Norman Fleming piggy-back while the Indians the Burkes and the Flemings had hired carried their luggage and Norman's wheelchair. Periodically, the Mounties called for everyone to stop and rest for a few minutes.

By noon, under a clear blue sky and a bright sun, they reached the Scales. Luggage was opened, and they all munched on the food they had brought along.

In spite of the sunshine, the air was bitterly cold, and some of the women and children were already complaining of fatigue and frostbitten toes. Staring up at the fifteen hundred stairs that seemingly led to nowhere, a few of the climbers were so disheartened, they decided to go back to Dyea. Some planned to catch the next available ship and head back home. Others chose to stay in Dyea for a while, and when the weather warmed up, they would try it again.

Just ahead of the Burke family, a small, middle-aged man turned to his wife and said, "You know what…I'm just not up to this right now. Maybe we ought to go back to Dyea until the weather warms up."

Elaine Burke listened as the man's wife said, "Whatever you decide is fine with me, dear. When it gets warmer, we can try it again. It'll be easier when it's not so cold."

Elaine smiled to herself. *What an encouraging wife she is. I need to take a lesson from her.*

She watched as the man told the two Eskimos he had hired that they were going back to Dyea. The four of them turned around and headed south along the trail they had just covered, joining the others who were returning to Dyea.

The Mounties called for those who remained to follow them, and soon an unbroken line headed upward on the ice-chipped stairs toward their dream of gold.

Matt Holden positioned himself between his parents so if either should slip or simply need a hand, he could help them. Matt had also asked Livia Bray and her mother to climb just ahead of him so if they needed help, he would be close by.

Not far behind the Holdens were the Burkes and the Flemings, with Dale Burke carrying Norman Fleming on his back.

As the travelers and their hired men climbed the steep stairs, the Mounties up front signaled for them to pause and catch their breath every few minutes.

The afternoon sun gleamed off the snow that blanketed the mountains all the way to the jagged peaks.

When the climbers had been making their way upward for almost two hours, they took an extra few minutes to rest. The Holdens and their hired men were some six hundred steps from the bottom. Matt glanced up ahead and saw Livia leaning over her mother, who was sitting on a frozen step and panting, her breath forming clouds of steam.

Matt told his parents he was going to check on Livia and her mother. When he drew up to the step where Martha was sitting, he said, "Are you all right, ma'am?"

"I just asked her the same thing, Matt," Livia said. "She's a bit winded, but she says she's fine."

Martha took a deep breath. "But it sure feels good to sit down and rest. These stairs are awesome. We're not even halfway to the top. It's going to take some doing to climb them all, but I'll make it."

Livia smiled. "Sure you will, Mama."

"I've come this far, and I'm not going to leave this north country until I find out for certain what has happened to your father."

Matt bent down and looked Martha in the eye. "That's the spirit, Mrs. Bray. And I'm right here to help you and Livia any way I can."

"I appreciate that."

Matt stood up straight. "Well, ladies, I guess I'd better get back to my parents. It's about time to start climbing again."

Livia gestured to the side of the Golden Stairs. "Matt, have you ever seen such beautiful scenery as this?"

He turned and took in the jagged mountains and the valley below. "Don't think I ever have. God's handiwork is marvelous, isn't it?"

Livia nodded. "That's for sure."

Matt moved down to where his parents were, ready to resume the climb.

"Are they okay, son?" Cleve asked.

"Yes, Dad. Mrs. Bray was just a bit out of breath."

Maudie started to say something, but her words were cut off by a sudden thunderous roar from above, and someone higher on the stairs shouted, *"Avalanche!"*

Men cried out and women screamed as they looked up to see great waves of snow cascading down the side of the mountain. Most of it was sliding straight down, but some of it slid at an angle, heading dangerously close to a portion of the Golden Stairs.

Matt glanced up the stairs and caught sight of Livia slipping on the edge of the icy step she was on, desperately trying to get to her mother. Suddenly she lost her balance and fell, arms flailing and eyes bulging in terror.

As Livia dropped into the deep snow below the stairs, Matt said to his parents, "I'm going after her!"

Martha Bray was crawling toward the edge of the step, screaming her daughter's name.

When Matt reached Martha, he saw that Livia was lying faceup on the snow some fifty feet below the step she had fallen from. Her eyes were wide open, and she saw Matt leap from the stairs toward her.

Just as Matt hit the snow next to Livia, they both heard

another roar from higher up. A great wall of snow was coming straight toward them alongside the Golden Stairs.

Matt flung himself on top of Livia and wrapped his arms around her. Suddenly they were carried downward by the snow, buried completely. Down and down they fell, and after what seemed like an eternity, they came to a sudden stop beneath what seemed to be tons of snow.

When the roar stopped, Matt and Livia found themselves in almost total darkness, though from somewhere above them, a tiny sliver of light was getting in.

Matt released Livia from his grasp and looked at her. "Are you hurt?"

"I…I don't think so. The snow was soft where I landed when I fell. I'm not hurting anywhere."

"Oh, thank God," he said.

She looked up toward the thin beam of sunlight. "I'm amazed at that light. How is it getting in here? And why are we not suffocating?"

Matt looked around them. "Somehow we landed in a low spot and the snow didn't fall right on top of us."

She swallowed with difficulty and nodded.

Matt raised up on his knees and looked above him, noting that the space where they were was little more than four feet high. "We're trapped, but at least we have air to breathe." He reached above him and clawed at the snow. "Oh, boy. It's packed solid and hard as a rock. There's no way we can dig our way out."

Livia sucked in a shuddering breath and reached for Matt. "No-o-o! No, we've got to find a way to get out!"

Matt took hold of her shoulders. "Try to stay calm. Let me think on this."

The sound of his voice did something to calm her. She gripped his forearms and closed her eyes. A moment later, Livia opened her eyes and saw Matt looking up at the sliver of light and turning an ear in that direction. "What are you doing?"

"I was trying to catch any sound out there."

Livia listened. "Nothing. Oh, Matt, what if my mother was caught in the avalanche? What if she's dead?"

"Please, Livia. Don't think like that."

Her eyes were wide. "But it *could* be! Maybe your parents are dead, too! There's no sound out there. Maybe everybody on the stairs was buried in the avalanche!"

"Right now, there's no way to know. But somehow we're going to get out of here and find out. Maybe the snow didn't come down far enough to reach your mother or my parents. Since we don't know, we must try to be optimistic."

Livia's whole body was trembling. "I'm trying, Matt. But...but we're all but buried alive! Do something! Oh, please do something!"

Matt tightened his grip on her shoulders and gave her a gentle shake. "Livia, please try to calm down."

Livia shut her mouth on what would have been a loud wail. Tears brimmed in her eyes and fell down her cheeks. "I'm—I'm sorry, Matt. I'm scared for Mama and your parents and everyone else out there. And I'm scared for you and me. How are we going to get out of here? We'll die if we don't get out! What are we going to do?"

Matt let go of Livia's shoulders and took both of her hands in his. "I'll tell you what I'm going to do. I'm going to pray. I am God's child, and He cares for His own. I'm going to pray that He will get us both out of here."

Livia's brow furrowed. "You don't think God is going to come down from heaven and dig us out of here, do you?"

"No. But if He wants us to survive, He'll make a way for our escape. Prayer is all I have, but it can be enough."

Livia bit her lips and wiped tears from her cheeks. "Okay. Pray, Matt. It sure can't hurt to do that."

Matt put a strong arm around her shoulder, then poured out his heart in prayer for Livia's mother, his own parents, and everyone on the Golden Stairs. He asked, if Mrs. Bray and his mother and father were still alive, that God would protect them and keep them alive. He asked that somehow the Lord would help Livia and him to get out of their snow trap alive. He closed in Jesus' name, thanking the Father above for giving him peace in his heart.

Livia began to weep, and Matt sat down beside her, put an arm around her shoulder, and did his best to keep her from panicking.

Hours slipped by, and finally the sliver of light above them darkened.

Livia clung to Matt in fear. "It's night now, Matt. Even if rescuers with lanterns are looking for people buried in the avalanche, there'd be no way they could know that you and I are down here. Everybody has to die sometime. Maybe this is our time."

Matt took hold of both her hands. "You're right, everybody does have to die sometime. And if this is God's time for us to die…I know I'll go to heaven. Will you?"

There were a few seconds of silence, then Livia said in a shaky voice, "I sure hope so. I've tried to live a good life and live by the Golden Rule. I've always tried to treat people as I want to be treated."

"But Livia…do you know Jesus Christ as your Saviour?"

"Well, I believe in God and I believe in Jesus. And as I said, I've tried to live a good life."

"You've tried? You mean you haven't always done so?"

Livia sighed. "No, I haven't. I've failed quite often."

"And because of this, you say you *hope* you'll go to heaven."

"That's the best I can say, yes. You said you *know* you'll go to heaven. How can you know you've done enough good works to outweigh the bad? Doesn't the Bible say that all of us are sinners?"

"Yes, it does. Romans 3:23, 'For all have sinned, and come short of the glory of God.' And Matt Holden is a sinner, Livia. But since I've received Jesus as my personal Saviour, my sins have been washed away in His precious blood, and I'm a forgiven sinner. I've been born again, which Jesus said I must be in order to go to heaven. Do you believe that Jesus died on the cross for sinners, Livia, and that he came back out of the grave as He said He would?"

"Well…yes, I do."

"Then do you understand that it's turning to Jesus in repentance of your sin, trusting only Him for salvation, and opening your heart to Him that saves you from hell and makes you a child of God?"

"I didn't before, but I do now. So it doesn't depend on what good works a person does at all, does it?"

"No. Ephesians 2:8 and 9 says, 'For by grace are ye saved through faith; and that not of yourselves: it is the gift of God: Not of works, lest any man should boast.' We're saved by God's *grace*, Livia. Grace is getting something good when all we deserve is something bad. Grace is going to heaven when we deserve to go to hell."

Matt heard Livia sniff, and her voice quavered as she said, "Will you help me, Matt? I want to call on Jesus to save me right now."

Matt's heart pounded with joy. "Yes, Livia, I'll help you."

Tears flowed down Livia's cheeks as Matt had the joy of leading her to Jesus.

When Livia had called on the Lord for salvation, she gripped

Matt's hand and said, "Oh, I have such peace! I've never known peace like this. I'm God's child now, and if I should die this very night, I know I'll go to heaven!"

"Praise the Lord!" Matt said. "Now, I want to pray."

They held hands and bowed their heads in the darkness. Matt thanked the Lord for Livia's salvation, then asked Him to deliver them from their snow trap.

When he said his "Amen," Livia said it, too. Then to keep her mind occupied, she asked Matt about his life in Chicago. She learned that he had been a professional boxer until he became a Christian, and she was impressed at what he had accomplished in the boxing world. She asked about Matt and his parents coming north to search for gold, and he explained why they left Chicago to come to Yukon Territory.

After a while, Livia relaxed and fell asleep in Matt's arms. Soon Matt was asleep, too.

Hours passed, and suddenly both of them were awakened when they heard a loud rumbling sound. They saw that somehow the snow that had trapped them had shifted, and early morning light fell on them through a gaping hole above them.

Matt scrambled to his feet and looked out through the hole. "Oh, Livia! I can see people moving about on the Golden Stairs!"

She stood beside him, and he put an arm around her. Tears were in his eyes as he looked down at her. "Livia, the Lord did it! He caused the snow to shift so we could get out of here!"

Livia was wiping tears. "Oh, thank You, dear Lord! Thank You!" She raised up on her tiptoes so she could see better. "Matt, do you think my mother and your parents are all right?"

"Well, let's go find out!" As he spoke, he lifted her up in his arms.

Within seconds, they were out of the low spot, and Matt carried Livia toward the Golden Stairs through the deep snow. She hurriedly scanned the people moving about on the stairs. Suddenly she gasped. "Oh, Matt, I see my mother! She's with your parents! They're alive! Thank God they're alive!"

"Hallelujah!" Matt shouted.

Matt plowed through the deep snow as fast as he could while Livia shouted, "Mama! Mama!"

Livia caught the attention of her mother and of Matt's parents, as well as that of many other climbers.

Within minutes, Matt and Livia were on the Golden Stairs. There was much rejoicing as they had a happy reunion with Martha, Maudie, and Cleve, who had given them up for dead.

They sat down on the steps together, and between Matt and Livia, the parents learned how they were trapped in the avalanche and how they finally escaped.

Some of the Mounties came to Matt and Livia, expressing their relief that they were alive. They then told them that sixty-four of the climbers and their hired men who were higher up on the Golden Stairs were swept down the side of the mountain and buried in the snow. In spite of rescue efforts throughout the night, none survived.

One Mountie said, "Our count of the dead was sixty-six until we saw you carrying Miss Bray toward us up the mountainside, Mr. Holden."

At that moment, Tom and Peggy Varner approached Matt and Livia, who quickly rose to their feet.

Peggy took hold of Livia's hand. "Oh, I'm so glad you and this young man are all right!"

Livia squeezed Peggy's hand, looked at Matt, and said, "I want you to meet Tom and Peggy Varner. I don't know them well, but they're missionaries who are going to Dawson City to start a church."

They were immediately in conversation about spiritual

things, and Livia told the Varners that when she and Matt were trapped beneath the avalanche, Matt showed her God's way of salvation and led her to Jesus.

"I know that if I had died down there under the snow after I received Jesus as my Saviour, I would be in heaven now," Livia said, a wide smile adorning her face.

The Varners and the Holdens rejoiced with her, and Martha Bray, who had heard every word, stepped close to Livia and said, "Honey, I'm so glad for you. I—I want to have that same assurance of salvation, too."

Tom took his small Bible from his coat pocket, and he and Matt had the joy of leading Martha to the Lord.

Soon the Mounties called out for everyone to get ready to start the climb again.

Matt and Livia quickly ate some dried biscuits and drank some cold coffee, and once again an unbroken line of humanity headed upward toward their dream of gold.

EIGHTEEN

It was just past noon when the travelers reached the top of Chilkoot Pass. The Mounties who were leading them announced that they were now crossing into Canada.

A feeling of excitement ran through the weary travelers as they sat down on snow-covered rocks to eat a quick lunch. Everyone was eager to head down the pass.

The Varners had found a spot where they could sit close together. Rebecca sat quietly toying with the food her mother had put on her plate. Peggy noted this from the corner of her eye as she sat next to her. She looked down at her daughter. "Becca..."

The seven-year-old raised her eyes, her gaze meeting that of her mother. "Yes, Mama?"

"You're not eating. You're pushing your food around on the plate. Hurry up, now. We need to get moving. We have a long way to go yet today."

Rebecca looked down at her plate. "I'll try, Mama. But I'm getting tired of the same ol' food. I'll be glad when we get to Dawson City and can have something different to eat."

"I know eating the same kind of food every day gets a bit

boring, sweetheart, but think of all the people in many countries of this world who have hardly anything to eat. We're very much blessed. The Lord has given us food to fill that empty spot each one of us has in our tummy. We must be grateful, even though we're not eating fried chicken and mashed potatoes. God says He will supply our needs. He doesn't say He'll supply our *wants*."

Rebecca smiled. "Okay, Mama, you're right." She picked up a small piece of bread that was folded over a dry slice of cheese, smacked her lips, and bit into it.

Soon lunch was over, and the Mounties led the long line of travelers down the north side of Chilkoot Pass. The snow-laden trail zigzagged down the steep side of the mountain, giving reasonably solid footing because of its rocky base and a generous supply of small broken tree limbs.

By four o'clock, they were at the bottom of Chilkoot Pass, where more Mounties greeted them and pointed out a large number of dogsleds for hire to transport them the fifteen miles to Lake Bennett. The Indians and the Eskimos placed the luggage and gear on the dogsleds, and thanked the travelers as they were paid for their labor. The Mounties who had led them from Tent City bid them good-bye and headed back up the pass with the Indians and the Eskimos.

The sun was lowering over the western horizon by the time the long line of dogsleds pulled up to the south shore of Lake Bennett, which at its north shore was the mouth of the Yukon River. The reflection of the sun danced on the surface of the water.

More Mounties were there to greet the travelers and show them a number of large boats for hire that would carry them north across the lake and down the Yukon River nearly four hundred miles to Dawson City. The Mounties explained that even though it was now spring, there were still chunks of ice in the

Yukon River. They assured them, however, that the boats could sail safely in the river.

Matt Holden hired a boat large enough to carry his family, Martha and Livia Bray, and the Tom Varner family, and all their luggage and gear. Everyone was told that the boats would pull out at eight o'clock the next morning.

The travelers pitched their tents for the night, and were supplied wood for building cook fires along the edge of the lake. Soon the delicious aroma of food cooking permeated the grounds where the tents were pitched.

It was a quiet group as they began eating. Everyone was exhausted from the strenuous day of climbing and trudging through the snow. The children were exceptionally tired, and many a little head drooped over a plate as the meal progressed.

Jess Colgan ate supper with Jack London, Laird Thompson, and Heath Caldwell. He listened with interest as Laird answered questions Jack asked about wolves. Dale and Elaine Burke, with their three children, ate supper with Norman and Margo Fleming. And Hank Osborne and his four sons ate their meal just a few feet from where the Holdens, the Varners, and Martha and Livia Bray were eating together.

The Osbornes listened as the small group talked about the Lord, often referring to or quoting Scripture. Martha and Livia both spoke joyfully about their newfound salvation.

Cleve Holden told how he had believed in evolution before he became a Christian, and as the group talked about God's wonderful work of creation, the Osbornes exchanged looks of disgust.

Finally, after listening to this for several minutes, Russell Osborne stood up and walked over to the Christian group. "We've been listening to all this talk about creation long enough," he said as they looked up at him. "You people are fools to believe that creation folly. Charles Darwin was right when he wrote that there is no God, that the universe came into being by a giant explosion."

"Well, Mr. Osborne, you're saying there is no God, eh?" Tom Varner said.

Hank Osborne stepped up beside Russell, with his other sons following. "I'll speak for Russell, preacher man. That's correct. There is no God."

"Let me ask a question," Matt Holden said. "Will you gentlemen agree that every effect has a cause?"

The Osborne brothers now flanked their father, two on each side of him. All four looked at him as he said, "Of course an effect has a cause. So what?"

"This big explosion Charles Darwin says happened. Was it an effect?"

"It was," Hank said.

"All right, then tell me. Who lit the fuse that caused the explosion?"

The Osbornes looked at each other blankly.

Tom Varner took out his pocket watch and held it up. "You know, gentlemen, at a watch factory in New York, there were all these watch parts in various boxes and containers in the storeroom. Somebody threw a lighted stick of dynamite into the storeroom, and *bang!* my watch came together. It keeps perfect time, too!"

Hank scowled at him. "You're insulting my intelligence."

Tom said, "Well, you insult *my* intelligence when you tell me the big explosion happened without a cause. You also insult the living God who created the universe by speaking it into existence. There *was* no explosion. God Himself is the cause of creation. He *spoke* the universe into existence."

Hank and his sons muttered among themselves that the explosion in the watch factory was a foolish way for Tom Varner to try to promote his argument.

"Let me ask another question," Matt said. "Does the earth in its orbit around the sun keep perfect time?"

The Osbornes exchanged glances, but no one replied.

"Well? Does it?"

Hank cleared his throat. "Yeah."

"Okay. And this earth and all the planets and heavenly bodies up there in the sky, which keep perfect time in their orbits, came from an explosion?" Matt chuckled. "And you call Tom's argument with his watch foolish?"

While the Osbornes were trying to think of something to say, Tom said, "So we're fools to believe in Almighty God, the Creator, as the cause of all this effect?"

Hank nodded stiffly. "You sure are."

Tom gave them a thin smile. "Well, twice in the Bible it says, 'The *fool* hath said in his heart, there is no God.'"

Hank Osborne gave Tom an angry wave of his hand, looked at his sons, and jerked his head toward the spot where they had been sitting. They followed in silence.

The next morning, long before time to leave, the campers were awake and making preparations for breakfast, as well as packing their luggage and gear. Breakfast was devoured by 7:30, and soon thereafter, everyone was waiting to step aboard the boats to begin another leg of the long, arduous journey.

Johnny and Rebecca stood with their mother and watched their father carrying luggage to the boat. The sky was a brilliant blue with a few white, fluffy clouds floating in the breezes overhead.

Rebecca, as usual, was hopping from one foot to the other when suddenly she pointed toward a bank of clouds and exclaimed, "Mama! Mama, look at that big cloud up there! It looks just like a huge Eskimo! See his furry coat and hood?"

Peggy looked where her daughter was pointing and squinted her eyes.

Johnny was trying to see what his sister saw, but was unable to make it out. All he could see was a shapeless, white, puffy cloud. "Becca," he said, "your imagination is making you see things that aren't there. It's because you're so caught up with Eskimos that you see them everywhere. Even in the clouds."

Rebecca gave her brother a perturbed look. "Oh, Johnny, I can't help it if you have no imagination! You see the Eskimo, don't you, Mama?"

Peggy was still looking toward the sky. "Well, I'm looking at the cloud you're talking about, honey, but I think maybe Johnny's right. It does take quite a bit of imagining to make it into an Eskimo." She looked down at her daughter. "But if that's what you see, that's all that matters. I'm sure, where we're going, there'll be a lot of real Eskimos. That's one of the reasons why we're going to Yukon Territory; to be missionaries to them as well as the settlers and gold miners there."

Peggy took hold of Rebecca's hand and squeezed it. Rebecca continued to stare at the cloud until the high winds changed it into another shape.

At eight o'clock, the boats carrying the travelers and their luggage and gear pulled away from the south shore of Lake Bennett and headed to the north side of the lake. As the boat in which the Holdens, the Varners, and the Brays were traveling made its way across the sunlit lake, Matt Holden was at the pilot's side, talking to him.

After a few minutes, Matt moved back to where the others were seated and sat next to Livia. From his coat pocket, he produced a small Bible and handed it to her with a smile. "This is my spare Bible that I kept in one of my travel bags. I want you to have it so you and your mother can read and study it. I have no idea if a Bible can be purchased in Dawson City."

"Why, thank you, Matt," Livia said. "Mama and I will spend a lot of time in it."

Tom Varner leaned close and said, "Matt, if Bibles aren't available in Dawson City, I'll have some shipped there from San Francisco. I expect to see many people come to the Lord, and I'll certainly want to give them Bibles."

"You had best order a good supply of them," Matt said with a smile. "I have no doubt that the Lord is going to bless your ministry."

While Matt and Tom went on talking, Martha was very much aware of the glances that had been going on between her daughter and Matt Holden. *I'd have to be blind not to see the interest they share in each other. He is such a nice young man. He's so loving and caring toward his parents, and that in itself says a lot.*

Martha glanced at her daughter once more, and Livia was looking at Matt while he was talking to Tom. There was definitely love light in her eyes.

A few minutes later, Johnny and Rebecca were excitedly pointing to the surface of the lake, crying out that they saw fish jumping. Matt excused himself to Livia, saying he wanted to go join the children in their excitement.

She giggled and said, "Why, of course. All you children need to encourage each other!"

Matt playfully tweaked her nose and headed for Johnny and Rebecca.

Martha leaned close to her daughter. "I've noticed the way you look at Matt, honey. Are you feeling toward him what it seems that you are?"

Livia blushed. "Mama, it's only a friendship thing between us."

"Oh, really? Well, I've also noticed the way Matt looks at *you*. I see more than friendship there."

"You do?"

"Most assuredly. It looks like love to me."

Livia smiled at her mother. "Well, Mama, I have to admit that I've never met anyone quite like Matt."

Martha smiled and nodded. "Aha."

"He always puts others ahead of himself, and that's so different from Nate. It's a very nice difference, too. And Matt cared enough about me to tell me about Jesus. That in itself makes him extra special. We'll see where all of this goes, but I will tell you this: He makes my heart beat faster whenever he's near. And that's a good sign, don't you think?"

"I know the feeling well, sweet girl. It *is* a good sign."

Moments later, Matt returned and sat beside Livia. At that instant, the boat's pilot lifted his voice and said, "Well, folks, we're nearing the north side of the lake. We're about to enter the Yukon River, and the current is quite swift, so I want you to be very careful moving around on the boat once we're on the river. It's going to rock from side to side some, and it'll bounce up and down quite a bit, too. I don't want anybody falling overboard."

The pilot noted that everyone was nodding that they understood, and he saw Tom Varner whispering a warning to his children.

The pilot then said, "When we approach a place on the river called Miles Canyon Rapids, and later a place called Whitehorse Rapids, I'll let you know. At that time, I want everybody to stay seated when I warn you we're coming up on the rapids. It would be dangerous to be walking on the deck then."

The pilot heard Johnny Varner ask his father why Whitehorse Rapids had that name. "Son," the pilot said loudly enough for everyone to hear, "the rapids are named Whitehorse because the white, foamy water looks like the manes of wild, white horses running in the wind. You'll see."

Looking around at all of his passengers, the pilot added, "Once we're past those two rapids, the Yukon River will remain relatively calm all the way to Dawson City, which I remind you is the heart of the Klondike."

Matt patted Livia's hand. "I'll keep you safe when we're passing through the rapids."

"I'm sure you will," she said. "However, you must care for your parents as well, since your father has that broken collarbone."

"Oh, not to worry. There's enough of me to go around."

Livia and Martha laughed, and Martha said, "Indeed there is, young man, indeed there is. And it's all muscle!"

Matt's features flushed.

Moments later, all the boats had left Lake Bennett and were moving northward on the Yukon River.

Hank Osborne and his sons were in the same boat with Jess Colgan, Jack London, Laird Thompson, and Heath Caldwell. As they moved down the river, the Osbornes laughed among themselves about their earlier conversation with the missionary and the former boxer, and the others heard them.

Hank Osborne looked at Jess Colgan and said, "What do you think about the Bible and all that heaven and hell stuff those Bible-believers talk about?"

Jess thought about his conversations with Chaplain William Glaxner and Fred Matthis at the prison. He adjusted himself on the seat and said, "Right now, Mr. Osborne, I'm not interested in any of it. All I can think of is finding lots of gold and becoming a multimillionaire."

Everyone laughed, and the subject was dropped. From that moment on, the men in that boat talked strictly about how rich they were going to be.

NINETEEN

The boats sailing down the Yukon River from Lake Bennett passed through the Miles Canyon Rapids and the Whitehorse Rapids, safely but with much excitement. Averaging some forty miles an hour, they arrived at the waterfront of Dawson City at six-thirty that evening. They knew they had plenty of daylight left to get their gear off the boats, to pitch their tents on the outskirts of town, and to eat supper at a café or a restaurant. At that time of the year, the sun set at 10:00 o'clock and rose at 4:00.

Mounties moved among the travelers as they unloaded their belongings from the boats, answering questions and offering assistance as needed. At the spot where Matt Holden, his parents, the Varners, and the Brays were, a young Mountie with one stripe on each upper sleeve stopped by.

Livia Bray turned to her mother and whispered, "Let's ask him if he knows Papa."

Livia took Martha by the hand and led her up to the Mountie. "Excuse me, ah...*Private*, is it?"

"Yes," he responded with a smile. "I'm Private Virgil Woodring. May I help you?"

"I hope so. My name is Livia Bray, and this is my mother,

Martha. Do you happen to know a miner by the name of Weldon Bray?"

Private Woodring shook his head. "No, I don't. He must be a relative."

"Yes, he's my father. Mama and I have come here from San Francisco to find him."

Virgil's brow furrowed. "You mean—"

"My husband left San Francisco over six months ago to come up here and mine for gold," Martha said. "The shipping company he used confirmed that he arrived at Dyea, but we haven't heard from him at all."

"Tell you what, ladies," Virgil said. "You should go to the Mountie post, which is just a mile south of town, and talk to the chief officer, Captain Lee Jensen. He might be able to help you locate Mr. Bray."

Martha nodded and looked at her daughter. "Let's go there first thing in the morning. Right now, we need to get our tent pitched, eat some supper, and get some sleep."

"Mrs. Bray, I'll pitch your tent for you," Matt Holden said.

Martha smiled. "We'll take you up on that. Ah…Matt, I want you to meet Private Virgil Woodring."

Matt extended his hand to the young Mountie. "Glad to meet you, Private Woodring. My name's Matt Holden."

As they shook hands, Martha said, "Matt, Livia and I were explaining to Private Woodring about Weldon. He said we should go to the Mountie post just south of town and talk to the chief officer there. He might be able to help us find Weldon."

Matt's face brightened. "Oh, I hope so."

"Livia and I will go talk to Captain Jensen in the morning and see if he might know Weldon's whereabouts."

Private Woodring was thanked for his help, and after he walked away, Matt pitched the tent for Martha and Livia right next to the tents he had pitched already for his parents and himself.

While the travelers were getting settled, a fresh set of Mounties moved among them, explaining that they would be leading the newcomers to the gold fields the next day to help them legally establish their claims.

The Mounties also said there were many experienced men in the gold fields who—for a price—would teach them how to mine. They also explained that there was an assay office in Dawson City where they could go with their gold to have its value tested, and that there was a Canadian government mint where they could have their gold made into coins. They were also advised that Dawson City had three banks and a telegraph office.

The sun was still shining high in the Canadian sky at seven-thirty that evening when the Holdens, the Varners, and the Brays sat around a pair of tables at the Gold City Café in Dawson City. Johnny and Rebecca were standing at a nearby table, talking to some children they had become acquainted with on the journey from Tent City.

When the waitress hurried away with the orders, Peggy said, "Someone has put a lot of time and effort into this place."

Maudie Holden and Martha and Livia Bray looked around and agreed.

"There are even curtains on the windows that match these blue and white checked table cloths," Peggy said. "It makes it seem so warm and homey."

Martha smiled and nodded. "Yes, it does. And I, for one, enjoy the look of *home*."

"Don't we all?" Maudie said.

Soon Johnny and Rebecca returned to the table and sat down

at their places. Rebecca looked up at her mother. "What did you order for Johnny and me, Mama?"

Peggy smiled. "You'll just have to wait and see."

Just then, the waitress appeared pushing a cart. She first placed Rebecca's plate in front of her, then did the same for Johnny.

Rebecca looked wide-eyed at her food. "Oh, Mama! Roast beef, mashed 'tatoes, and gravy! Wow! I've been so hungry for a meal like this!"

"Me, too!" said Johnny, his eyes fixed on his plate.

Tom smiled. "Well, let's ask the blessing so these ravenous children can eat!"

The adults relished their meals as much as the children did theirs, and lingered a while over coffee and warm apple pie.

When they were finished, Matt stifled a yawn and said, "Well, I guess we'd better head for our tents. Tomorrow is going to be a busy day."

The group stood up to leave, happy, tired, and satisfied. Even exuberant Rebecca was quiet, her full tummy making her sleepy.

Tom picked her up, and she laid her head on his shoulder as he carried her toward the door. By the time they had stepped outside, Rebecca was asleep.

Tom looked at his sleeping daughter and grinned at Peggy and Johnny.

"Well, that's one down," said Peggy, taking Johnny by the hand. "And I imagine big brother won't be far behind his little sister into dreamland."

The next morning, with the sun shining down on the snow-laden land, the new crowd of prospective miners gathered at the south edge of Dawson City where a large number of dogsleds were waiting, as well as several Mounties with their horses. The Mounties were ready to accompany them to find available claim sites and register them so all was legal.

Jess Colgan, Hank Osborne and his sons, and Jack London, Laird Thompson, and Heath Caldwell all hired dogsleds, and Jack, Laird, and Heath hoped they could find claims close to each other.

Elaine Burke, along with Barry, Susan, and Ernie, was at Dale's side as he hired a dogsled. When the driver was ready to go, Dale hugged his wife and children, saying he would see them that evening.

As Dale turned to board the dogsled, Barry said, "Papa, I want to go with you!"

Dale laid a hand on his shoulder. "Son, you'll have to wait until the claim site is settled and I start digging for gold. You can help me then, okay?"

Barry grinned up at his father. "Okay."

Nearby, Matt Holden hugged his parents and said, "I'll be back early enough to eat supper with you. I really believe that the Lord has a productive claim site ready for me."

Maudie raised up on her tiptoes and kissed his cheek. "I'm just as confident of that, too, son."

Moments later, the dogsleds pulled away, gliding on the snow-covered ground. The Mounties rode their horses just ahead of the sleds.

It was a few minutes after nine o'clock that morning, and Captain Lee Jensen was in his office at the Mountie post just south of Dawson City. There was a tap on the door.

"Captain, may I see you?" came the voice of Corporal Harold Mickelsen.

"Sure. Come on in."

Mickelsen opened the door. "Sir, you remember that missing man from San Francisco, Weldon Bray?"

"I do."

"Well, his wife and daughter are here. They came with that large group of prospective miners who arrived here yesterday. They'd like to talk to you."

"Of course. Bring them in."

Martha and Livia Bray were ushered into the captain's office and found Captain Jensen standing behind his desk, smiling at them. "Good morning, ladies." He gestured toward two chairs in front of the desk. "Please come and sit down."

Corporal Mickelsen introduced them to the captain, and Martha and Livia sat down. The corporal left the room, closing the door behind him, and Captain Jensen eased onto his desk chair. A solemn look settled on his face. "Mrs. Bray…Miss Livia…I wish I had some good news for you, but there has been no sign of Weldon since Colonel Steele at Fort Selkirk alerted me that Sheriff Beckett had sent him a wire inquiring about him."

When despair showed in the women's eyes, Jensen said, "Of course, that does not mean he isn't in the gold fields, but he certainly hasn't made himself known to anyone my Mounties have talked to. They've done a thorough search for him."

Martha took hold of Livia's hand and sighed. "Honey, we can't give up. We're staying right here until we find your father. If he's out there in those gold fields, he must come into town now and then. We'll have to keep our eyes open until we see him."

Livia nodded. "Yes, Mama."

Martha rose from the chair, and the other two stood as well. "Captain Jensen, thank you for letting us talk to you."

"Glad to oblige, ma'am. And I sure hope you find your husband."

As mother and daughter walked back toward town, they talked about their need to produce an income while they were staying in Dawson City. When they entered the town, they talked to a number of business owners and quickly learned that with the population booming and so many men around without their wives, there was a need for a good laundry in Dawson City.

So Martha and Livia began to look for a building that might be available to house a laundry. On a side street just off Main Street, they came upon a small house with a For Sale sign in front of it. A small building next to it was also part of the property.

The sign told anyone interested in the property to see the neighbors next door to the south. Martha and Livia went to the neighboring house and knocked on the door. A woman in her midfifties greeted them, and when they asked the price of the house next door, they found it quite reasonable.

The woman said that the house belonged to an elderly couple who had moved to Calgary, Alberta, but had left it fully furnished. The small building next to it had been used as a gun shop. She assured them that if they needed to borrow money to buy the place, the Dawson City Bank and Trust would loan it to them. She then handed them the keys to both the house and the small building and told them to look the place over.

When Martha and Livia stepped into the house, they found it clean and well-kept. The kitchen was bright, and the cupboards were well-stocked with dishes and cooking utensils.

"Mama, this place is perfect!" Livia said. "It's all furnished, even down to the sheets and linens."

When they stepped into what had been the gun shop, they were pleased at its size and the way it was laid out.

"All we'll need to buy are some galvanized washtubs," Livia said, "and some soap, bleach, and starch, of course. We'll need a couple of irons, too, and ironing boards."

Martha nodded, smiling. "We can do that. I like the location here, just off Main Street. We'll put up a big sign that says Bray Laundry, and before long, everybody in town and those who pass through will know there's a laundry here. I have no doubt we'll be busy."

"Of course we will, Mama," agreed Livia, her eyes sparkling.

Martha took hold of both of her daughter's hands. "Honey, surely once we've made ourselves known here, your father will hear of Bray Laundry and come to us. Let's go to the bank and set up our loan, then we'll move our belongings into the house and buy what we need at the mercantile."

Livia's eyes were still sparkling. "Oh, Mama, isn't God good to us? We've only been here a day, and already He has supplied our needs!"

Martha hugged her. "Yes, our Lord has been very good to us!"

At Dawson City Bank and Trust, Martha and Livia had enough money with them to make a reasonable down payment on the property, and the bank gladly approved their loan. Then they went back to their tent and shared with Cleve and Maudie Holden what Captain Lee Jensen had told them and that they had purchased the house and small building. Martha then said that she and Livia needed to take their tent down and go to their new home. In spite of his injured collarbone, Cleve helped Martha and Livia take down their tent, then hired a man with a wagon to haul their tent and luggage to their new home.

At the same time Martha and Livia were riding the wagon to their property, Tom Varner and his family were in the office of Wiley Madison, the chairman of Dawson City's town council.

Tom was inquiring about the possibility of renting the town hall on Sundays, and if possible Wednesday nights, where he could hold church services.

Madison told them he would love to have a church in town, and he knew many other people would, too. He would have a meeting with the town council that evening and see if they would agree to rent the town hall to him.

While the Varners were in Wiley Madison's office, Norman and Margo Fleming were in the office of Dawson City's only real estate firm. They learned of several lots in town where a hotel could be built, and the realtor also gave them the names and locations of the two construction companies in town: Yukon Construction and Smith and Jones Construction.

Then, pushing Norman's wheelchair, the realtor took them to look at the available lots. They passed the Fairview Hotel and, just a block farther found a perfect lot to build their hotel on.

They returned to the real estate office, and papers were drawn up for them to purchase the lot. The realtor recommended the Smith and Jones Construction Company, which had built the Fairview Hotel for widow Belinda Mulroney.

The Flemings paid the purchase price for the lot, told the realtor they were going to name their hotel the Klondike Hotel, then went down the street to Smith and Jones Construction. In a short time, they had hired them to build the hotel, which included a restaurant, living quarters for themselves, and living quarters for the person they would hire to run the restaurant.

The Flemings then went to the Fairview Hotel, with Margo pushing Norman in his wheelchair. They wanted to meet Mrs. Mulroney and let her know they would be opening the Klondike Hotel.

They found that Belinda Mulroney lived up to her Irish name. She was a tiny lady with sparkling green eyes and a mop of silvery hair that still had some red streaks in it. Her smile was engaging and her energy seemingly boundless. Belinda told the Flemings she had no problem with them building another hotel. With the rapid growth of Dawson City, several more hotels would be needed.

The Flemings then headed back to their tent.

"Honey, now that our hotel is in the hands of the builders," Margo said, "it's time for us to find better living quarters. Living in the tent for any extended time is just not suitable."

"You're right," Norman said. "We need to go to work on that."

"Tomorrow I'll look around and see if I can find something more comfortable. The Mounties said there are several boarding houses in town. If we could find one with a decent-sized room on the ground floor, that would be best, don't you think?"

"That would be great," Norman said. "Whatever you can find, we'll make it work until we can move into the hotel."

"All right. I'll go out first thing in the morning, and by tomorrow night, we'll have a solid roof over our heads once again."

TWENTY

Matt Holden was aboard a dogsled owned and driven by a young man whose name was Art Donley. Just ahead of them on his bay gelding was Mountie Len Howson, who was leading them to a claim site.

Under a piercing blue sky, a biting wind blew across the rolling, snow-laden hills, lifting up spirals of snow like dust.

The dogs huffed and puffed, periodically letting out a low yipping sound, and the snow creaked under the hooves of the Mountie's horse.

Sergeant Howson led them up to a snow-covered bridge that spanned a frozen creek, which wound among the hills and was lined by claim sites. He pulled rein at the edge of the bridge, and Art Donley halted the sled. Howson pointed across the creek to a vacant site, which had a small shack on it.

"Mr. Holden, this site was previously owned by an older man who died of heart failure a few weeks ago while digging for gold. He did quite well in the eight months he worked this mine, and there's evidence that there is much more gold in the mine. You interested?"

"I'll take it," Matt said.

After they crossed the bridge, Howson said, "I'll walk you over the site so you can get a good look at it, then you can sign the necessary papers."

When the tour was completed, Matt was pleased with the prospect of the mine. He was glad he had made plans to return to town at the end of each work day. The shack was small and drafty. While he was signing the papers, a wagon loaded with mining equipment crossed the bridge and drew up.

Art Donley greeted the driver with a smile. "Hello, Keith. Looks like we've got you another student here."

"Good to see you, Keith," Howson said. "I want you to meet the new owner of this claim site. Matt Holden, from Chicago."

By this time the wagon driver was on the ground, and he shook hands with Matt, saying, "I'm Keith Landon. I serve as an instructor to teach new miners how to mine for gold properly. If you're interested, the schooling period is only two or three days, and my fee is two dollars an hour. I also have the equipment you'll need in my wagon, and Sergeant Howson here will tell you that my prices are quite reasonable."

Matt arched his eyebrows. "You can teach me in only two or three days, eh?"

"That's right."

"Well, Mr. Landon, you're hired! And I'll buy whatever equipment I need at your reasonable prices."

Howson stepped up to Matt and shook his hand. "Well, my friend, I must get back to Dawson City and turn in your papers. It's been a pleasure dealing with you."

"Thank you, Sergeant. I hope we run into each other again."

"I'm sure we will."

Art Donley was standing beside the sled, where he had placed Matt's canvas bag. "Mr. Holden, I'll be back to pick you up at five o'clock," he said.

"Okay. See you then."

Keith Landon guided Matt up to the wagon and was showing him the equipment he would need for mining gold when the man who worked the claim on the south side of Matt's came out of his cabin, heading for the mouth of the mine. He spotted Landon and waved. "Howdy, Keith. New student?"

"Right. Come on over and meet your new neighbor."

The miner made his way along the edge of the frozen creek and drew up. Matt noted a bit of gray in the hair and sideburns he could see beneath the man's hat. He judged him to be in his midforties.

"Matt Holden, shake hands with your new neighbor, Roger Whitson," Landon said. "Roger has done quite well with his claim site."

Matt smiled as he shook his neighbor's hand. "Hey, that's good to hear. How long have you been working this mine, Mr. Whitson?"

"Almost six months, now. So far, I've taken just over a hundred thousand dollars worth of gold out of the mine."

"Hey, that *is* encouraging!"

"I hope you do even better, Mr. Holden," Whitson said. "Where you from?"

"Chicago, sir. And you? Do you have a family back home?"

"I'm from Kansas City, Missouri, and I have no family. My wife and daughter are both dead."

"Oh. I'm very sorry, sir."

Whitson nodded. "I'm here in the Klondike to pile up enough money to last me the rest of my life, then I'll go back to Kansas City."

"Okay, Matt," Keith Landon said, "let's get started teaching you how to mine gold."

"Glad to make your acquaintance, son," Whitson said. "Nice

to see you again, Keith. Well, I've got to get back to work. The gold is calling me."

As he entered his mine, Roger Whitson whispered to himself, "Martha and Livia might as well be dead. I'm never going to see them again."

Keith took Matt into the dark mouth of his mine as they carried the needed tools and a lighted lantern with them.

Once inside, Keith said, "Matt, much of the gold in these mines is found near bedrock, some twenty to two hundred feet under the permanently frozen surface of the ground. The miners dig deep shafts into the ground by building bonfires. I'll show you how to do it."

Matt shook his head. "I never even thought about the ground being frozen so deeply."

"You'll see. With the bonfires burning, the ground beneath will slowly thaw each day, and you'll gain another foot of depth. I'll show you how to build and control the fires, and within a few days, you'll be digging gold out of the ground."

"I'm sure glad I have you to teach me, Mr. Landon."

"My pleasure. Now, something else. The creek over here...in about six weeks, it'll thaw out and the water will be running swiftly."

"Yes, sir?"

"I'll come back then and teach you how to use a sluice box to also mine gold from the creek."

Keith showed Matt how to build and control the bonfires. And some of the ground was thawed enough for him to also show Matt how to dig out the gold. Keith said that by every indication, there was a lot of gold left in the mine.

When it was nearing five o'clock, Keith led Matt out of the mine. When they stepped into the light, Art Donley was already there with his dogsled.

"So, did you learn much about digging for gold?" Art asked.

"He knows a great deal more than he did before we started," Keith said. "Okay, Matt, I'll meet you back here at nine in the morning."

At the same instant, two men came out of the mine in the claim site just north of Matt's and headed for their nearby cabin.

Keith Landon hollered at them. "Mr. Harris…Mr. Ziegler…come meet your new neighbor."

Both men came over, and Keith introduced them to Matt. Harris and Ziegler welcomed Matt to the gold fields as they shook hands with him. Matt said he was glad to meet them and hoped to get to know them better, then climbed on the dogsled, eager to tell his parents and Livia about his claim site.

Just as Matt sat down on the sled, Art said, "I have to pick up one other miner at a claim site about a half mile from here. His name is Jess Colgan."

"Oh, I know him. Not well, but we learned each other's names while climbing Chilkoot Pass."

"Well, the driver of the sled Jess rode to the gold fields this morning got sick during the day and had to head back to town. You don't mind sharing a ride with him, do you?"

"Of course not. There's plenty of room on here to carry another passenger."

A half mile from where Matt Holden boarded Art Donley's dogsled, Jess Colgan was talking with Laird Thompson, who had the claim next to his. Jack London and Heath Caldwell each had a claim just the other side of Thompson's. While Colgan and Thompson were talking, the dogsleds that had carried London, Caldwell, and Thompson to the gold fields that morning glided up.

"Jess, do you need a ride?" Thompson said.

"Thanks for the offer, but there's a sled on its way to pick me up."

Thompson nodded. "Okay. See you tomorrow." London, Caldwell, and Thompson climbed aboard their sleds, and the barking dogs headed toward Dawson City.

Jess Colgan saw Art Donley's sled coming across the snow-covered hills, took off his hat, and waved it at Art. Art waved back, and a few minutes later, guided his dogs up close to Jess and pulled rein.

When Jess saw Matt Holden, he smiled and said, "Hello, Matt. Fancy seeing you here. Did you find yourself a good claim site?"

"Sure did. How about you?"

"I got a good one, too."

Jess boarded the sled, sitting just ahead of Matt, and Art put the dogs in motion with a loud "Mush!"

Jack London marveled at the strength of the dogs as they pulled the sled so swiftly over the snow-covered ground. He turned to the driver and said, "Wayne, those dogs amaze me. With you and me and all this equipment on this sled, it's plenty heavy, yet they pull it over these hills like it was all made of cardboard!"

Wayne smiled at him. "You're really interested in sled dogs, aren't you?"

"That I am. I just might write about them someday. I can't get over how strong they are."

"Well, Mr. London, you don't know the half of it. You'd really be amazed if you could watch just one dog pull this sled."

Jack's jaw sagged. "*One* dog? Are you telling me that *one* of these dogs could pull this sled by himself?"

"I am. Of course, not as fast as it's going now with the whole team pulling, but just the same, one dog could pull it over these hills."

Jack shook his head in wonderment. "I'll take your word for it. I've had a special interest in wolves for quite some time, but you've intrigued me, and I want to find out more about these sled dogs."

"Well, there's plenty to learn, believe me."

On the sled Matt Holden and Jess Colgan were riding together, Jess said, "Matt, I overheard a couple of men in town talking about you. They said you were once a professional boxer."

Matt nodded. "That's right, I was."

Jess began asking about his boxing career, including what well-known boxers he had fought. Jess had heard of most of them and was impressed. He was even more impressed when he learned how many bouts Matt had won.

Jess's brow furrowed. "Could I ask you a personal question?"

"Sure."

"Since you were doing so well, why did you give up boxing?"

"Well, Jess, I had the privilege one time of hearing the famous evangelist, Dwight Moody, preach. I learned from him that God says if I die without putting my faith in Jesus to save my sinful soul, I'll spend eternity in hell."

Jess was looking at him askance.

Matt went on. "When I made Jesus my Saviour, I lost the killer instinct a successful fighter must have, and I no longer wanted to fight for money. According to the Bible, all of us are sinners before God, and unless we repent and receive His Son as our Saviour, we have no hope of heaven. That includes *you*, Jess."

Jess turned and looked out across the snow-laden hills.

"Jess, every person has to die, right?"

Jess did not reply. He only stared across the hills.

Matt went on. "You know very well that every person has to die. Nobody knows how long they'll live. You need to be prepared to die, and only in Jesus can you be properly prepared."

Jess scrubbed a glove across his mouth. "Matt, I don't mean to insult you, but I don't see it that way. I have my own beliefs about life and death. I'm not interested in this Bible stuff, and I don't want to hear any more."

Matt nodded, his heart heavy.

Soon the dogsleds arrived in Dawson City. When Matt Holden got off where his tent and that of his parents stood, he looked at Jess and said, "Please think about what I told you."

Jess looked upset but did not reply.

The sled pulled away just as Cleve and Maudie Holden came out of their tent, smiling at their son.

"Did you get a good claim site, son?" Cleve asked.

"Sure did, Dad. I'll tell both of you all about it over supper. But…what's happened to the Bray tent?"

"Something wonderful happened to them today," Maudie said.

Cleve and Maudie first told Matt about what Captain Jensen had told Martha and Livia about Weldon Bray, then they told him of the property the Brays had purchased in town so they could open a laundry.

"So they've already moved there?" Matt said.

"That's right," Cleve said. "They're expecting us to show up there any time now. They want us to see it."

A smile spread over Matt's face. "Well, let's go!"

∽

When the Holdens drew near the house that Martha and Livia now owned, they found them sitting on the front porch in their heavy coats, waiting for them. Both rose to their feet, and as the Holdens drew up to the porch, Livia's smile warmed Matt's heart, and he smiled back at her.

"Hello, Matt," Livia said. "I assume your parents told you what the Lord did for us today."

"Yes, and I'm really glad for you…though I'm sorry Captain Jensen had no good news about your father."

Livia nodded solemnly. "If Papa's in the gold fields, we'll find him, Matt."

Martha moved up beside her daughter. "Now, we'll show you sweet people the building that will be our laundry, then we'll give you a tour of the house. By that time, supper will be ready, and you'll be the first guests to eat a meal with us in our new house. We've got chicken and dumplings on the stove!"

Cleve sidled up beside his son with Maudie on his arm and elbowed him in the ribs. "I'll go for chicken and dumplings, won't you, son?"

"You better believe it, Dad!"

TWENTY-ONE

When the dogsled Dale Burke had hired drew near his tent, he saw Elaine and the children standing in front of it. They had been waiting for his return and began waving to him. The sled soon came to a halt, and Dale stepped off the sled and hugged his family.

"Papa, were you able to get a claim site?" Barry said.

Dale smiled down at him. "Yes, son. I got what looks to be a very good one." He paused and looked at Elaine. "There's just one problem."

"What's that, dear?" Elaine said.

Dale cleared his throat. "Well, the claim has a small cabin on it, but it's *very* small. There's room for only one person in it. I figure to successfully mine the claim, I'll need to stay there and work day and night. So, I'll have to find some place here in town for you and the children."

Elaine felt a knot in her stomach. She wanted to object, but she knew the gold fever that had caused her husband to quit his good job in Omaha still held him in its grasp.

Dale pressed a smile on his lips. "I'll find you a nice place. I learned a whole lot about mining gold from one of the professional instructors today. I'll soon be producing our fortune!"

At that moment, the Burkes saw Margo Fleming pushing Norman toward them in his wheelchair, coming from town. When the Flemings drew up, Norman smiled and said, "How about Margo and me taking the Burke family to supper at one of the cafés? Some things happened today that we want to tell you about."

Dale looked at Elaine, then at the Flemings. "We'll just take you up on that!"

When the Flemings and the Burkes were eating at the Snowbird Café, Norman and Margo told the Burkes about purchasing the choice lot for the Klondike Hotel and hiring Smith and Jones Construction to build it.

Norman said, "Margo and I also decided that instead of living in our tent until the hotel was completed, we'd look for a place in a boardinghouse."

"I was going to take a walk through town tomorrow and find us one," Margo said, "but as we were heading here to our tent, Norman spotted a two-bedroom house with a For Rent sign in the front yard. We stopped and looked at it. We really liked it, so we rented it on the spot. We'll take down our tent and move in this evening."

"We'll help you carry your things there," Dale said.

"Oh, that would be wonderful," Margo said.

"My brothers and I will help!" Susan said.

Norman patted her cheek. "That's awfully sweet of you and your brothers, honey."

"I'm so glad you found the house to rent," Elaine said. "When will the hotel be built and ready for occupancy?"

"It'll be ready in late July or early August," Norman said. "The company has a large crew and will get right on it."

Norman then looked at Dale. "Were you able to get a claim site?"

"Oh yes! And I learned today from one of the instructors how to mine gold from the frozen ground. The site has a small one-man cabin, so I'll be staying there and working the mine day and night."

Margo noted the pained look in Elaine's eyes. "Dale, will you come into town on weekends to be with your family?" she asked.

"I plan to be with them every Sunday."

"Elaine, dear," Margo said, "I need to go powder my nose. Would you like to come with me?"

Elaine nodded. "I think I could stand to do the same."

When the two women entered the powder room, no one else was there. Margo took hold of Elaine's hand. "Honey, are you upset because Dale plans to stay at the claim site six days a week?"

Tears filmed Elaine's eyes. "You remember that day you and I met at the hotel in San Francisco, and I told you I really didn't want to leave my home in Omaha and go to Yukon Territory?"

"Yes."

"I told you how Dale was caught up with gold fever and gave up his good job so we could come up here to the gold fields."

Margo squeezed Elaine's hand. "Yes."

Elaine sniffed and thumbed tears from her eyes. "Well, as you can see, that gold fever still has its grip on him. That's why he's going to stay at the claim six days a week."

Margo looked into Elaine's tear-filled eyes. "Honey, I understand why you're upset, and I don't blame you. But I can see that Dale's mind is made up. I think all you can do now is go along with it."

Elaine nodded. "I won't fight him on it, but it's sure going to be lonely for the children and me. At least he said he'd find some comfortable living quarters here in town for us."

Margo squeezed Elaine's hand again. "I have an idea how you might stay occupied so you won't be so lonely."

"What's that?"

"Well, Dale and your children have often said what a good cook you are. Would you be interested in running the restaurant in the hotel for Norman and me?"

Elaine's eyes brightened. "Do you mean it?"

"I sure do."

"Oh, I'd love to do that!"

"I know Norman will be as happy as I am to have you running our restaurant. And remember, we said we were going to have living quarters built in the hotel for whoever runs the restaurant."

"Oh! You *did,* didn't you?"

"So you'll have a home to live in. And since Dale is going to be spending so much time at his mine, you and the children can live with Norman and me in the house we just rented until the hotel is ready."

Elaine's brow furrowed. "Are...are you sure Norman will go along with all of this? Especially with the children and me living with you in the rented house?"

"Without a doubt."

"Oh, it will be wonderful for us! But..."

"But what?"

"Margo, are you sure you want those three little ones under foot all the time?"

"Honey, listen. The house we've rented is really quite spacious. Norman and I will love having all four of you living with us. You'll have to share one bedroom, of course, but we'll let you have the larger of the two. I'm sure you can make do. Norman and I were never able to have children, so having happy little voices fill our home will be a real joy. Is this proposal all right, then?"

Elaine smiled. "It's better than anything I could have hoped for! It's so kind of you to do this for us."

"The gain will be ours, dear."

Elaine hugged her. "Thank you, Margo. You've put my mind at ease."

Smiling broadly, the two women left the powder room and returned to the others. When they sat down at the table, Margo told Norman, in front of Dale and the children, what she had just offered Elaine.

Norman clapped his hands together. "Wonderful! Margo, you're a genius!"

Elaine looked at Dale, who smiled and said, "With you cooking the meals at the hotel's restaurant, all the other restaurants and cafés will go out of business!"

Everybody at the table laughed, then Barry looked at his father and asked, "Papa, will I still get to go to the claim site with you?"

Dale nodded. "Son, as soon as I get it going good, I'll take you to see it." Dale then ran his gaze between Margo and Norman. "Thank you so much for what you're doing for my family. This will free my mind to better dig for gold."

Norman chuckled. "We're glad to do it, Dale. We're the ones who are blessed."

That night as Jess Colgan was lying in the bedroll in his tent, he thought of how Matt Holden had preached to him that day just as Chaplain William Glaxner and Fred Matthis had done when he was in prison.

This made him angry all over again. He clenched his teeth

and growled, "So there's a burning hell where the bad people go when they die. Well, Mr. Matt Holden, I haven't done anything bad enough to put me there!"

Jess flipped from one side to the other, and his thoughts ran to guard Howard Ziegler. He touched the scars that Ziegler's whip had left on his back. "Ziegler, if I knew where you were, I'd find you and kill you!"

He pictured Ziegler's face in his mind, and the burning hatred made him shake all over. Jess recalled how people had warned him many times to get a grip on his temper…that one day it would destroy him if he didn't.

Finally, he put his mind on his new claim site and thought of the riches that were going to be his. And after a while, he dropped off to sleep.

The next morning, when the dogsleds were gathering at the south edge of Dawson City to take the miners to their claim sites, Matt Holden was standing alone, watching for Art Donley's sled. A few yards away, Jess Colgan was talking to Jack London, Laird Thompson, and Heath Caldwell. Matt picked up that Laird was talking about wolves and that Jack, especially, was taking it in like a thirsty man drinking cool water on a hot day.

Soon Matt saw Art come over a small hill and aim his dog team straight for him. When Art drew the sled to a halt, he smiled at Matt and said, "Jess Colgan's driver is still sick. Do you mind if I take Jess to his claim site this morning and bring him back this evening?"

"I don't mind at all, Art."

Jess had noticed Art and was looking toward him.

"Jess, I'm taking you to your site and picking you up today," Art said "Your man is still sick."

Jess hurried toward Art's sled. "Do you mind if I ride with you again?" he said to Matt.

Matt gave him a smile. "Of course not. Let's get going."

Both men climbed aboard the sled, and Jess's attention was drawn to the revolver holstered on Art's hip. As he sat down, he kept his eyes on the gun.

"Something wrong, Jess?" Art said.

Jess shook his head. "Oh, no. I noticed that gun on your hip yesterday and was going to ask you about it, but didn't get around to it."

"What is it you want to know?"

"Well, I was just wondering why a sled driver would need to wear a gun."

"Well, my friend, sometimes when I'm driving the sled, big hungry bears will suddenly appear, wanting to kill and eat my dogs. I can put grizzlies or any other kind of bear down with a bullet between the eyes."

"I didn't realize bears were a threat in this area. I just hadn't noticed any other sled driver wearing a gun."

"That's because they use rifles, which they keep handy on their sleds. Personally, I like the revolver because I can whip it out faster."

Art called out "Mush!" to his dogs, and soon the sled was gliding over the snow-covered hills toward the gold fields.

Matt leaned close to Jess and said, "Have you given any thought to our conversation on the way back to town yesterday?"

"No. I've heard plenty of that Bible stuff in my life. I have my mind fixed on one thing, Matt, and that's getting rich on my gold mine. I'll think about death and eternity when I get old."

"Just remember, Jess, lots of people never live to get old."

Jess's face flushed. "Look, Matt, I appreciate your letting me ride on your sled, but I don't want to hear any more of your Bible talk."

"Jess, I can't force salvation on you," Matt said in a kind tone, "but remember what I told you yesterday. Only in Jesus Christ can you be properly prepared to die. Without Him as your Saviour, you'll spend eternity in hell. Jesus said, 'I am the way, the truth, and the life: no man cometh unto the Father, but by me.'"

Jess went silent and stared off into space.

Some three miles ahead, Keith Landon was at Matt Holden's claim site, waiting to give him his first full day of mining instruction. Roger Whitson had come from his claim site to the south and had struck up a conversation with Keith. As they talked, they saw the two men at the claim site on the north appear.

Landon called out, "Good morning, Mr. Harris...Mr. Ziegler!"

Both men returned the greeting and walked over and joined Landon and Whitson, chatting about how the mining was going.

Art Donley's sled continued over the rolling, snow-covered hills, and soon Matt spotted his claim site a quarter of a mile away. He noted that four men were standing in front of it. He also saw two Mounties leisurely riding their horses just ahead, moving in the same direction as the sled.

Art slowed the dogs slightly as the sled passed the Mounties and called out, "Good morning, Sergeant Miller! Good morning, Corporal Webb!" Art then put the dogs back to their regular speed, and soon the sled drew up to Matt's site.

As Matt was getting off the sled, Art greeted the four men by name.

When Jess Colgan heard Art say the name *Ziegler*, his head came up, and it took him only a second to see the familiar face. His heart jolted, and he covered his mouth to stifle his shocked intake of breath. *Howard Ziegler! What is he doing here, of all places?*

Blood flushed the sides of Jess's neck. He jumped off the sled, snatched Art Donley's gun from its holster, snapped back the hammer, and pointed the gun at Ziegler. "Ziegler!" Jess shouted.

When Ziegler heard his name, he looked around at the man who was pointing the gun at him.

"Take a good look at this face!" Jess Colgan hissed. "Remember me?"

Ziegler shook his head. "I don't remember you. As far as I know, we've never met before."

"You remember me, all right!" Jess said. "I was in prison at San Quentin when you were a guard there!"

Ziegler frowned. "I was never a guard at San Quentin. That was my twin brother."

"Liar!" Jess growled, and fired the gun.

The slug hit Ziegler in the chest, and he went down.

The two Mounties, who had heard the commotion and rushed to the scene, slid from their saddles, guns in hand.

"Drop that gun!" Sergeant Alfred Miller shouted at Jess.

Jess Colgan cocked the gun and whirled, bringing it to bear on the Mounties. In the same split second, both Mounties fired.

When the two slugs hit Jess, he jerked to one side, and the gun in his hand went off. The slug hit Roger Whitson, who collapsed in the snow. Jess fell flat on his back.

Burt Harris dropped to his knees beside his friend, touched the side of his neck, and let out a whimper as he looked at the Mounties and said in a choked voice, "He's dead."

Matt Holden was kneeling in the snow beside Jess Colgan, noting the two bullet holes on the left side of his chest.

Gritting his teeth, Jess looked up at Matt. "Is—is Howard Ziegler dead?"

Harris heard him and moved to the spot where Jess lay in the snow. "The man you shot wasn't Howard Ziegler! His name's Holton Ziegler, and like he said, he was Howard's twin brother! Howard's never been up here in Yukon Territory!"

Jess's eyes closed, and his face pinched in agony. He gasped for breath, and looked up at Matt, who still knelt beside him.

Matt bent down close, his eyes fixed on the dying man.

Jess gasped once more and said hoarsely, "Matt…Matt…I—I—"

His face was without color as he drew his last breath.

TWENTY-TWO

A deep sense of sorrow gripped Matt Holden as he rose to his feet beside the lifeless form of Jess Colgan. Both Mounties drew up beside Matt as he ran his gaze to the other two dead men lying nearby in the snow.

"This one's dead, too?" Sergeant Alfred Miller said.

Matt sighed. "Yes, sir."

"Was he a friend of yours?" Corporal Dean Webb asked.

Matt shook his head. "We were barely acquaintances. Tell you what...there's a missionary in Dawson whom I know quite well. He came here from California to start a new church and is an ordained preacher. His name is Tom Varner. I'm sure he would conduct the burial services for these men."

Sergeant Miller turned to Art Donley. "Art, we need to get the bodies into town so they can have a proper burial. Would you transport them on your sled for us?"

"Of course," Art said.

Sergeant Miller looked at Matt. "Since you know the preacher in town, would you go with us and ask him if he'll conduct the burial services?"

"Certainly." Matt turned toward Keith Landon, who was close by. "Mr. Landon, since I'm needed in town, could you take up instructing me tomorrow morning?"

Landon smiled. "Of course. I'll be here first thing in the morning."

"Thank you. I appreciate it."

"Since the sled is going to be full," Corporal Webb said to Matt, "you can ride with me on my horse into town."

In Dawson City, Martha and Livia Bray were walking along the snow-covered gravel sidewalk, headed for the Comstock Grocery Store, where they would purchase soap and supplies for their laundry service. As they drew near the store, they saw Tom Varner headed toward them on the sidewalk.

When they drew up to each other, Martha said, "Good morning, Pastor Varner."

"Good morning, Pastor," said Livia, smiling.

Tom touched his hat brim. "Good morning to both of you. You must be getting real close to opening up your laundry service."

Martha nodded. "That we are. In just a couple of days."

"I'm sure the Lord will bless your business. I'm about to meet with Wiley Madison, the chairman of the town council. He's supposed to let me know how the meeting went last night about our church being able to meet in the town hall."

"I sure hope they'll let us," Livia said.

"I'll know shortly, ladies. Nice to see you both."

Mother and daughter entered the grocery store, and Tom made his way on down the sidewalk to Wiley Madison's office. When he opened the door and stepped in, Madison was sitting at his desk. He smiled and said, "Good morning, Preacher. Come sit down."

Tom eased onto a chair in front of Madison's desk. "So how did the meeting go, sir?"

Madison's face lit up with a smile. "It went *very* well, I'm happy to say! The councilmen voted unanimously to allow you to hold Sunday morning and evening services in the town hall, as well as Wednesday evenings."

"Wonderful! Our people will be happy to hear this."

Madison leaned forward on his elbows. "And guess what? They also voted to let you use the town hall at no charge."

"Oh, hallelujah!"

Tom rose to his feet, and Madison did the same. Tom offered his hand, and when Madison gripped it, Tom said, "This is an answer to prayer, sir. It was your excellent leadership and kindness toward us that God used to bring the council to this decision. Thank you so very much!"

"Just thank the Lord," Madison said. "Mrs. Madison and I will be there for the very first service."

"And you will be *more* than welcome!"

They shook hands again, and Tom hurried out onto the sidewalk eager to tell Peggy and the children the good news. He was about to head toward his family's tent when he heard a familiar voice call out, "Pastor Tom! Pastor Tom!"

He turned to see Matt Holden riding double on Corporal Dean Webb's horse, riding beside Sergeant Alfred Miller, and followed by a dogsled bearing the lifeless forms of three men. The Mounties and the dogsled drew up, and Matt slid to the ground. Both uniformed men dismounted quickly.

People on the street and looked on, wide-eyed.

Matt gave Tom Varner the details of the shootout that took place in front of his claim site. "I told Sergeant Miller and Corporal Webb, here, about you coming to Dawson City to start a new church, and that I was sure you'd be willing to conduct the burial services for these men. They asked that I come and talk to you about it."

"Of course I'll do it," Tom said.

At that moment, Martha and Livia Bray came out of the Comstock Grocery Store, carrying paper bags of soap and washing supplies. Wiley himself was now part of the crowd.

"Look, Mama," Livia said, "there's Matt with Pastor Varner and those Mounties!"

Martha nodded. "Something's happened, honey. Matt's supposed to be at his claim site."

They hurried toward the small crowd that was gathered on the street in front of Wiley Madison's office. As they drew nearer, Livia said, "Mama! Those three men lying on that sled…"

"They're dead, honey. Something terrible must have hap—!" Martha stopped in her tracks a few feet from the sled, dropped all of her packages, and gasped. "Livia! It's your father!"

Livia moved up a step and broke into sobs.

Matt Holden stepped up and took hold of Livia's hand. "This one is your father?"

"Yes! Papa's dead, Matt. He's dead!"

Matt looked around at the people, pointed to the one Livia had called her father, and asked, "Do any of you know this man?"

One of the men in the crowd said, "I do, sir. His name is Roger Whitson. He's—he *was* a miner out in the gold fields. I'm vice president of the Royal Bank of Canada down the street. My name's Charles Blevins. Mr. Whitson has an account with us."

Martha tried to speak to Blevins, but her throat was tight and she couldn't make the words come out.

Livia said, "My mother is trying to tell you, Mr. Blevins, that this man—was her husband, my father. His name is Weldon Bray. He came up here from our home in San Francisco many months ago, but we never heard from him. Mama and I came up here to try to find him."

Matt said, "Mrs. Bray…Livia…this man who called himself Roger Whitson has a claim site right next to mine. When I met him yesterday, he told me he was from Kansas City and that he had a wife and daughter who were both dead. I sure had no idea he was the man you were looking for."

Charles Blevins ran his gaze between mother and daughter. "Ladies, the bank will have to have some kind of proof that your husband's name was actually Weldon Bray, and that you are his wife and daughter."

Matt turned to the two Mounties. "Gentlemen, as you can see, I know these ladies personally. I met them in Tent City and got to know them quite well while we were climbing the Golden Stairs. Can you help them lay legal claim to whatever money Weldon Bray has in Mr. Blevins's bank and whatever gold he might have dug up and kept at the mine?"

"Do you ladies have anything with you that will prove this man is your husband and father," Sergeant Miller said, "and that his name is Weldon Bray?"

"We have a few photographs of him, my daughter, and me together, Sergeant," Martha said. "Some of them are from when my daughter was a little girl, others when she was eleven or twelve, and some are more recent. That won't prove what his name is, but it will show what I'm telling you about him being my husband and Livia's father."

Charles Blevins spoke up. "Sergeant, if these ladies have pictures of themselves with this man that cover a few years in time, those pictures will be proof enough for the Royal Bank of Canada. If they have papers of any kind that confirm their identity, we'll transfer what funds there are in the account to them."

"We have such papers, Mr. Blevins," Martha assured him.

"Then we're in business, ma'am."

"Good," Sergeant Miller said. "Mrs. Bray, once Corporal Webb and I see those papers and the photographs, we'll check out the claim site and let you know if there's any gold stashed there. We won't be able to do it until tomorrow."

"That's fine. Livia and I will go to our house and bring the photographs to Mr. Blevins."

"I'll be in my office at the bank, ma'am," Blevins said.

"Corporal Webb and I will be waiting with Mr. Blevins at his office, Mrs. Bray," Sergeant Miller said.

Martha nodded.

"In the meantime," Tom Varner said, "I'll need some help digging graves for these men. We'll have the burial service at the cemetery at three this afternoon."

"We'll see that you get that help, Pastor," Miller said.

Martha and Livia, accompanied by Matt Holden, carried their personal papers and the photographs into the Royal Bank of Canada. After the Mounties and the bank officers had examined the papers and the photographs, they believed Martha and Livia and told them that "Roger Whitson" had over $60,000 in his account. The account was then transferred to Martha and Livia Bray.

Matt accompanied Martha and Livia to the other banks in town, but none had an account in the name of Roger Whitson.

At precisely three o'clock that afternoon, Tom Varner conducted the burial service at the town's cemetery. Matt and his parents and Peggy Varner were at the graveside to comfort Martha and Livia as best they could. When the burial was over, the Varners and the

Holdens went with Martha and Livia to their house and stayed for a while. After about an hour, everyone left except Matt.

Martha watched Matt's parents and the Varners walk away from the house, then closed the door. Matt and Livia were standing right behind her. When she turned around, tears filled her eyes, and she reached for both Livia and Matt. They held her close, and mother and daughter wept for several minutes with Matt's arms around them both.

When their emotions were once again under control, Martha rubbed her eyes and said, "I'll leave you two alone, now. I've got to lie down for a while."

Livia kissed her mother's cheek. "I'm glad you're going to get some rest, Mama. I'll be here in the parlor when you get up."

Matt and Livia headed for the parlor, and Martha made her way to her bedroom.

As Martha lay on her bed looking up at the ceiling, tears blurred her vision and slid down the side of her face. "Weldon," she whispered, "I don't understand how this whole thing happened. I had no idea that you were an unhappy man. You were never terribly affectionate to me, but you seemed to love me. I thought you loved Livia, though you weren't always openly affectionate toward her, either. If there was a problem between us, Weldon, why didn't you talk to me about it? We could have worked it out."

Martha took a shuddering breath and sniffed. "Where did I go wrong as your wife? What should I have done to keep this awful heartache from happening?"

She broke into sobs, and after a few minutes her head was pounding. She looked up toward heaven, wiped at her tears, and said, "Heavenly Father, I'm so glad that both Livia and I belong to You, now. I recall a Scripture Matt quoted not long ago: 'As for God, his way is perfect.'"

Martha wiped more tears from her face. "Lord, I am truly at a loss in all of this that's happened, but You say in Your Word that Your way is perfect. Please help me to cling to that fact, and to trust You as You lead in our lives."

Only a few seconds had passed when Martha felt a sweet peace flow into her heart, and it found a welcome place there.

Downstairs in the parlor, Livia and Matt were sitting together on the sofa. Livia had been talking about her father, then broke into sobs and wept for several minutes. Matt put his arm around her shoulder and held her close as she wept.

After a few minutes, Matt said, "Livia, I'm so sorry that it turned out like this with your father."

"Thank you, Matt. I know Mama is having a hard time dealing with this, and so am I. My father was never a demonstrative man, but I always felt that he loved us. Then he upped and left us, apparently not planning to ever contact us again. Matt, how could that happen?"

"Well, I didn't know your father, Livia, but I do know that gold fever has ruined many a man and his family. It can completely take over a man's heart and mind so that no matter how much gold he lays his hands on, it's never enough. As Solomon says in Ecclesiastes, '*There is no end of all his labour; neither is his eye satisfied with riches.*'"

Livia nodded and brushed a stray tear from her cheek. "That must be what got hold of my father."

Matt squeezed her tightly and said, "I know this jolt over your father's death has been difficult for you, but at least now you know he was indeed here in Yukon Territory."

"Yes, at least that mystery is solved. I just wasn't prepared to find him dead. You've been such a help to Mama and me, Matt. I don't know what we would've done without you."

Matt looked into her sky blue eyes. "I'm glad I could be here for you."

"I wonder if Mama will want to go back to San Francisco. Oh, I hope not. We're just getting settled here."

"Well, let's take this one step at a time. As long as I'm here, at least, I would love to have you here, too. We'll let the Lord guide us."

Livia managed a smile. "I know He will work everything out in our lives, Matt. Even though I'm young in my Christian life, the Lord has already shown me that He never makes a mistake, and that He will never leave us nor forsake us."

"That's right."

She managed another smile. "Matt, thank you for being such a good friend to Mama and me."

Matt squeezed her against him again. "Livia, I want to say something to you. I feel a tender friendship between your mother and me...but I feel more than friendship toward you."

Livia studied his dark brown eyes, her heart pounding. "Matt, I feel the same way about you. It's more than friendship."

Matt shifted his position on the sofa and folded her into both his arms. "Livia, the first time I saw you, something wonderful happened in my heart. I've never felt this way toward anyone else."

"Oh, Matt, the same thing happened to me the first time I saw you!"

He pulled her closer and said, "Sweet Livia, the Lord will show us if He has chosen us for each other."

She eased back in his arms and looked once again into his eyes. "Yes, He will. He will."

၁

The next morning when Matt arrived at his claim site, he found Keith Landon there, as well as a Mountie he knew well, Sergeant Dewey Blanding. With them was a man Matt did not know.

Sergeant Blanding introduced the stranger as John Nordstrom, who had arrived at Dawson City the day before, along with nearly three hundred other gold seekers. Blanding explained that Nordstrom had been assigned the claim site that had belonged to Weldon Bray.

As Matt Holden and John Nordstrom shook hands, Nordstrom said, "Mr. Holden, since we're going to be neighbors, let me tell you a little about myself. I emigrated from my native Sweden three years ago and settled in Seattle. I was working a farm just outside Seattle when I heard about the gold strike in Yukon Territory. My big dream is to establish a large department store in the growing city of Seattle, and I hope to find enough gold so I can realize my dream."

"Well, Mr. Nordstrom, I hope you see your dream come true," Matt said, smiling.

As time passed, more gold seekers arrived almost daily in Dawson City. By the first of September, Dawson City's population had grown to just over thirty thousand. The Klondike Hotel had opened in mid-August, and was already running consistently full. Margo Fleming was busier than she had ever imagined, but she loved it. Norman was occupied as well, handling all the accounting and bookkeeping.

The Flemings were pleased that their restaurant was also doing well with Elaine Burke as chief cook and manager. Elaine and her children enjoyed their living quarters at the back of the restaurant. Dale's claim was producing moderate amounts of gold, though he worked sometimes seven days a week.

Matt Holden had found a good vein in his gold mine and had a beautiful house built in Dawson City for his parents. On the lot next to it, he had a nice log cabin built for himself. Cleve had been left somewhat handicapped by his broken collarbone and the damage done to his shoulder, but he occasionally went with his son to the claim site and helped in the mine as best he could.

The church that met in the town hall was doing quite well. Many souls had come to the Lord, and Christian gold seekers from the United States and other English-speaking countries attended regularly. Pastor Tom Varner had been asking his people to pray that the Lord would provide the church with enough money to purchase property and erect their own building.

Pastor Varner had a burden on his heart for a young man in his early twenties whose Christian father had been bringing him to the services, but the young man was openly rebellious. After much prayer, Pastor Varner went to the home to talk with the young man, and had the joy of leading him to the Lord.

The father's gold mine had just paid off in a big way, and in appreciation for the change in his son's life, he gave the church enough money to purchase property in Dawson City and erect a new building. He also had a parsonage built next to the church for the Varners. They moved into the house the last week of August, and the church was to hold their first service in the new building on Sunday, September 4.

❧

As the sun was setting on September 2, Margo and Norman were enjoying a quiet evening in their own quarters. A small fire glowed in the fireplace. Even the early September nights in Yukon Territory were quite cool. Margo was seated in an over-stuffed chair, and Norman was in his wheelchair, facing her.

"You know, sweetheart," he said, "when we first started on our venture into this north country, I was a little hesitant. But it has turned out to be even more than we had ever dreamed."

A soft smile lit up Margo's face. "I know this change in our lives has been tough for you. It has for me, too. But I'm so glad we came. I feel like this is right where we belong. To me, it's home."

Norman grinned. "I agree, love. It indeed is home!"

Because of the money Weldon Bray had in the Royal Bank of Canada, and an additional five thousand dollars worth of gold that was found in his cabin on the claim site, Martha and Livia Bray had opened a clothing store and had a new house built. They had hired two widows to run the laundry, and they let them move into the small house.

Obsessed with becoming multimillionaires, Hank Osborne and his sons worked hard on their claim, but so far had banked only a little over thirty thousand dollars.

Jack London's claim was not doing well, but he kept working hard, hoping to strike a rich vein. He shared a three-bedroom house in Dawson City with his friends, Laird Thompson and Heath Caldwell, whose claims were doing quite well.

TWENTY-THREE

On Sunday morning, September 4, the auditorium of the new church building in Dawson City was nearly full. Most of the crowd was made up of regular members, but a good number were visitors from the town and the gold fields who the members had invited to this special service.

Most visitors had come to please friends who invited them, and others were there as a matter of curiosity. In the curious group were Hank Osborne and his sons, who had never been in a church service.

As the song service began, Livia Bray, who was sitting with Matt Holden, noticed that he was singing with unusual enthusiasm. Between songs, she leaned close to him and whispered, "You're really excited about the new building, aren't you?"

He smiled and whispered back, "Yes, I'm excited about the new building. But I'm even more excited about something else."

"Oh? What's that?"

"I'll tell you later today, when we can have some time alone."

When it was time for the sermon, Pastor Tom Varner walked to the pulpit and introduced the man who had been sitting beside him on the platform—Wayne Dukart from San Francisco.

Pastor Dukart moved up beside Tom and greeted the crowd, saying he was delighted to be there. He put an arm around Tom and said, "This man was my assistant pastor for many years, and it was hard to let him go, but what a blessing his ministry here in Dawson City has become to our church and to me. I'm so proud of him, and so glad for the way he has allowed the Lord to use him to reach so many souls for Christ here in Dawson City."

Pastor Varner then returned to his seat, and Pastor Dukart stepped to the pulpit and opened his Bible. He preached from several passages about the emptiness and uncertainty of riches, and told of a heaven to gain and a hell to shun by receiving Christ as Saviour. He warned those who had come to Yukon Territory seeking gold not to let the gold be their god, as so many have done the world over. He closed his sermon with Paul's exhortation in 1 Timothy 6:17 to "charge them that are rich in this world, that they be not highminded, nor trust in uncertain riches, but in the living God, who giveth us richly all things to enjoy."

When he gave the invitation, several men, women, and young people walked the aisle to receive Christ as Saviour, for which the congregation gave praise to God.

When the service was over, Pastors Varner and Dukart stood at the door and shook hands with those who were filing out. From the corner of his eye, Pastor Varner saw Hank Osborne and his sons in the line. He had spotted them earlier in the crowd and was pleased to see them there. He wondered what they were thinking now.

When Hank approached the two preachers, Pastor Varner said, "Hello, Mr. Osborne. I'm so glad you and your sons were here for the service."

Hank did not comment.

Pastor Dukart shook Hank's hand. A sardonic grin formed

on Hank's features as he said, "You might as well know what Varner already knows."

"And what is that, sir?"

"I'm an atheist, and so are my four sons, here."

Pastor Dukart's brow furrowed. "Do you know what the God you say doesn't exist says in His Word about atheists?"

Hank only stared at him blankly.

"God says, 'The fool hath said in his heart, There is no God.'"

Hank laughed. "That's wrong, preacher. Only fools believe there is a God! When I was in my twenties and thirties, I used to give lectures in meetings of atheist clubs. I showed in my lectures that people who believe that God exists, and who believe all this Bible stuff, are the *real* fools!"

People in the crowd were pressing close, wanting to see how Pastor Dukart would handle the situation. Pastor Varner smiled at the crowd, having seen his pastor handle atheists before.

"Mr. Osborne, your telling me about the lectures you gave reminds me of something," Pastor Dukart said. "An evangelist I know conducted revival meetings in New Jersey a few years ago. He had learned one evening that there were some atheists in the crowd, so in the sermon, he said that he could prove to the satisfaction of any atheist within ten minutes that the atheist was a fool.

"The next morning while the evangelist was out walking, a man accosted him on the street and said, 'I was in the church service where you preached last night, and I heard you say that you could prove to the satisfaction of any atheist within ten minutes that he was a fool. Well, I'm an atheist, and I say all this Christianity nonsense is false. I'm also in the newspaper publishing business, and if you don't prove to my satisfaction in ten minutes that I'm a fool, I'll see that it's published in all the city newspapers that you're a liar!'

"The evangelist said, 'Then you're saying that there's no truth in the Bible or Christianity.'

"'I do, sir,' the atheist said. 'I have studied and traveled and delivered lectures against Christianity for more than twelve years. I say there is no God, and I say of Christianity, there is nothing in it.'"

"The evangelist said, 'You're certain there is nothing in it?'"

"'Yes, sir. There is nothing in it.'

"'Then will you please tell me,' my evangelist friend said, 'if a man who will lecture twelve years against *nothing* is not a fool, what in your judgment would constitute a fool?'

"The atheist turned away in a rage. The evangelist, drawing his watch out of his vest pocket, insisted he still had six minutes, but the atheist stomped away in anger. And let me tell you this. My evangelist friend was not published in the city newspapers as a liar, either."

Hank Osborne raked Pastor Dukart with a malevolent glare and stomped away, his sons following.

Matt Holden and the other people who had gathered at the scene shook Pastor Dukart's hand, telling him it was a great story.

Pastor Varner said, "I hope what you said will make them think long and hard about their atheism, Pastor."

"We'll just pray that the Lord will use this morning's sermon and that story to turn them to the Lord," Matt said.

That afternoon, the Holdens had Martha and Livia Bray over for dinner at their home. After the meal was over, Matt excused Livia and himself, saying he needed to talk to her alone.

The September air was quite cool, and Matt and Livia put on their coats and went out on the front porch. When they sat down together on the porch swing, Livia said, "Am I going to hear that 'something else' you are so excited about?"

Matt smiled. "Yes, you are."

"Well, I'm waiting!"

Matt chuckled. "I haven't told you this, but a few months ago I set myself a goal that when I had banked a hundred thousand dollars from my gold mine, I would then feel confident that I could provide a good life for you, and I would ask you to marry me. Just this past Friday, I deposited gold coins in my bank account that ran the balance slightly over a hundred thousand dollars."

Livia's eyes widened as Matt left the swing, went down on one knee, took both of her hands in his, and looked into her eyes. "Livia, sweetheart…will you marry me?"

Her heart pounding and her eyes dancing, Livia said, "Matt, you are so kind and considerate of me. I would marry you even if you never took one gold nugget out of that mine. I love you, and the Lord has already shown me that you are the one He has chosen for me. That's what really matters."

Still holding both her hands, Matt said, "And He has shown me that you are the one He chose for me, praise His name. But since I *do* have that money in the bank, I can take care of my parents and your mother too, when she can no longer manage the clothing store and the laundry. You and I will need to have our own home built before we marry, which we can now afford." He squeezed her hands. "But I thank you for saying you would marry me even if I didn't have this money. God is so good and has blessed us in so many ways."

"Yes, He has, Matt."

A grin spread over his face as he let go of one hand and said, "Just for the record, may I hear a yes in answer to my question? Will you marry me?"

Tears filmed Livia's eyes. "Yes, my darling! I will marry you!"

From his shirt pocket, Matt took out a diamond engagement

ring he had bought at Dawson City's only jewelry store and placed it on her left hand. They enjoyed a sweet kiss, then Matt rose and sat beside her once again. They talked about how long they should wait to marry after announcing their engagement, and agreed it would be proper if they waited till next spring.

"How about April?" Matt said. "I say that because it was this last April that I had the privilege of leading you to Jesus when we were trapped in the avalanche by the Golden Stairs."

"Oh yes! I have such wonderful memories of the Golden Stairs!"

"Okay, we'll set the exact date later."

"All right. Now, could we go inside and tell Mama and your parents that we're engaged?"

"Yes, but let's pray together first."

They held hands as Matt led them in prayer, thanking the Lord for bringing them together, and asking Him to bless their future as husband and wife.

When they went inside and broke the news to Martha and the Holdens, there was much rejoicing. Martha, Maudie, and Cleve all agreed that they had known for some time that the Lord had chosen Matt and Livia for each other.

Unable to wait any longer, Matt and Livia went to the parsonage and shared the good news with Tom Varner and Peggy. Pastor Varner agreed that they would set the date for the wedding for sometime in April 1899.

The next day, Tom Varner and his family said goodbye to Pastor Wayne Dukart at the edge of the Yukon River as he boarded a boat to head for home.

That evening, just after supper, there was a knock on the front door of the parsonage. Tom opened the door to find Hank

Osborne and his youngest son, Vernon, on the porch.

"Pastor Varner, Vernon and I would like to talk to you," Hank said.

"Of course. What about?"

"The sermon your pastor preached yesterday morning and the story he told us about the atheist fool have been bothering Vernon and me all day. We realize how wrong we've been and…we want to talk to you about our need for salvation."

"All right," Tom said, his heart pounding. "Let's go over to my office in the church building." He heard a sniffle and turned to see Peggy standing behind him, wiping tears.

"I'll be back in a little while, honey." he said.

After three hours of talking with Hank and Vernon and reading passages together from the Bible, Pastor Tom Varner had the joy of leading both men to Christ. They promised to be at church the next Sunday to be baptized.

When the new converts were about to leave, Tom said, "I assume your other sons weren't touched by the sermon and the story like you two were?"

Hank shook his head. "No, they weren't. But Vernon and I will do all we can to live as God would have us to, and we'll trust that one day they'll follow our example."

Tom smiled. "I like your attitude. I'll help you all I can to be the testimonies to Russell, T. J., and Lou that the Lord would have you to be."

When Tom returned to the parsonage, he knew the children had already been in bed for a couple of hours, but was not surprised to see Peggy waiting for him in the parlor.

She jumped out of her overstuffed chair, eyes wide, and said, "Did they open their hearts to Jesus?"

Tom wrapped her in his arms. "They sure did, sweetheart! And they're going to be baptized next Sunday morning!"

She clapped her hands together. "Oh, praise the Lord!"

Tom and Peggy were so thrilled with what God had done in the lives of Hank and Vernon Osborne, they had a hard time getting to sleep that night.

The weeks passed, and winter came to Yukon Territory with its subzero temperatures and snowstorms.

Matt Holden and Livia Bray fell more and more in love, though most days they had only a little time together. Matt's claim site was still producing gold in generous amounts. Early in November, they set their wedding date for Saturday, April 8, 1899.

Hank Osborne and his youngest son continued to grow in their spiritual life, and because the Osborne mine was doing so well, both men gave to the church from their shares of the gold. Russell, T. J., and Lou still held onto their atheism, though they did not persecute their father and Vernon for their Christian principles.

Life went on for everyone in Dawson City and the gold fields. The freezing temperatures and heavy snowstorms did not slow down the gold rush. By mid-November, Dawson city's population had grown to over thirty-three thousand.

On Monday, November 21, Elaine Burke was busy in the kitchen at the restaurant in the Klondike Hotel, along with two women the Flemings had hired to work under her supervision. All three women were preparing food for that day's lunch menu when they looked up to see Margo Fleming open the kitchen door.

"Honey, may I talk to you in private?" Margo said to Elaine.

Elaine smiled. "Of course."

Margo led Elaine to the hotel office, and when they sat down, she said, "Elaine, dear, Dale still hasn't come home, has he?"

Elaine bit her lower lip and shook her head.

"So it's been over three weeks since you've seen him?"

"Yes. Twenty-four days to be exact."

"On Friday you told me you were going to go talk to the Mounties if Dale hadn't come home by Sunday. Are you ready to talk to them now?"

"I doubt anything has happened to him, Margo," Elaine said, her voice quavering. "Like I told you on Friday, the gold fever has captivated Dale. In September and October, he seldom came home to be with the children and me. It was like he was losing huge amounts of gold if he came home. He's done reasonably well in his mining, but he can never seem to get enough."

Margo started to say something, but Elaine cut her off. "But since something may have happened to him, I'll go to the Mountie post outside of town and see if they'll go to the gold fields and make sure Dale is all right."

"That's what I was going to suggest, honey. It'll be best if you know for certain that he's okay."

"As soon as the lunch rush is over, I'll let my ladies clean up the kitchen while I go to the Mountie post."

At the Mountie post, Elaine was met by Corporal Harold Mickelsen when she entered the building. When she told him her situation, Mickelsen said he would have her talk to an officer newly assigned to the post, Lieutenant Brent Sawyer, since Captain Lee Jensen was in Dyea at the moment.

Moments later, Elaine was seated in Lieutenant Sawyer's office, and explaining the situation to him.

Sawyer had a frown on his face. "This isn't good, ma'am."

"I know, Lieutenant," Elaine said. "I'm afraid something might've happened to Dale. Could you send a Mountie out to the gold fields to check on him for me?"

"I'll do better than that, Mrs. Burke. I'll ride out there myself and check on him. It won't be hard to find some Mounties out in the gold fields who know where your husband's claim site is. I'll let you know as soon as I return."

Elaine headed back to the hotel, chewing on her lower lip and telling herself Dale was all right.

TWENTY-FOUR

It was late afternoon when Lieutenant Brent Sawyer stood in the knee-deep snow at the gold fields, and two Mounties pointed out Dale Burke's small cabin on his claim site some seventy or eighty yards away.

"Would you like us to go over there with you, Lieutenant?" one of the Mounties asked.

"Thanks, but that won't be necessary," Sawyer said. "If he's not in the cabin, I'll go into the mine and find him."

Sawyer swung aboard his horse and aimed it toward the claim site. As the gelding trudged through the snow, the lieutenant looked around the hills and noted that the snow clung to the trees, filling the notches of branches and crevices of winter-dead bark. A slight wind whistled across the snow-clad slopes, and Sawyer noted miners moving about their claim sites, their breath coming hard and sharp against the wind.

When he drew up to the small cabin, its roof heavy with snow, he noted that there was no smoke coming from the chimney. He figured Dale Burke was probably still in the mine, but decided he would start by knocking on the cabin door.

Dismounting, he made his way up to the door and noticed

that it was slightly ajar. He pushed it open and called out, "Mr. Burke, you in here? I'm Lieutenant Sawyer from the Mountie post at Dawson City."

Just then he saw the figure partially under the covers on the bed. He closed the door and quickly stepped up to the bed. Dale Burke's eyes were open and staring into space. Bending low over him, Brent said, "Mr. Burke, can you hear me?"

The man was very thin, and he had not shaved for several weeks. He did not look at the Mountie.

Brent laid a hand on his shoulder. "Mr. Burke, your wife asked me to come and see if you were all right. She said it's been too long since they've seen you. I'd like for you to come to town with me so your wife and children can see that you're alive."

There was a flicker of response on Dale's cheeks, and he finally focused on Brent Sawyer's face. In a hoarse voice, he said, "I don't…I don't have time to go see my family. I must keep digging for gold. The most important thing is the gold."

"If you're up to it, Mr. Burke, you can come back and resume your mining. But Mrs. Burke and your three children need to see you. Please, come with me. We can both ride my horse."

Dale's head rolled slowly back and forth. "No. As soon as I get a bit rested up, I've got to get back into the mine."

"But isn't your family important enough to—"

"My family will have to wait. I must dig for more gold. Now, leave me alone."

That evening at the hotel restaurant, Elaine Burke was placing plates of food on the counter at the large kitchen window when she saw Lieutenant Brent Sawyer coming toward her. "I'll be with you in a moment," she said.

A few minutes later, Elaine and the Mountie were alone in a

small room just off the kitchen. He told her what he had found, and that Dale had refused to come to town with him.

Elaine's eyes were misty as she said, "Lieutenant Sawyer, I appreciate you doing this for me. I'm glad to know that Dale is alive." Her throat tightened, and she choked as she said, "I…I can't understand why he won't come home."

"It's the gold fever, ma'am."

Elaine sighed and nodded. "Has to be. Do you go to the gold fields often?"

"I've been at the Mountie post for only a short while, but I've been to the gold fields almost every day since I was assigned here."

"Will you look in on Dale for me next time you're out there?"

"Be glad to, ma'am."

Two days passed. On Wednesday evening, November 23, Elaine Burke and her children were in their living quarters a short while after the restaurant's closing time. Elaine was just saying that Barry, Susan, and Ernie should be getting ready for bed when there was a knock at the parlor door.

The children looked on as their mother opened the door and said, "Well, hello, Lieutenant Sawyer. Please come in."

The children had been eager to meet Lieutenant Brent Sawyer ever since their mother had told them about him. They came running and were quickly introduced to him by their mother.

The lieutenant hugged each child, then Susan looked up at him and said, "Is my Papa all right?"

Brent looked at Elaine. "I—I have something to tell you. Maybe you and I should talk alone, first."

Elaine frowned. "Is it bad news?"

"Yes, ma'am. I just—"

"Has something happened to Dale?"

He glanced down at the wide-eyed children, then looked at Elaine and nodded.

"Lieutenant, I think it's best that Barry, Susan, and Ernie hear it from you."

Brent swallowed hard. "All right. Could we sit down?"

Elaine guided him into the small parlor, and he sat in an overstuffed chair as mother and children occupied the sofa, facing him.

Dale explained that he had gone to the gold fields early that afternoon, and when he went to Dale's claim site to check on him, he found him dead in the bed inside the cabin.

Elaine broke into sobs, and the children also wept. After they had dried their tears, Brent explained to Elaine that he had found a small amount of gold in a sack in the cabin. It was in his saddle-bag outside. He said he had hired a dogsled to carry Dale's body to the town's undertaker, who volunteered to conduct the burial service for Mr. Burke. The burial would be tomorrow morning at eleven. Brent told Elaine that he had already paid the undertaker the full fee for the burial.

Brent then told them that his wife and two children had been killed some two years before in a train wreck near their home in Edmonton, Alberta. Brent choked up as he told the story, and Elaine, Barry, Susan, and Ernie showed him their sorrow in his loss.

That night after tucking her children into their beds, Elaine looked into the sack of gold nuggets Brent had left with her, then poured herself a steaming cup of tea and sat at the kitchen table close to the stove. A chill ran through her. She quickly left the chair and grabbed a shawl from a peg by the door and draped it around her shoulders.

Once again seated at the table, she held the cup in both hands for its warmth. After taking several sips of the hot tea, Elaine eased back on the chair and let her mind wander.

She thought back to the day she met Dale and how she instantly knew that he was the one for her. Dale made it clear that he felt the same, and shortly thereafter they were married. They were young and in love, and were excited abut their future together.

Elaine let her mind take her to the birth of each of their three children, and to the good life they had in Omaha. Barry, Susan, and Ernie were healthy, happy children. Dale had a good job and all was well with the Burke family. Who could ask for anything more?

Then came that fateful day when Dale learned of the gold strike in Yukon Territory, and nothing was the same after that.

Elaine sipped more tea and looked around the kitchen. "I really lost my husband a long time ago," she said to the empty room. "Gold fever claimed him, and eventually destroyed him. Oh, Dale, I wish we had never heard of this place."

She poured herself another steaming cup of tea, then sighed and spoke again to the empty room. "I guess I could take the children and return to Omaha. But…but I really don't think I care to make that long, arduous trip again, especially without a man to help me. I have a good job here that pays well and that I enjoy. The children are happy, and because of the Flemings, we're well cared for. We now have many close friends, and as much as I fought coming here, it really does feel like home now. I don't want to disrupt the children's lives any more than has already been done. So we're staying put."

Elaine drank the last of her tea and placed the cup on the

cupboard. She banked the fire in the big black stove, picked up the lantern from the table, and headed down the hall. She paused to look in on her sleeping children, then moved to her own bedroom. While getting into her nightgown, she said to herself, "At least I have a purpose now, and I'm settled in my mind what my babies and I are going to do."

She doused the flame in the lantern and crawled under the covers, pulling them up to her chin as she sank into the feather bed.

A sigh escaped her lips as she realized the enormous task ahead of her to be both mother and father to her precious children. "But we will make it, my dears," she whispered, and soon was fast asleep.

The next day, Lieutenant Brent Sawyer stood in the deep snow next to Elaine and her children as the town's undertaker conducted the brief graveside service. On Elaine's other side was Margo Fleming. Because of the snow, Norman was not able to attend. Several of Elaine's new friends were there also, along with the four Mounties who had dug the grave. They also lowered the coffin into the frozen ground after the undertaker had finished the service.

When the burial was over, and Margo and the other friends had expressed their condolences to Elaine and her children, Brent Sawyer turned to Elaine and said, "I have a question."

Elaine wiped tears from her cheek as she looked up into his face. "What's that?"

"Is it all right if I come to your quarters at the hotel and check on you and these precious children from time to time?"

"Of course," said Elaine, smiling through her tears "You'll be more than welcome."

The following Saturday, November 26, Jack London and his friends Laird Thompson and Heath Caldwell decided to take the weekend off from their gold mines and just spend some time in Dawson City. They went into the El Dorado Saloon for drinks and headed for the door an hour later.

When they stepped out of the saloon, they found a crowd gathered around two dogsled owners who were arguing about which one had the strongest dogs. Jack and his friends soon learned that the owners were John Thorne and Rafe Matthews.

Matthews bragged that his lead dog, Ruff, a 150-pound husky, could start the sled in the ice and snow all by himself with five hundred pounds on it, plus his weight as he drove the sled. The sled had been standing there on the street for about two hours, and the runners were frozen fast to the hard-packed snow.

"The sled has a thousand pounds of flour on it in twenty-five-pound sacks," Matthews said. "I'll take off half of them, and I'll bet you a thousand dollars, Mr. Thorne, that Ruff can start the sled with that load and pull it a hundred yards down the street."

Thorne laughed. "Tell you what, Mr. Matthews, *my* dog, Jack, is a 140-pound St. Bernard and Scotch Shepherd mix, and Jack can start your sled by himself, just as it is, with one thousand pounds on it, plus my weight as I drive. And Jack can pull it a hundred yards. I'll bet you a thousand dollars on it."

The crowd applauded and people dared Matthews to take the bet. When Matthews said he would, people in the crowd started betting with each other whether Jack could do it or not.

The team of eight dogs was unhitched, and John Thorne's dog, Jack, was hitched to Rafe Matthews's sled.

It seemed that Thorne's dog had caught the excitement of the crowd, and when his master stepped on the rear of the sled and shouted, "Mush, Jack!"—the gallant dog hunched his back, dug in, and broke the sled and its weight from the ice and snow. He pulled it down the street with the crowd shouting, and Jack London was almost beside himself as he waved his hat and shouted for Jack.

When the sled reached the one-hundred-yard mark, Thorne turned the sled around and drove it back to the crowd. There was a big cheer for Jack, and another cheer went up when Rafe Matthews unhappily paid Thorne the thousand dollars. Bets in the crowd had to be paid off, too.

As Jack London and his friends walked away from the scene, London said, "I am definitely going to write some novels about this frozen northland, and wolves and dogs. As you know, my digging for gold hasn't gone as well as I'd expected. I'll stay at it till early spring, then I'm going back to California and become a writer. And when I start writing, I'm going to use what you've taught me about wolves, Laird, for my first book. The second one will be about a gallant St. Bernard and Scotch Shepherd mix who loves his master enough to win him a bet on how much weight he can pull. Only I won't call him Jack. I'll call him Buck."

Laird chuckled. "Jack, ol' friend, I can hardly wait to read your novels!"

On March 20, 1899, the first day of spring, Mountie Brent Sawyer visited Elaine Burke and her children in their living quarters. He hugged Barry, Susan, and Ernie, who had come to love him dearly, then he said, "I need to talk to your mother alone for a little while. Would you go play in your room while I do that?"

Barry flashed his mother a knowing grin, than flashed it at Brent. "Sure, we'll do that. C'mon, Susie. C'mon, Ernie."

When they were alone, Brent sat down on the sofa beside Elaine and took her hand in his. "Elaine, I think you can see that I've fallen in love with your children."

"Yes, and they have also fallen in love with you."

He squeezed her hand. "I want you to know that I have fallen in love with you, too, only in a different way. I think Barry knows it, too."

Elaine smiled as tears misted her eyes. "Well, Barry also knows that his mother has fallen in love with *you*, Brent."

Brent folded her in his arms and kissed her tenderly. He then looked into her misty eyes. "Elaine, will you marry me?"

With her heart fluttering, Elaine smiled and wiped tears from her eyes. "Yes, Brent, I will marry you."

He kissed her again, then said, "In hopes that you would accept my proposal, I put a deposit on a four-bedroom house here in Dawson City yesterday."

She wiped away more tears. "Oh, Brent, you darling! This is wonderful!"

"How about you becoming a June bride, and we'll move into the house right after we get married?"

"Sounds just right to me!"

When the children were called in and told the good news, they jumped up and down with excitement and hugged their mother and their future stepfather.

On the same day, Pastor Tom Varner met in his office at the church with Matt Holden and Livia Bray. When they were comfortably seated, Tom said, "Since your wedding date is set, I have something I need to tell you."

Matt and Livia both showed concern at his words, but sat still as he explained that he had received a wire two days previously from Pastor Wayne Dukart in San Francisco. Pastor Dukart said in the wire that he had developed tuberculosis and must resign as pastor of the church. The congregation had voted unanimously for Tom Varner to come back and be their pastor.

Tom said that he and Peggy had prayed about it and agreed that it was God's will for them to do this. Tom wired Pastor Dukart back and told him they were sure it was God's will for them to come back to the church. In a return wire, Pastor Dukart told them there was a young man the church would send to be pastor of the mission church in Dawson City. He was married to a godly young woman, and she was for it a hundred percent.

When Matt and Livia told Tom that they could see God's hand in it all, he said, "Peggy and I plan to leave Dawson City on April 6, which will put us in Dyea to meet a ship on April 9 that will take us home to San Francisco. Since your wedding is set for Saturday, April 8, would you be willing to change it to the Saturday before so I can still perform the ceremony?"

Matt and Livia looked at each other and smiled, then Matt said, "Pastor, we had talked about getting together with you because we had something to tell you. So, this seems as good a time as any. After much prayer, Livia and I have decided to leave Dawson City and make our home in her hometown of San Francisco. We have over two hundred thousand dollars in the bank, which will give us a good start in our marriage. We're already asking the Lord to help us decide about a business to start in San Francisco. We've discussed this move with my parents and Livia's mother. Mrs. Bray already has a wealthy man who has been asking her to sell the clothing store and the laundry to him."

Pastor Varner grinned and shook his head. "This is really something. So you're going to take the Holdens and Martha with you to San Francisco?"

"That's right," Matt said. "We were going to leave right after we got married, but now I have an idea. With the schedule you've just mentioned for you and your family, if we left at the same time, we would cross Chilkoot Pass on April 8, the day we had set for our wedding. Since it was at the Golden Stairs where by God's grace I was able to save Livia's life in the avalanche and had the joy of leading her to Jesus, why not have the wedding ceremony on the Golden Stairs?"

Livia clapped her hands together, laughing, and said, "Oh, Matt, that's a wonderful idea! I'm all for it!"

Matt took her hand, kissed it, and said, "I thought that might appeal to you."

"It appeals to me too," Pastor Varner said. "We'll have the wedding as scheduled, only on the Golden Stairs!"

The plans went as scheduled, and at two o'clock in the afternoon on April 8, 1899, Matt and Livia stood together before Pastor Tom Varner on the Golden Stairs just below the south side of the peak on Chilkoot Pass to take their wedding vows. The temperature was ten degrees above zero.

Although the conditions did not allow Livia to wear a white wedding dress, she was clad in a white fur coat, which was a gift from Matt. The sun shone down from a clear sky. The only thing brighter was the glow on Livia's face.

Looking on as Pastor Varner conducted the ceremony were Martha Bray, Cleve and Maudie Holden, and Peggy Varner and Johnny and Rebecca…as well as a number of fellow travelers who were headed down the ice-chipped stairs toward Dyea, Alaska.

After the vows had been made and Tom Varner had led in prayer, asking God's blessing on the newly married couple, Tom said, "Matt, you may kiss your bride."

Matt held Livia close, kissed her soundly, then looked into her sky blue eyes and said, "Sweetheart, because you are now my wife, every day of my life will be like walking on Golden Stairs!"

EPILOGUE

By the fall of 1899, Dawson City's population had grown to over forty-two thousand as more gold seekers flooded the area. The mass movement of gold seekers tied the northern wilderness to the rest of the world in a positive way. It has not stood empty since. The Klondike Trail from Seattle to Dawson City is now an International Historical Park. Visitors from around the world come to walk in the erstwhile dreams of the gold seekers, which lasted from 1897 until 1902. Every year more than a million people visit exhibits in Seattle, Skagway, and Dawson City. Each summer some four thousand people follow the promise of adventure and climb Chilkoot Pass.

Of the forty thousand-plus people who made it to the Klondike gold fields, only about four hundred found enough gold to become rich. The lure of the Great North Country led thousands to the Juneau-Skagway area in the years that followed, laying the groundwork for Alaska's statehood.

One of the men who did well in the Yukon Territory gold fields was Swedish immigrant John Nordstrom, who in our story was assigned the claim site previously worked by Weldon Bray, alias Roger Whitson. Just after the turn of the century,

Nordstrom left the Klondike with sufficient funds to return to Seattle and follow his dream. There he started a small shoe store, which was the beginning of a highly successful nationwide retail corporation known as Nordstrom, Inc.

Jack London left Yukon Territory in mid-1899 after an unsuccessful attempt to get rich in the gold fields, and returned to his birthplace, San Francisco. As London had planned, he took up writing novels in early 1900. His first published book, *The Son of the Wolf* came off the press that same year. His next novel, *The Call of the Wild*, which he wrote as planned about a 140-pound St. Bernard and Scotch Shepherd mix dog named Buck, came off the press in 1903. He also wrote *White Fang*, which was published in 1906, and *Burning Daylight*, which was published in 1910—all four having to do with Yukon Territory and Alaska.

London continued to write novels, and many were successful. However, his constant drinking finally turned him into a helpless alcoholic, and in a deep depression, he committed suicide on November 22, 1916, at the age of forty.

GOLD GLIMMERS, AND THE RUSH IS ON!

NEW DREAMS OF GOLD TRILOGY
By Al & JoAnna Lacy

WINGS OF RICHES–BOOK ONE

Get in on the first book in a new trilogy by master narrators Al and JoAnna Lacy. Set in North America's nineteenth-century gold country, the tales are adventure filled and gripping!

ISBN 1-59052-389-X

THE FORBIDDEN HILLS–BOOK TWO

Jim Bannon leaves his family's Wyoming farm in hot pursuit of gold in the Black Hills of Dakota Territory. Will he secure the wealth that is his ticket to marry the love of his life?

ISBN 1-59052-477-2

THE GOLDEN STAIRS–BOOK THREE

Livia does not expect to meet anyone like Matt Holden on the Golden Stairs. While he saves her life, no one knows if her father has been as fortunate…

ISBN 1-59052-561-2

Frontier Doctor Trilogy

ONE MORE SUNRISE–BOOK ONE

Young frontier doctor Dane Logan is gaining renown as a surgeon. Beyond his wildest hopes, he meets his long-lost love—only to risk losing her to the Tag Moran gang.

ISBN 1-59052-308-3

BELOVED PHYSICIAN–BOOK TWO

While Dr. Dane gains renown by rescuing people from gunfights, Indian attacks, and a mine collapse, Nurse Tharyn mourns the capture of her dear friend Melinda by renegade Utes.

ISBN 1-59052-313-X

THE HEART REMEMBERS–BOOK THREE

In this final book in the Frontier Doctor trilogy, Dane survives an accident, but not without losing his memory. Who is he? Does he have a family somewhere?

ISBN 1-59052-351-2

Hannah of Fort Bridger Series

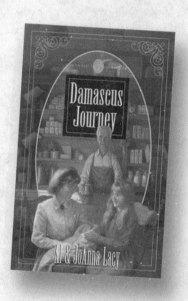

Hannah Cooper's husband dies on the dusty Oregon Trail, leaving her in charge of five children and a general store in Fort Bridger. Dependence on God fortifies her against grueling challenges and bitter tragedies.

Angel of Mercy Series

Post-Civil War nurse Breanna Baylor uses her professional skill to bring healing to the body, and her faith in the Redeemer to bring comfort to thirsty souls, valiantly serving God on the dangerous frontier.

Shadow of Liberty Series

Let Freedom Ring
#1 in the Shadow of Liberty Series

It is January 1886 in Russia. Vladimir Petrovna, a Christian husband and father of three, faces bankruptcy, persecution for his beliefs, and despair. The solutions lie across a perilous sea.

ISBN 1-57673-756-X

The Secret Place
#2 in the Shadow of Liberty Series

Popular authors Al and JoAnna Lacy offer a compelling question: As two young people cope with love's longings on opposite shores, can they find the serenity of God's covering in *The Secret Place?*

ISBN 1-57673-800-0

A Prince Among Them
#3 in the Shadow of Liberty Series

A bitter enemy of Queen Victoria kidnaps her favorite great-grandson. Emigrants Jeremy and Cecelia Barlow book passage on the same ship to America, facing a complex dilemma that only all-knowing God can set right.

ISBN 1-57673-880-9

Undying Love
#4 in the Shadow of Liberty Series

19-year-old Stephan Varda flees his own guilt and his father's rage in Hungary, finding undying love from his heavenly Father—and a beautiful girl—across the ocean in America.

ISBN 1-57673-930-9

Journey of the Stranger Series

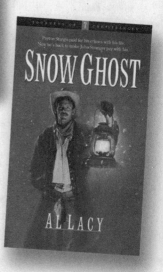

One dark, mysterious man rides for truth and justice. On his hip is a Colt .45…and in his pack is a large, black Bible. He is the legend known only as the stranger.

Battles of Destiny Series

It was the war that divided our country and shaped the destiny of generations to come. Out of the bloodshed, men, women, and families faced adversity with bravery and sacrifice…and sometimes even love.

The Orphan Train Trilogy

THE LITTLE SPARROWS, Book #1

Kearney, Cheyenne, Rawlins. Reno, Sacramento, San Francisco. At each train station, a few lucky orphans from the crowded streets of New York City receive the fulfillment of their dreams: a home and family. This orphan train is the v i s i o n of Charles Loring Brace, founder of the Children's Aid Society, who cannot bear to see innocent children abandoned in the overpopulated cities of the mid–nineteenth century. Yet it is not just the orphans whose lives need mending—follow the train along and watch God's hand restore love and laughter to the right family at the right time!

ISBN 1-59052-063-7

ALL MY TOMOROWS, Book #2

When sixty-two orphans and abandoned children leave New York City on a train headed out West, they have no idea what to expect. Will they get separated from their friends and siblings? Will their new families love them? Will a family even pick them at all? Future events are wilder than any of them could imagine—ranging from kidnappings and whippings to stowing away on wagon trains, from starting orphanages of their own to serving as missionaries to the Apache. No matter what, their paths are being watched by Someone who cares about and carefully plans all their tomorrows.

ISBN 1-59052-130-7

WHISPERS IN THE WIND, Book #3

Young Dane Weston's dream is to become a doctor. But it will take more than just determination to realize his goal, once his family is murdered and he ends up in a colony of street waifs begging for food. Then he ends up mistaken for a murderer himself and sentenced to life in prison. Now what will become of his friendship with the pretty orphan girl Tharyn, who wanted to enter the medical profession herself? Does she feel he is anything more than a big brother to her? And will she ever write him again?

ISBN 1-59052-169-2

Mail Order Bride Series

Desperate men who settled the West resorted to unconventional measures in their quest for companionship, advertising for and marrying women they'd never even met! Read about a unique and adventurous period in the history of romance.

#1	Secrets of the Heart	ISBN 1-57673-278-9
#2	A Time to Love	ISBN 1-57673-284-3
#3	The Tender Flame	ISBN 1-57673-399-8
#4	Blessed Are the Merciful	ISBN 1-57673-417-X
#5	Ransom of Love	ISBN 1-57673-609-1
#6	Until the Daybreak	ISBN 1-57673-624-5
#7	Sincerely Yours	ISBN 1-57673-572-9
#8	A Measure of Grace	ISBN 1-57673-808-6
#9	So Little Time	ISBN 1-57673-898-1
#10	Let There Be Light	ISBN 1-59052-042-4